# THE ARRANGEMENTS

ORLY KONIG

Next
Chapter Books

# ALSO BY ORLY KONIG

*The Distance Home*

*Carousel Beach*

Published by Next Chapter Books, LLC

www.orlykonig.com

Cover design by EBookLaunch.com

E-Book ISBN: 979-8-9906906-4-6
Print ISBN: 979-8-9906906-5-3

## LOVE IS THE FLOWER YOU'VE GOT TO LET GROW.

— JOHN LENNON

# 1

## FLOWERS ARE THE MUSIC OF THE GROUND. FROM EARTH'S LIPS SPOKEN WITHOUT SOUND.

— EDWIN CURRAN

I was born invisible. Or at least, that's how it felt. *Feels*. I'm not ugly and I'm not trolling for compliments. What I am, is plain. Forgettable. Vanilla without even the zing of the bean.

Which is one of the many reasons I love flowers. Flowers are never invisible. Flowers have a language of their own for those who have the presence to listen. Flowers are magic.

Any flower. Every flower. It's impossible not to smile at such beauty or find peace with a single inhale of a flower's pure fragrance.

Most people assume I became a florist because I was named for the calla lily. Fun fact, I wasn't named for a flower. Or at least, not intentionally.

There are two things in this world my mom loves above anything else—opera and Maria Callas. My father wasn't a fan of the name Maria and he put his foot down on Callas (thank you, Dad!). They compromised on Calla. In ancient Greek culture, the calla lily represents magnificent beauty. Thank you, gods of irony.

Becoming a florist was more of an eventuality than a conscious decision. For one, I grew up "working" in a flower shop. And two, except for when I'm with my best friend Nate, it's only in the company of flowers that I truly feel like me.

The store phone rings but I let it go to voicemail. It's after hours, long after hours, and I'm done peopling. We're two days from Valentine's Day and the store has been a non-stop hive of busyness. Here's another fun fact about me: I am not a fan of Valentine's Day.

"Hello? Hello?" says a raspy voice. "This is Lawrence Preston. I'm calling to make sure you have my order. Hello?"

Mr. Preston. Bless him. Mr. Preston is 87 years old and for 71 years has given his valentine sixteen lavender roses. Sixteen because that's how old they were when they met. Lavender because that's her favorite color.

The Prestons moved into the retirement home two blocks from the store six years ago after Mr. Preston fell and broke his hip and Mrs. Preston forgot she put eggs to boil and exploded a dozen extra-large free-range brown eggs all over the kitchen. Rumor has it the furnishings they took with them to the retirement home still smell of eggs.

"All set, Mr. Preston," I answer the now silent answering machine.

Lavender roses were my father's go-to as well.

He never tired of telling the story about how he fell in love with my mom the first time he saw her. That she was the only woman for him until I was born. From the moment the nurse handed me to him, all blotchy and cranky, he was smitten. Love at first sight.

"First and forever," my father used to say.

*First and forever.* First maybe, but certainly not forever. He did, after all, leave without so much as an explanation. And left on Valentine's Day. The Valentine's Day before my 16th birthday.

I'd asked Mr. Preston once if he'd fallen in love with Mrs. Preston at first sight. "Oh my, yes," he'd answered. "She came into my pop's drug store with a couple of friends to buy lip gloss. I reorganized the feminine hygiene shelf three times before I realized they were giggling over what I was doing. Lucile smiled at me, and I just knew. Of course, I was far too embarrassed to speak to her, especially holding an armful of lady products. But the following day, she came back to the store alone and this time, thank goodness, I was in the gift card section. The rest is, as they say, history."

Lavender roses for love at first sight. They deserve more credit on a holiday like this. I finger the soft petals and the rose responds by releasing the softest, sweetest perfume.

My phone dances on the worktable and I peer down. Nate is FaceTiming me. I tap accept without picking up the phone.

"Hey," I say.

"Hey. Why am I staring at the ceiling?"

"Because I'm working."

"So?"

"I'm not an octopus, I only have two hands."

"But you can position the phone so I'm looking at something more appealing than the ceiling."

I pick up the phone, make a face at Nate, and lean the phone against a vase. "Better?"

"Slightly. By the way, there's a stain on the ceiling you guys should pay attention to."

I look up. "It's a shadow."

"Nope, it's a stain. Isn't that where the bathroom is in your apartment?" I live in the apartment above the store, owned by Maggie Cameron, mother of my best friend and my mother's best friend since they were in middle school.

I look up again. "Hmm. Maybe?"

"What do you mean maybe? Don't you know the layout of your own apartment?"

"Did you call just to make fun of me because I don't know where my bathroom is?"

"I called to see if you're still grumpy."

I glare at him through the smudged screen of my phone.

Nate cocks his head, brows raised and I feel the corner of my lips curl into a smile. Nate is the human equivalent of a support animal. My support animal. Bonus, he doesn't poop on my carpet or need to be walked.

Nate's been my best friend since day T-9 months. My mom and Maggie took the whole best friends to the next level. We were born on the same day, in the same hospital, two hours, and two rooms apart. We became Nate and Callie, Callie and Nate. Despite having different parents, everyone treated us like twins. Down to the matching outfits for the first days of school. At least until we were old enough to object.

Nate's seen me through every upheaval, every downslide. He's cheered me on and propped me up. It was Nate who sat up all night with me after my dad left. Nate who convinced me to go to prom with Robbie Harris so we could double date then ended up dancing with me and driving me home after Robbie disappeared ten minutes after arriving at the dance. It's Nate who I call with every update on my life.

He knows how to push every one of my mood buttons and how to nudge those buttons back into place. We've spent our entire lives sharing the good, the bad, and the too embarrassing to repeat out loud.

And Nate is the one person I've spent every holiday and every birthday with. Thirty-two years of holidays and birthdays.

"So, about Valentine's Day," Nate says with a slow hedging drawl.

"Ah yes. Indian or Thai?"

"Actually, that's what I want to talk about."

I glance quickly at the screen, mid-trim on yet another rose stem. Nate shifts and I'm suddenly looking at his ceiling.

"Hey, ceiling."

"Sorry." But when he adjusts the camera back on him, he wears the look of someone about to deliver the lamest of excuses.

"Seriously?" My fingers clench the stem in my hand. The rose retaliates by stabbing me with a thorn.

"Seriously what? You don't know what I'm about to say." He looks defensive because he knows I know exactly what he's going to say. He's going to flake on me.

And I have no intention of letting him off easy. Flaking on a Wednesday dinner, fine. Flaking on a weekend movie-binge, I can live with. But Valentine's Day, New Year's Eve, and our birthday are non-negotiable. "You've signed yourself up for a vegan anonymous bootcamp and can't make our dinner-movie marathon night."

"Okay, so you do know what I was going to say."

"Don't do it. Trust me on this one. Burgers are your friend."

Nate pretends to think about what I've said, then says, "Okay, you've convinced me."

"Good. So burgers it is. Not very Valentiney but neither are we." The burger joint will probably be the least packed of all our favorite spots.

"Actually, I can't do Monday."

"But Monday is Valentine's Day." Like I said, not open for negotiation.

"I know and I'll make it up to you."

"So, what, you have a hot date you're ditching me for?" Unlike me, Nate is a dater. Unlike me, Nate is perfect. Gorgeous, funny, smart, kind. He's the perfect specimen (with apologies to Chris Hemsworth who will forever remain the sexiest man alive for me).

Nate has always been popular. I became semi-popular by association—I came as a package deal with Nate. Girls wanted to hang around me to get front row access to Nate. And the guys wanted to be my friend because of all the hot girls who hung around me because of Nate. I was the velcro strip you don't see but is needed to keep the picture secured to the wall. The invisible velcro strip.

All I need is the look of guilt on his face to elicit another "Seriously!" This one delivered with the emphasis of we-don't-do-this.

"I've been kinda seeing someone and she sort of invited me for dinner."

"You've *kinda* been seeing someone? And she *sort of* invited you?" I'm not sure if it hurts more that he's ditching me on my least favorite day or that he hasn't said anything about this someone he's sort of seeing. We don't keep secrets and he's kept a secret. A big one.

Obviously, she's not his first girlfriend. But I can't help feeling the ever-present twinge of "will this be the one who takes him away from me."

"Yeah. I was going to mention it but, I don't know." He squints at something past me, and I find myself turning to see what's back there.

"What the hell, Nate." I'm lacking both sass and a sense of humor at this time of night.

"I'm sorry." He blinks at me from under the forelock of dark hair he's forever brushing aside and, as I've done since we were in diapers, I forgive him.

Almost. "I can't believe you're doing this to me," I pout to prolong his punishment.

It would be a lie to say I don't care about being single, especially on holidays created expressly for coupledom, but I always had Nate. And Nate always had me. Sure, there'd been girlfriends, a couple even potentially serious ones, but he never let those relationships get between us.

"Here's a wild and crazy idea," Nate says, leaning closer to the phone before finishing his wild and crazy idea in a whisper, "why don't you ask someone out?"

I lean back with a look of not-so-mock disgust. "You want me to call some random dude to ask him out? It's like you don't even know me."

I change the trajectory of the conversation back to familiar territory. "Tell me about this person you're sort of seeing."

"She's nice."

*She's nice.* It's the most non-committal answer, and the most damning. If he'd gushed about how amazing she is, how gorgeous, how something, I'd shrug it off as another Nate fast-and-furious crush. It's what he does. The women he dates are wonderful until they're not. Our lack of commitment to other people has come up often in conversations. Between us, between us and whoever we may be dating, and between us (individually) with Nate's mom, Maggie.

The reason is easy: we're both waiting for "the one." For Nate, he's waiting for what his parents had. The kind of love that you only find once and only if you've landed in a field of four-leaf clovers. For me, it's my belief that whatever "great love" is out there is fleeting, so why bother, despite Nate's parents' example.

I raise a skeptical eyebrow. "She already has one strike against her. I'm now solo on the worst night of the year because of her."

"I'll make it up to you."

"How?"

"Tomorrow night?"

"The only thing I'm going to want to do tomorrow is soak in the bathtub then go to sleep for what will, no doubt, be the shortest night of my life. Your mother agreed for us to do flowers for a wedding as well."

"Ouuf. Sorry."

"You should be. She's your mom."

"She's your boss."

"She was your mom first."

We're mature like that.

"Tomorrow?" Nate asks again.

"Tomorrow."

"Yay."

"Yay?"

"Get over yourself."

"It's you I can't get over."

"Tomorrow. And we're going to talk about our birthday. The double three." He tilts his head and bats his lashes at me.

"Oh yeah, our birthday." I pretend to not have remembered.

"Oh please, you have it on the calendar so that no one forgets what day it is." He's grins at me.

"Guilty." I grew up in the shadow of a former Miss Maryland, a woman who commands attention by her mere presence on this earth. I may not have inherited her looks or love of being in the spotlight, but the day I share with Nate is an exception to all my troll-like instincts.

"We have something important to discuss," he says. I hear his phone ping with a message. "Hey, I need to go. I'll see you tomorrow."

Before I can grill him about the important topic he wants to discuss, Nate blows me a kiss and hangs up. I'm left staring at my reflection in the black screen of my phone.

Staring back is my nineteen-year-old self and I'm transported to our freshman year of college. Nate had been dating some hot psychology undergrad and I'd just started seeing an engineering friend of Nate's. With our birthday a week away, we threw a party, significant others and all. Because, for the first time, we both simultaneously had significant others.

The party had been a rollicking success. Until we walked into the kitchen of the house Nate shared with three other guys to find our significant others in a lip lock that was more full-body lock.

We spent the rest of the night on the roof outside Nate's bedroom window, drinking beer and dissecting where we'd gone wrong. Somewhere around 4:00 a.m., we clinked empty bottles and sealed a pact. If we were still single when we turned 33, we'd get married.

"Holy shit," I whisper into the quiet store.

2

___________

# IN JOY OR SADNESS, FLOWERS ARE OUR CONSTANT FRIENDS.

— OKAKURA KAKUZO

"How do you never have food in here?" Nate is standing in front of the open refrigerator. He bends, peering at the bottom shelf, again, then twists to look at me accusingly.

"Did you come over to criticize my domestic skills?"

"You don't have domestic skills."

"I hate you."

"Doesn't change the fact that there's nothing to eat."

"Maybe because it's, oh, almost Valentine's Day and I've been working non-stop."

This morning, at the crack of unholy-not-even-light-yet, Alex, my favorite of the flower vendors we buy from, arrived with a truck full of lilacs, calla lilies, and ivy for the wedding arrangements Maggie agreed to a week ago. A week before Valentine's Day. A week after I forbade her from accepting any new orders. White Calla Lilies for innocence, purity. Lilacs for the pop of purple to signify first love. Ivy for fidelity in marriage. And to prove to myself and Maggie and the universe that I'm not a total romance scrooge, I arranged for the flower girl to present the bride and groom with sprigs of lavender which, according to folklore, brings good luck.

It had taken every minute of the day, not counting the three unavoidable potty breaks, to get all the orders filled. Luckily, Maggie and Julia, the part-time assistant Maggie and I couldn't live without, came through with helping on the Valentine's orders. Although I suspect part of their motivation was keeping me away from the stuffed bears after I almost beheaded one over the "special request" on an order form. In all fairness, it wasn't the bear's fault but seriously, who specifies the length of the stems down to the eighth of an inch?

"Fine, we'll order something," Nate says, closing the fridge. "Any cravings?"

Lulu figure-eights between his legs and meows up at him. "I wasn't asking you." He reaches down and scratches her on the top of the head. She coos and gives his legs an extra hop-bump of love.

"Nope," I answer, which is a total lie but I know better than to admit a craving to Nate. The trick is to make him suggest what I'm craving. And I've been dreaming about the Thai noodles Julia had for lunch.

"You twitched," Nate says.

"I did not."

"You did. So what is it?"

"I seriously don't care."

Lulu meows again.

"Even she doesn't buy it, but fine. How about Mexican. I could go for an enchilada."

I feel my face scrunch before I can stop it. "We had that last week."

"Your point?"

"No point." We have a habit of getting stuck on a favorite-for-now food and binging it until we can't stomach one more bite. Which usually only lasts for a couple of months. Except

Mac & Cheese. The night I moved in here, we bought some from the hot bar at the grocery and ate it sitting cross legged on the bed since it was the only furniture I owned at the time. It was so good (and we were so lazy) that we ate it every day for two weeks. Neither of us could walk past the hot bar for almost a year after that without feeling a bit sick.

"How about Thai?" I suggest, hoping my tone sounds breezy and not like I've been obsessing about Thai Kitchen's drunken noodles for the last seven hours.

"I knew it." Nate laughs. He taps at his phone. "Indian?"

I groan. "Why do you do that?"

He frowns. "Do what?"

"You ask what I want then offer a counter suggestion."

"I don't."

"You do."

"I do?"

I nod. "You do. Is it just with me or with girlfriends as well?"

The creases between his eyebrows blur into one. "Just you I think. At least, no one else has called me out on it."

"Interesting," I say, grabbing for his phone. I tap through the options in the food delivery app, click on Thai Kitchen and put in my order. Drunken noodles with tofu and two Thai teas. I hand Nate his phone back. "Decision made."

"You're a bully," Nate teases.

"Only with you." What I really am is a people pleaser who makes a Golden Retriever look fickle.

"Two teas?" Nate gapes at me. "You're going to be up all night."

"No, I won't."

"Yes, you will. And you'll be bugging me at 3 a.m. when you can't sleep."

He's not wrong. Last time we ordered Thai, and I gave in to the two-tea craving, I was, indeed awake half the night. And I had, indeed, texted Nate at 3 a.m. whining that I couldn't sleep.

When he hadn't answered, even though I knew thanks to notification settings that he'd read my messages, I FaceTimed him.

Once we've placed the order, we each grab a beer (those I do have in the fridge) and move to the couch, taking our usual spaces. I twist so I'm partially facing Nate, with my legs stretched across the couch on his lap. Something we do every time we're together. Something I've only ever done with him though.

"So, you have a date tomorrow?" I ask, pointing my toes and poking him in the side.

Nate studies his beer for longer than necessary before taking a pull. "Yeah," he finally says.

I push my toes deeper into his side. He's holding back and whatever he's holding back has just nudged the air between us to the muggy discomfort of a greenhouse in the summer. I wipe my palm on the leg of my jeans even though I'm not actually sweating and attempt to lighten the moment. "That was enthusiastic. She must be super special."

His left eyebrow twitches up in a you're-not-going-to-let-this-go expression. I shrug. I'm not going to.

"Why don't you want to talk about her?" I sip at my beer and study his face. He repositions deeper into the corner of the couch, looking very un-Nate-like uncomfortable.

"I don't know," he admits. "Maybe because she's different from other women I've gone out with."

"Different as in?" And because I can't help teasing him, I whisper, "Does she have three eyes? Three boobs? Oh, oh, webbed feet?"

"You're a jerk." He laughs, releasing whatever unease has built between us. "She's smart and serious and she makes me laugh."

"Hey, that's me you've just described. And yet you're ditching me for her."

Lulu, hearing my slightly raised voice jumps into Nate's lap and eyeballs me.

"Don't mess with me or my attack cat will have to teach you a lesson." Nate laughs, running a hand along Lulu's back and making her promptly loose interest in me.

"She does and she's not getting dinner." I boop her nose which earns me a slap with an only partially retracted claw.

Nate's phone buzzes and he frowns at it. "Sorry Princess but the food is here. Priorities." Lulu flicks her tail as Nate sets her down on the couch. Any other time, he would've used the cat as the excuse to send me to answer the door. He really doesn't want to talk about this new lady friend.

Back on the couch with our dinner, Nate flips the TV on. I turn it off. He glares at me. Lulu glares at me.

"Both of you can just go suck on a noodle."

"You are so weird," Nate says, shaking his head. He picks up the end of a noodle and puts it in his mouth, then slurps it in slowly.

"You're gross. Has she seen you eat?" There's the eyebrow again. I'm rewarded, though, when the other end of the noodle slaps him on the chin.

"You said yesterday that you wanted to talk. So talk." I suddenly want to get off the kinda girlfriend topic.

He takes a bite of his pad thai, using the chew time as think time. I know this trick. Nate is the master of the "can't talk, eating" stall tactic.

I watch as he chews until I'm certain there's nothing left to chew. "Now?" I ask.

"I guess with our birthday coming up and Beth, I've just been thinking about the future," he finally answers. "Don't laugh, but I had a dream about us being married."

*Beth.* Her name is Beth.

"Us, married? Eww." Standard response.

We were six when Nate's dad died. After the funeral one of

the neighbors casually commented that Nate and I were destined to be together and we both answered, "Us, married? Eww."

There's never been a version of my life that didn't include Nate. Even with the pact, though, I never considered marrying him a "real" option. Because he's Nate.

"What was the dream about?" I prompt.

"We were arguing over what to have for dinner."

I laugh. "We do that several times a week already. So where did the married part come in?"

"I don't know. We just were."

"So, basically this." I gesture at us.

"Yeah. Except we weren't living here."

"Hm, okay then." Then after a pause and a sip of my Thai tea, I add, "I had one of those dreams not long ago. We were married but it wasn't us except we were living together but there was nothing romantic although we were definitely in love. It was confusing."

"Not that confusing. We do love each other just not in that way. I mean look at us." We're sprawled with legs intertwined, a cat acting as a chaperone on the middle cushion with a possessive paw on Nate's thigh. "We definitely act like a married couple."

"And yet you're ditching me for another woman on Valentine's Day." I'm so not letting this go.

Nate takes the remote from the coffee table and flips to reruns of The Big Bang Theory. My best friend the nerd. As kids his favorite entertainment involved anything space related. While I fussed with flowers and squealed if I came across anything slithering in the dirt (even if it was only an inch long), Nate gazed at the stars and built rockets. As adults, I can now say that my best friend is, literally, a rocket scientist.

"Do you think we'll ever get married?" I ask.

"You mean we as in you and me? Or as in we're both married but to other people?"

I purse my lips the way my mom used to do when I asked a stupid question. Because, yes, there really are stupid questions despite what some people would have you believe.

"I hope so," Nate says, ignoring the look.

I pop a piece of tofu in my mouth. "You hope so meaning you and me? Or each of us with other people?"

"Whichever comes first." Nate smirks.

"Well," I play along, "Our birthday is two months away."

Nate stares into his take-out container. Finally, he says, "Do you ever wonder why we always find some fatal flaw in anyone we date?"

I think for a minute before answering. "You mean like Roy who ordered food like he was channeling Sally from When Harry Met Sally? 'I'll have the salad but only if the lettuce is locally grown and the dressing on the side but only if it's made with 10-year aged balsamic.' Or Megan who laughed at everything you said like you were the funniest man alive."

Nate glares at me. "Rude. I am the funniest man alive."

"Ehhh. Luckily, neither of us has a fatal flaw," I say.

"Oh, we do. We were just born with the ability to see past each other's flaws."

He's right, of course. Which makes that one of his flaws. He's always right.

"You mean like the way you never use a coaster?" I move his beer to rest on the coaster five inches from where he'd set it down.

"Fair. Or the way you sleep like a dying starfish?"

"Once. I did that once." Once that he called me out on. Who knows if I actually do it every night since no one ever sleeps in bed with me except Lulu.

Nate holds up three fingers.

"Liar."

He laughs. "Hey, Cals, promise me one thing."

"K," I hedge.

"Regardless of who we end up marrying, promise this will never change."

"It'll never change," I say. "Anyway, we turn 33 soon and you know what that means." I watch him from behind a strand of hair that's fallen loose from my unruly bun.

"Yup. It means I better act fast or I'll be stuck with you forever."

# FLOWERS DIDN'T ASK TO BE FLOWERS AND I DIDN'T ASK TO BE ME.

— KURT VONNEGUT

I have a bone to pick with whoever scheduled Valentine's Day during the winter. It's a cruel reminder for those of us who are single that if we had the ability to attract another human, we'd be at home snuggling instead of freezing our behinds off walking to get takeout for one.

I bury my face into my scarf, wishing I'd given in to the temptation to order in. Except the only place that had less than an hour and a half wait was a chain pizza joint. No offense to greasy pizza, but not today.

Today calls for something special. Even if I am eating alone. Unless Lulu forgives me for giving her the wrong can of cat food this morning.

The market square is busy with couples, hand-in-gloved-hand or arms around each other. Everyone a reminder that I'm alone, on my way to pick up enchiladas. Don't judge.

I have to step off the curb to avoid a couple standing in the middle of the sidewalk discussing which restaurant to try.

I do a quick survey of the guy. He's probably the type who

comes into flower shops half an hour before closing assuming we've kept the largest bouquet of perfect red roses just for him.

We had one of those today. I let Maggie help him. More precisely, she wouldn't let me out of the back, knowing full well I'd reached my end with people and their ridiculous requests. He left with a bouquet that wasn't perfect red roses. Maybe next year he'll remember to order early.

Inside the pocket of my coat, my phone buzzes. I pull my hand out just enough to catch a glimpse of the screen but not expose my hands to the cold.

Nate: Thinking of you. What are you up to?

Me: About to have the time of my life with Pedro. You?

Nate: Tell him hi. And nothing.

Me: Nothing?

Nate: Well …

Me: STOP

Nate: I was going to say waiting for Beth to finish dinner.

Me: What's for dinner?

Nate: Fondu

Me: How romantic

Nate: You say romantic, I say fussy

Me: Does she know you are romance challenged?

Nate: I brought olives from the grocery store.

Me: Olives? From the grocery?

Nate: Olives. From the olive bar.

Me: In the plastic container?

Nate: Yeah?

Me: face palm emoji

Me: Olives?

Nate: Yeah!

Me: Did you at least take some flowers to go with the olives?

Nate: The flowers in the grocery were all picked over.

Me: a row of face palm emojis

Nate: Gotta go

Me: Say cheese

Nate: You're so weird

Nate: heart emoji

Me: But I'm your weird

Me: heart emoji

I don't begrudge Nate having a date and I'm hella curious about her. But I'm also feeling oddly, newly grumpy about this woman he's spending tonight with instead of keeping our tradition of take-out and movies.

I drop the phone back into my coat pocket and pull open the door to Pedro's Cantina.

The hostess is quick to retrieve a bag with my name on it from a shelf behind her. I see a handful of bags in addition to mine and for a sad second I consider asking if any of them are a single meal order. Maybe I should hang around and offer to eat together. Not that I'd actually do it, but I find the thought amusing.

Lulu doesn't greet me when I walk in. She doesn't even lift her head although her tail waves reproachfully from where it's draped over the cat perch by the window.

"Hey, Lou," I say even though she's made it clear she has no use for me today. Who knew seafood stew instead of cowboy medley was such a grievous offense.

She stands, stretches into an elegant downward cat pose, then turns and lays back down with her back to me.

I bypass the kitchen and immediately settle on the floor of my living room, turning the TV on in the process. Not that I care to watch any of the sappy shows playing, but I need noise. A second later, I'm up and removing a box from the bottom of my bedroom closet.

The box is decorated with hearts of all sizes in an assortment of pinks and reds. I made it when I was five. It was a class project, meant to be a "mailbox" for the valentine's cards we'd been instructed to give to each other.

I ease back onto the floor and open the lid. Lou immediately hops off her perch and saunters over to see what she can steal from me. I remove a stack of cards tied together with a red ribbon, ignoring the pile of postcards held together by a crumbling rubber band.

Every Valentine's card Nate has ever given me is in this stack, starting with the generic card with the piece of candy glued to it from that first exchange when we were five. There are a handful of loose envelopes from other guys: the 3$^{rd}$ grade card from Rickie Winters with the scribbled "want to hang out?" and accompanying yes/no boxes. Of course, it turned out that Rickie Winters wanted to hang out because he figured it would involve Nate and the trampoline in Nate's back yard. But Rickie had been my first crush, hence saving the card.

There's the card from Elliot Patterson, my first serious boyfriend the year after college, or so I'd thought. We dated for five months, and I'd been smitten. Until he gave me the Valentine's card with a platonic "you're awesome" message scribbled inside. No personalization, no "love" or even a "fondly" salutation.

That was the night before Valentine's Day. He'd left after dinner, claiming an early morning. The following day he posted a picture on social media of him on a plane bound for the Bahamas. Next to him in first class was his model-gorgeous ex, the one who'd broken up with him five months before.

Elliot was the first guy I'd given my heart to. I'd trusted him, believed him. When Nate asked if I was sure, really, *really* sure about Elliot, I'd given him a hug and said, "really, *really* sure."

I pick another card from Nate out of the box. The one he gave me the same day Elliot stomped on my heart. A slip of paper falls out. I unfold it and read: "You're too good for him. You are amazing. Don't forget that."

Inside the box are hundreds, thousands, of tiny paper scraps in all shapes and sizes, each with a quick note from Nate. *You look nice today. That's a good color on you. Hey Sunshine.* There are notes with smiley faces or doodles of flowers or miscellaneous other drawings. Each note is Nate's little way of reminding me that there's someone who thinks I'm special.

I run my fingers through the collection of paper, letting them slip through like grains of sand. Silly maybe to keep all of them but they cushion my heart.

Not to mention that they conceal the stack of postcards. I snap the rubber band on the postcards. I haven't touched it in sixteen years and one snap is all it takes to make it crumble. There are 38 postcards from locations around the United States. Every card has the same handwritten message: "Thinking of you, every minute. All my love, Dad."

I fan the edges of the postcards, a quick trip through the life my father chose instead of staying with us. How could he have been thinking of me for even a single minute, when he never reached out to talk to me?

A card falls out of the stack. The Atlanta Botanical Garden. The picture on the front is of the Parterre Fountain and the Chihuly glass sculpture. From the first time I saw a magazine article about Chihuly, I became obsessed with his garden installations. I read every article I could find and even made my dad take me to a glass blowing class. The fire scared me, but my fascination didn't flame out. I begged to go to any and every exhibit where I could see Chihuly sculptures in the wild. The Parterre Fountain remains a dream destination.

My father promised we would, one day, go together.

He went without me.

My phone rings and I reach for it assuming it's Nate. The number on the phone, however, isn't Nate's. I let it go to voicemail. The last thing I need tonight is a heart-to-heart with a robocall voice or, worse, a live telemarketer with nothing else to do but call on Valentine's Day.

I slip the postcard back into the stack. For a full year after he left, Dad sent postcards. Never explaining the progression from one location to another, never explaining why he left on this mission. And then one day, the postcards stopped.

My phone buzzes, announcing a voice message.

"Hey, Callie. It's Dad. Wow, I can't believe how amazing your voice sounds. I'm sorry, that sounded weird. I'm nervous. Am I allowed to confess that? It's been a long time. Too long, I know. And you have every right to be angry with me. I was hoping you'd answer, but I think I'm actually relieved you didn't. It is Valentine's Day though and I've been thinking about that dinner at L'Auberge. God I've missed you. We have so much to talk about. Please, Butterfly, call me back."

*Butterfly.*

He gave me this nickname to remind me that there's beauty in all of us. I clung to that idea throughout my childhood, waiting for the transformation from common, colorless cater-pillar to exquisite butterfly. I mean, seriously, look at my mom.

The transformation never came.

I replay the message, sure it's some sick joke or hallucination. It's not. He may sound older, more tired, but I'd know that voice anywhere. Seventeen years of hurt and confusion burst to the surface. Because what could have made today suckier?

# 4

## ALL THE FLOWERS OF THE TOMORROWS ARE IN THE SEEDS OF TODAY.

### — INDIAN PROVERB

"How many calls is that?" Nate asks two days later.

"Three."

"Three that you haven't bothered to return?"

"Three that I don't *care* to return."

Nate rolls his eyes and I return the stare-down with a get-over-it look. He knows how I feel about my father.

The night my father left it was Nate who sat with me on the old swing set in our backyard in the uncomfortable temperature of a mid-February night in Maryland. And once my mother stopped smashing dishes in the kitchen and the night fell silent, we'd stayed silent as well. There was nothing to say. No insight into why my father would leave his family without warning.

Or at least not a warning that I saw. The only indication that Mom hadn't been caught as off-guard as me was the "just go already then," she'd yelled before hurling a soup bowl with its uneaten matza ball after my father.

It was Nate who helped me paint his older brother, Leo's

room when I moved in with them after my mom checked herself into a wellness center two weeks after my father's exit.

And it was Nate who convinced me to keep the postcards from my father. "Someday you'll want the story behind each of these," he'd said. I'd reluctantly listened.

"You could call him for me," I say, trying for a casual air that's about as easy-going as the Tasmanian devil on a triple espresso.

"Why would I do that?"

"Because you're my best friend and you love me."

"I am your best friend and I do love you, which is why I'm telling you, *again*, to call your father back." I'd been slightly (very) taken aback at Nate's suggestion that I return the call after that first message. It wasn't just me Dad hurt when he left. Nate had loved him like a father.

"I don't want to hear his excuses," I say.

"It's been sixteen years. Maybe it's time to forgive and move on."

I stare at him as though he's just sprouted a second head. "It's been *seventeen* years. And no."

I inherited my mom's stubborn streak. And the grudge-holding gene. Not to mention the sometimes-immature responses to suggestions I don't want to hear.

"There might be a good reason he's reaching out now," Nate says.

I study Nate suspiciously. Does he know something about Dad's sudden reappearance? "I'm sure there is. And I'm sure I don't care."

The stove dings and, thankfully, Nate turns his attention to extracting the lasagna. I've been given a reprieve, at least for a couple of minutes. Nate sets the hot Pyrex onto the stovetop and turns off the oven. The smell reminds me that I've barely eaten today.

"Let's eat," Nate answers my rumbling stomach.

I take the plate he holds for me and cut myself a square of lasagna. For a couple of minutes, the smell and heat wafting from the pan make me forget about my father and whatever reason he has for calling after so many years of silence.

"Want to watch a movie while we eat?" Nate asks as he prepares his plate with a portion double the size of mine.

"Sure," I answer. My dad would not approve of to the way Nate and I do Wednesday dinners.

Wednesday dinners were Dad's thing. He was an enthusiastic cook, thankfully because the only culinary skills my mom had were making coffee and ordering take-out (apparently, I inherited that from her, as well). Every Tuesday, dad and I would leaf through cooking magazines and pick a recipe, then Wednesday he'd pick me up from school and we'd go to the grocery together. While I did homework on the kitchen island, dad would cook. It was our time together, and I loved every minute.

When I first moved in with Maggie and Nate, I asked to continue the tradition. Yes, I know ... if I was so angry at my father for leaving, why would I continue a tradition he established? Obvious, isn't it? I thought if I kept at it, I wouldn't completely lose him. If I kept up with his weekly dinner tradition, he'd eventually come back for one of them.

Voicemails seventeen years later was not exactly how I'd imagined this working out.

Despite not wanting to care, I care. "What reason would he have for reaching out now after all this time?" I ask, following Nate to the couch.

"I don't know but David always had a solid reason for everything he did. Why would this time be any different?"

I hate that answer. It means that there was a good reason he left in the first place. And then didn't return.

"Maybe he had a decent reason to leave, but I don't understand why he didn't call or come back even for a visit. Not one call or one surprise appearance, not even on our birthdays or when we graduated. That makes zero sense. That's not the man I grew up with." I fall silent.

None of this new. It's the same mixed up free-flow of emotions I go through every year at this time. Or anytime my thoughts travel to my dad.

"The only way to find out is by asking him."

It is. But asking him means learning the truth and learning the truth will mean ripping open wounds that aren't entirely healed.

Nate scrolls through the movie choices. He nixes my rom-com choice and I nix his sci-fi choice.

We end up with Apollo 13 because, well, rockets. We've seen it so many times we can recite pretty much any line. And usually do. But tonight, Nate stares at the screen as though he has no idea how it'll turn out, as though if he doesn't give it 100% of his attention, the mission will fail.

While NASA and the people of the 1970s breathlessly wait for the astronauts to re-enter the earth's atmosphere, Nate says, "I'm sorry about Monday."

It takes me a minute to switch from the movie to real life. "Sorry because you left me alone on Valentine's Day or sorry because you wish you'd spent Valentine's Day with me?"

"D, all of the above."

"Funny."

He flashes a toothy grin then snaps back to the movie.

I nudge his thigh with my foot. "You like her," I prod.

Nate leans forward, his eyes glued to the TV where the capsule has just appeared and the parachutes have deployed. I wait for it and ... there ... he exhales and sinks back into the couch. Now that we know the astronauts are safe, he allows a smile to spread.

"Yeah, I kinda do."

"Wow." The word pops out half playful, half stunned. I

mean, I figured he *kinda* liked her if he agreed to go out with her on Valentine's Day, but this has the feeling of something I haven't seen with him before.

"Are you going to finally tell me about her?" I ask when Nate doesn't offer more.

Nate's posture tightens, confirming my suspicion. "Just feels weird talking about it."

"It?" I tease but there's now a pit in my stomach that the teasing tone has a hard time getting around.

"The relationship," he corrects himself.

"Why?" I ask. He's never held back. Not with Sheila Underhill who he was convinced he'd spend the rest of his life with until he met Danielle Kipp two months later. Or with Terri Dunberry who wasn't very subtle in her desire for wedded bliss.

"What did you end up doing?" Nate detours the conversation.

"Mexican," which he already knows. "And I watched Sleepless in Seattle for the bazillionth time and got weepy in all the usual spots."

"I can't leave you alone for a minute, can I?" Nate shakes his head in mock disbelief. If he'd been with me, he would have teased but he'd be sniffling right along with me.

"What can I say, I'm predictable that way."

"You're predictable in every way."

"Am not."

"Are too."

"Take that back." I cross my arms and pout. I did mention how mature we can be, right?

"Name one surprising thing you've done recently," Nate challenges.

When it takes me too long to come up with an answer, he adds a smug, "That's what I thought."

After a couple of minutes of quiet while I try to come up

with a smart comeback (and fail), I ask, "You really think I should call him back?"

"I really do. If not for him, then for yourself."

"For myself? The better thing for me would have been if he'd never called."

Nate purses his lips but lets it drop.

Protecting myself is what I do best. I've perfected the leaving-before-left approach and I can't imagine why I would willingly open the door and let someone back in after they've trashed my heart once already.

Nate starts the movie he'd vetoed earlier, You've Got Mail, keeping with my Meg Ryan, Tom Hanks streak, and holds his arm up for me to snuggle next to him. I scoot closer without a second thought. Only once I'm tucked under his arm, head resting on his chest and a blanket wrapped around both of us does the thought that he may have done this very same thing with Beth yesterday flits through my brain.

I shove the thought away and snuggle deeper against Nate.

# 5

# BE HONEST, BE NICE, BE A FLOWER NOT A WEED.

— AARON NEVILLE

There are days, like today, when I'm extra grateful for my down-the-stairs commute. Somewhere around 2:00 a.m. it started raining and hasn't let up yet. It's as dark outside at noon as it was when Nate texted at 5:30 a.m. to complain that the thunder woke him up. The real reason he texted at 5:30 was to check on me. Thunderstorms scare me, always have.

When I was little, I'd crawl into bed with my parents. Dad would usually carry me back to my room and snuggle with me until I fell asleep again. If Nate was sleeping over, he'd slip down from the top bunk to shield me from the storm monsters. And if he wasn't at my house, all I had to do was look out my bedroom window to see him waving from his window.

He still checks on me. He's even shown up "to hang out" when storms are in the forecast.

Lulu isn't a fan either. Storms are one of the few times she lowers her standards and leaps into bed with me. Usually she'll sleep at the edge of the bed and attack my feet if I move too much (maybe there's something to that whole starfish thing after all). But storms get her tucked next to me under the blanket.

I don't usually allow Lou to wander around the store when we're open, but I didn't have the heart to leave her upstairs this morning. We've been open for two hours and not one person has come in. Not that I'm complaining.

Another crack of lightning rattles the window and Lulu skitters to my side.

"It's okay, baby. We're safe in here." I run my hand from the top of her head to her tail and she leans into me. Here's the upside to storms, my cat finally appreciates me.

I wasn't lying to Lulu, we are safe here. Fancy Fleur is where I feel most at peace. It's where I can be me. There's an energy and a stillness when I'm among flowers that only exists here. The store is the one place where I can, usually at least, push aside the headaches and heartaches of real life.

Maggie let me start "working here" when I was little. Back then, she paid me with the flowers that weren't up to snuff for customers and an end of the week ice cream bonus. Fancy Fleur became the place I escaped to when I needed an emotional boost and mental peace. Even before I learned about the hidden language of flowers, I sensed their magic. They talked to me. And I learned to communicate through them.

It was only a matter of time then before my influence on the store became more obvious. It started with the wood and iron shelves I found at a flea market. Shelves that now showcase local artists. I hung strings of firefly lights that crisscross the ceiling and, on days like today, create a cozy, magical space. Maggie happily allowed me to add my personal touch to the space. The only thing that caused a rumble from Maggie is the painting on the far wall of the store.

I saw the drawing in a dream that had jumped from a tender, sweet kiss with some nameless man who could have been Nate or Chris Hemsworth even though they look nothing alike, to running to catch a bus despite never having taken public transportation my entire life, to ordering a coffee in a café and having my father appear as the waiter. The coffee mug had an ivy pattern painted along the bottom and there'd been a picture of ivy on the side of the bus. I never could figure out the connection with the kiss (although I'd insisted we watch Thor that night and spent an uncomfortable amount of time staring at Nate until he called me out).

But the ivy had stayed in my brain, and I found myself doodling it. Nate found one of the drawings and convinced his mom it belonged on the wall. I look now at the ornate lettering spelling out "Leaf an impression," ivy entwined around the letters and sprites and fairies and cupids woven among the leaves. It's playful, surprising, and never fails to elicit a smile.

Lulu nibbles at a sunflower petal. "Don't do that." I shoo her aside and replace the chewed stem with a fresh one. Into the cooler the vase goes before the arrangement becomes salad for the cat.

"You better get off the table before Maggie gets here or we're both in big trouble." Lulu responds by swishing her tail and walking away, only to sit at the other end of the table just out of my reach. So much for me being her support person.

"What are you going to be in trouble about once I get here?" Maggie's voice comes from behind me.

I whirl around, heart pounding. "Shit you surprised me. I didn't hear the alarm."

"Obviously or you would've sent that fur ball flying from the table." Maggie glares at me then gives Lulu a loving scratch on the chin. Lulu accepts the affection, then repositions, stretching a hind leg above her head and proceeds to clean the back of her leg.

"Manners," I whisper to the cat as I scoop her up and deposit her on the floor.

"Anyone come in?" Maggie asks.

"Nope. Do you blame them?"

"God no. It's awful out there." For someone who's lived her entire life in Maryland with its unpredictably predictable crap weather, Maggie is the first to complain at every weather change. She hates the bitter cold of winters, despises snow, can't tolerate the hot muggy summers, and you don't want to hear her rants on the long drawn-out rainstorms.

Which is why I attempt to cut her off before she can launch into another weather tirade. "You could have stayed home. It's not like we have a ton of orders to fill and if this continues, the Friday walk-ins will be a handful of brave swimmers if we're lucky."

Maggie gives me the side-eye as she shakes out her hair. "I always come in."

That would be an accurate statement. I can count on both hands the number of times she's left the store in someone else's care for more than a couple of hours and on one hand the number of times she's actually gone away for a few days.

"Anyway," she continues, "I need to talk to you."

"Uh oh." I stop trimming the ends of the Gerbera Daisies that came in yesterday. The last time she announced we needed to have a talk, it turned out to be an intervention on my dating, or lack of. Despite staying single for more than 25 years, Maggie is a romantic at heart. She whole-heartedly believes that life is better with love. I don't disagree, I just don't think I'm destined to have that sort of love.

Lulu jumps back up on the table and bumps at Maggie's arms. "Hey, baby," Maggie coos. Lulu chirps. "Are you being a naughty little girl? Because you know you're not supposed to be up here." Lulu lets out another I-adore-you chirp.

"I swear that cat." I roll my eyes at her betrayal.

Before Maggie can switch her attention back to whatever she wanted to talk to me about, my phone buzzes with an incoming call and a new text. I stare at it until the buzzing stops and the screen goes black, only to light up with the silent scolding that I've yet again dodged my father.

Maggie is staring at me.

"What?" I demand.

"You don't answer your calls anymore?" From the set of her mouth, I see it, she knows exactly who it was.

"Not when it's someone I don't want to talk to."

"You should," she says. I detect an edge to her tone but she's bent over fussing on Lulu so I can't read her face. This is what she wanted to talk to me about.

"You've spoken to him." It's an accusation, not a question.

Maggie nods. "You should return his calls."

Seventeen years of hurt, of wondering, bubble to the surface. "Why? Why do I have to answer now? Because he finally remembered he has a family?"

Maggie straightens but her eyes remain on the cat. "That's not how this is, Callie." The fact that she appears to be siding with him fuels my anger. Of all people, Maggie is the last I'd expect to soften toward David Ecker. She took his leaving and the impact it had on us as a personal stab to the heart. He'd stepped in as the male role-model for Maggie's boys when her husband died. And he'd been the brother she'd always wanted.

He left all of us. Not just me.

"How is it then? The man walked out the door without a word of explanation. And for half of my life, only bothered to send a few dinky postcards. Now he wants to catch up and I'm supposed to run to him with open arms. Yeah, no."

"I know you're angry. I'm in no way suggesting that you blindly forgive him. But there comes a time when we need to move on. If not for him, then do it for yourself."

I've spent half my life wondering what made me so unlovable that even my own father hadn't stuck around. So no, I don't see why I need to open myself up to him again.

"Just think about it," Maggie says before pulling me into a

hug that snaps away the protective thorns I've planted around my heart.

❧

AFTER THE LONGEST of busy-being-not-busy days, I'm looking forward to an evening with Nate. At least until I walk into the restaurant and realize his invite hadn't been just a friendly, "let's hang out together because I've missed you and I know it's been a shitty day" invite. Sitting next to Nate at the high-top table in the bar, their knees touching, is the reason I spent Valentine's Day bribing my cat to snuggle with me.

I plaster on a smile as I make my way through the tables. Nate half-stands as I arrive and gives me a side-hug, the kind of hug you give a friendly friend, not your best friend who's known you since before you could feed yourself.

"I'm glad you could join us," he says, settling back on the bar stool, an inch closer to the pretty blonde as though to reassure her that she has top billing.

For once, I catch myself before any sassy remark escapes, because, yeah, what plans would I have? Take-out, a movie, and a cat. Two out of those three at least. Lulu is still holding a grudge after I put her back in the apartment when she ate the third yellow rose for an anniversary arrangement. Yellow rose for friendship, joy, and according to some cultures, enduring love. Can't blame Lou for wanting to nibble a reality check into overly cheerful flowers.

"Callie, this is Beth. Beth, Callie," Nate makes the introductions. I turn, ready to shake her hand from across the table, only to realize she's standing in my personal bubble and pulling me into a hug.

"I've been dying to meet you. I've heard so much about you. All amazing, of course." She doesn't pause for a breath until she pulls away.

Now that she's standing, I get the full picture of how ridiculously cute she is. Beth is a head shorter than me with glistening highlights in already shiny golden hair. Her features look like they were sculpted by an artist (and no, not a plastic surgeon artist; she's all nature made). And the worst part, she radiates an easiness that makes me want to beg her to be my best friend.

I can't decide if I want to love her or hate her.

"It's nice to meet you," I say, taking a step back into my personal bubble. Her gushing excitement makes me uncomfortable.

Then there's the way Nate beams at her.

I slide onto an empty seat at the high-top, surprised to find a gin and tonic waiting for me. It's my usual, need-a-fix drink but not something I order often. Nate clearly anticipated that this evening will require extra reinforcements.

"I have a confession," Beth says, reaching across the table and grabbing my hand. "I was in Fancy Fleur the other day."

Nate looks at her with the same surprise I feel. My mind hop-skips through the various customers who've come through, but I can't remember seeing her. She's the type of person you notice.

"You were working in the back," she adds as though reading my mind. Or my face? I feel the blush of embarrassment. "I wasn't trying to be creepy. Nate talks so much about the store and his mom, and you, obviously, and I was so nervous about meeting you. I just wanted to see you before we actually met. You know, sort of scope out the competition even though you're not *competition* competition but you know what I mean."

She was nervous over someone like me?

"You should have said hi," I say.

"You seemed very focused." She looks shy admitting that she'd been scoping me out. "And, I admit, I was mesmerized by the look on your face as you put the flowers together."

I feel instantly exposed and acutely aware of every imperfect feature. What do I look like to others, especially when I'm not actively trying to will my face into being less plain (not that will power actually helps, but you can't blame a girl for clinging to hope)?

"I have so much admiration for your creativity. I have ..." she holds up her fingers into a zero sign.

I'm totally judging this book by her cover, but I'd peg her as full of creative flair. From the scarf, casually and expertly looped around her neck and the unique earrings that could have only come from an artsy boutique, the unassuming beige sweater and the perfectly distressed jeans. I close my eyes, allowing the feeling to settle. Beth is a Gardenia. Refined, elegant, heady. A mystical flower associated with positive energy and attraction.

I struggle to find a question that won't give away the fact that Nate hasn't said much, anything really, about her. Yet he's talked to her about me. That tiny fact makes me incredibly uneasy.

"It takes plenty of creativity to teach high school," Nate says, sending me a lifeline. "Getting teenagers to take an interest in science and space is its own talent."

Science. Space. Of course.

"Another nerd," I tease. "I'm fascinated but it's over my head. Poor Nate gave up trying to draw me into his space world."

"Callie's hopeless," Nate agrees. He stretches his arm across the space between him and Beth, resting it on the back of her chair, and adds, "It's nice to finally be around someone outside of work who doesn't roll her eyes when I start talking about work."

They exchange a quick look before Beth dips her eyes to the drink she cradles in her hands. Umm, what just happened? I stare at Nate. Lust, I've seen. Infatuation, I've lived through with him. But this is a look that doesn't match anything I've witnessed with Nate before.

"How did you guys meet?" I ask, pulling my eyes back to Beth. It's the question everyone loves and hates.

"At a job fair, believe it or not," Beth says. She gives Nate the slightest of smiles, her eyes lingering on him for just the time it takes to make me squirm.

"Trying to decide what you want to be when you grow up?" I tease Nate.

"Ha, ha. They have different professionals talk to the kids about career paths. I was one of the lucky ones volunteered to attend by HR." He says this as though it had been a chore but the way his mouth twitches into a smile makes clear that it was a chore that had a good payoff in the end.

"I remember those job fairs," I say. "At least, I remember being fascinated by a flight attendant."

"You hate flying," Nate declares.

"I hate flying," I confirm to Beth.

"I don't mind it, but I much prefer road trips," she says.

"Now you're talking. Music, snacks, detours," I add.

"More pee breaks than actual driving," Nate grumbles.

I glare at him and Beth giggles.

"I drink a lot of water," I defend myself.

"Yeah, that's the reason."

"You suck."

Beth watches our exchange with the smile of someone who's getting a behind-the-scenes look into a favorite program.

"You guys are exactly like Nate described."

"Bickering siblings?" I ask.

"A combination of bickering siblings and an old married couple," Beth says with a laugh.

"Eww," Nate and I say at the same time.

Around us, the restaurant is filling up, the noise multiplying with each new arrival and every drink consumed.

Beth, I hate to admit, is easy to talk to and has a wicked sense of humor. I enjoy seeing her tease Nate as much as I enjoy doing it myself. After three rounds of appetizers and drinks, I'm still searching for something to dislike about her. The only thing I don't like is the way he's looking at her.

# 6

# THE OPTIMIST SEES THE ROSE AND NOT ITS THORNS; THE PESSIMIST STARES AT THE THORNS, OBLIVIOUS TO THE ROSE.

— KAHLIL GIBRAN

There are car people and then there's me. Don't get me wrong, I love a nice car as much as the next gal, but my criteria is more about comfort and looks. Of course, it has to be reliable and solid, but I don't care how many ponies gallop under the hood or how fast they get out of the gate. And the price is the price, right?

Six years ago, my old Toyota crossed the metal bridge and I'd dragged Nate in search of a replacement. The moment we walked into the Volkswagen dealership I'd fallen in love with a red Beetle with black leather interior. It had an upgraded sound system, heated front seats, and the cutest logo that doubled as the latch for the trunk.

"You don't buy a car because the logo is cute or the sales guy is nice," Nate had groused at me when I'd agreed to the quote because the sales dude said it was a great price and it was the only car with my wish list of features. It was within my budget and that logo!

Nate had stepped in, calling BS, and shuttled me out of the

dealership. I'd pouted until Nate showed me a listing for an identical car, $3,000 cheaper.

Today we're looking for a car for him. "What about that one?" I point at a red sedan.

"Really? Do I look like someone who would drive a little red car?"

"No, but I do." I bend to read the specs taped to the window.

"You're a girl."

"Are you saying only girls drive little red cars? This one has heated rear seats." I tap at the window.

Nate leans forward, cupping his hands around his face to get a better view inside a dark gray SUV. "Well, yeah. And why does it matter about the rear seats? You don't sit back there."

"What if I have friends with me. Or kids. And that's sexist." I slap at his upper body.

He flashes a cheeky grin. "Took you long enough."

I roll my eyes and continue down the line of cars. "Why again are you looking for a new car? Yours is brand new." Three years isn't technically brand new, but he babies his cars and compared to the 14 years I had my previous car, three seems pretty damn new. Unlike me, Nate is a car person. Unlike me, Nate pours over reviews and researches each new model within an inch of its rubber tread. And unlike me, Nate chooses his cars by ponies and speed and power and safety and reliability.

"Rhetorical?" He asks which, in itself, is rhetorical because we have this exact conversation every time his lease is up.

"I like this one," I say, wandering away from the SUV toward a sleek black coup.

"Of course you do. I'm looking for something more practical."

"What's practical about that?" I point at the SUV he's circling like a dog marking his territory.

He doesn't answer. It's another of those discussions we've

had many times over the years. I don't get his desire for large cars. He doesn't understand my aversion to them.

"Beth really enjoyed meeting you," Nate changes the subject as we shimmy between two packed rows of SUVs.

"You talked about me after I left?" A tingle of insecurity dislodges a bead of sweat. I know previous girlfriends have queried our relationship but Nate has never reported that any of them said they "enjoyed meeting" me. Some were jealous, some were dismissive, most thought our relationship was just weird. The concept of a platonic best friend dynamic between a man and a woman doesn't compute for most people.

"Of course." He stops to read the specs for an even larger SUV than the previous one.

"Keep walking. You don't need something that massive. Unless you and Beth are planning on getting married and starting your own soccer team?" I raise an eyebrow which isn't very effective behind my sunglasses. And despite the joking tone, the thought makes my stomach somersault. A feeling I will need to unpack at some point.

But first, I have to save Nate from himself. I make my way to a dark gray car that looks like a stunted SUV. "Did you look at this one? It's cute."

"You've gotta stop using the word 'cute' when talking to me about cars."

"But it is. Look at it."

"Do I really look like someone who would drive a 'cute' car?" He flexes his upper body.

I snort. Although he's not wrong, Nate defies the nerd stereotype. Not only did he get the smarts, but he's got a body that looks as though he could bench press the rockets he works on.

"Fine. How about his one, it's not cute." I lead the way to a compromise SUV, larger than the one I like, smaller than the ones he likes.

"Not bad," Nate concedes.

"What did she say?" I steer the conversation back to their post-dinner discussion about moi, curiosity getting the better of me. I do want to know what she thinks. Maybe because I enjoyed the evening more than I want to admit, maybe because there's power in knowledge. Probably just because I want to make a good impression.

"What do you think of Beth?" He's staring at the laundry list of features taped to the window of the car although I'd bet all $63,245 of that sticker price that he's not seeing it.

"Nope. You tell me first." I rehearsed what to say about her, more so because I needed to sort out how I felt versus how I wanted to feel. Everything about her seems different from anyone else Nate has ever dated and though he always asks what I think, this is the first time he really seems to want my approval.

Nate huffs his frustration at me. Or maybe at not finding the car he wants because he's leading the way to another SUV down the line. Finally, he says, "She thinks you're great."

I motion for him to continue. Not because I'm looking for praise, but because I can hear a but in there.

"But?" I prompt when he doesn't say anything.

"But nothing," Nate says, with an exaggerated eyeroll.

Sometimes I really do hate that he knows me so well.

Nate waves at a sales guy who's been hovering far enough away to give the illusion of minding his own business but close enough to claim us as his victory sale.

"Beth thinks you're nice," he emphasizes, then hesitates before adding, "but she thinks you won't approve of anyone I date because of our history."

I laugh. "Our history? She does know we were never a thing, right?" What should have been nothing more than a "duh" response on my end, feels oddly un-breezy.

"Of course. But she's not wrong, either. The fact that we've been best friends since the day we were born intimidates most people. We have a special bond."

"So special that you punched me the first day we met." Mom and Maggie love telling the story how they'd insisted the nurses put us in the same bassinet in the hospital and Nate backhanded me when I started to cry.

"I was establishing hierarchy."

"You were a bully."

"I was the big brother."

The sales guy marches over, hand extended. He pumps Nate's hand, but I duck to the other side of the vehicle before he can reach for me. Nate chuckles at my dislike of public displays of pleasantness with strangers. Weird for someone who works in retail, I know. It's why I rarely man the front of the store.

Finally, we settle into the car of Nate's dreams for a test drive. We barely make it out of the parking lot before he starts in on me again. "You didn't answer earlier."

"Answer what?" I know what he wants to hear. Beth is unarguably fabulous. Too fabulous. Is it possible that Nate has found his one? I should be happy for him. I *am* happy for him. Then why do I feel a tightening in my stomach that has nothing to do with the speed with which Nate just took the turn?

"How you feel about the truck," Nate deadpans.

"It's cushy," I answer, running my hand along the edge of the expensive leather seat. I open the window halfway, then close it, open it all the way, then close it. I fiddle with the temperature, then the vents.

"Stop touching everything. You're making me twitchy."

"I'm just making sure it meets our standards."

"*We* have standards?"

"*We* have standards."

Nate slaps at my hand when I reach for the radio dial. "Sit still will you. You're getting your grubby fingerprints all over."

"They'll wash it before handing you the keys. Relax."

"Why do I bring you with me?" He says this every time.

"Because you love me and you value my opinion." I say this every time, too.

"For better or worse. Mostly worse," Nate mumbles under his breath, knowing full well I heard what he said.

"For better, for worse, in sickness and in health." I steal a look at Nate.

"You forgot richer or poorer."

"How about love and cherish?"

"How about love and strangle?" Nate's mouth twitches into a smile.

"Till death do us part," I add with a verbal flourish.

For the first time in 32 years and 10 months, we fall into an awkward silence. The silly pact we made 13 years ago, the pact that was never a "real" reality yet always the inevitable reality, suddenly seems precariously positioned at the edge of the Beth cliff.

# 7

## WEEDS ARE FLOWERS TOO, ONCE YOU GET TO KNOW THEM.
### — A. A. MILNE

The front door of the store opens and Tish, the ceramic artist who sells some of her pieces through Fancy Fleur, lumbers inside under the weight of a box. She sets it on the counter and shakes out her arms. "I've been delivering orders all morning. My arms feel a foot longer." She chortles at her arm-foot joke. "I hope you'll like these. They're a bit different from others I've done."

Tish is an interesting combination of confident and socially awkward, flakey and brilliant. In the two years I've known her, I feel as thrown every time she walks into the store as that first time. Partly because of her looks, partly because of her insane knowledge of pretty much any topic.

She moved into the apartment above the art gallery on the other side of the courtyard from Fancy Fleur in a flurry of excitement and banging. Unlike our row of live-work units, the ones on the other side of the courtyard have detached garages in the back. With the arrival of Tish, the owners of the gallery transformed their garage to a pottery studio.

The neighbors were not amused. Not the elderly couple who own the yarn store to the left of the gallery or the people in the townhouses that share the alley. Drama ensued, the community management company got involved, sides were taken.

And Maggie, as one of the few remaining original owners of a live-work property in the community, found herself, of course, at the center of the hoopla. She'd sworn to shun the new arrival until said new arrival waltzed into Fancy Fleur with her mermaid-dyed hair and a box of the cutest ceramic vases, each different, each carved with a cute saying or image of a flower.

"Let's see what you've got for us," I say opening the box Tish brought in. Every delivery from her feels like the perfect marriage of Christmas and Hanukkah.

Maggie has tried ordering specific vases, but Tish claims the clay decides what it wants, not her. We've learned to expect the unexpected. She's never disappointed us.

Today's delivery includes a vase in shades from green at the bottom to cream at the top. Etched into the side are the words, *Flowers are happiness*. I unwrap another vase in a sunset of yellows and oranges with an etched outline of a sunflower.

"These are gorgeous," I say, removing the rest of the vases and lining them up on the counter.

Tish suddenly holds up a hand and cocks her head. I adjust my hearing, wondering what we're listening for. There's nothing strange coming from upstairs or the back room or outside as far as I can hear. Just the faint strains of music from the speaker under the counter.

"Rachmaninoff. Rhapsody on a Theme of Paganini. Variation 17, I believe," Tish says, punctuating the 'I believe' with a pointer finger. "You know he performed it himself for the premier? In Baltimore of all places. November 7, 1924. I wish I could have been there for that. Well, I wish I remembered being there. I know my previous incarnation was there."

My mouth drops and I force it shut. (A) How did she know all of that, and (B) previous incarnation?

Tish shrugs. "What? I know my music. Most people assume I'm a rocker or I don't know what they assume." She gestures at her appearance which today includes hot pink hair, a tight black crop T-shirt, ripped black jeans, and combat boots. Coupled with dramatic black eyeliner and bright red lipstick, she could easily pass for an anime character. "There's so much chaos in the world already that I don't feel it necessary to add more into my head. I find classical music inspiring and grounding."

That explains the music part.

Hard to disagree with the chaos in the world and the grounding effect of classical music. Although as a kid, I disagreed plenty. Mostly about opera though. And mostly because my mother loved it so much.

Granted, Mom works in the opera world, but she also seems to live that world. My mother takes on life with the intensity of opening night at the Kennedy Center. That very ferocity that drives her passion often overflows into life. Like the time she palmed a handful of laxatives because the size four cocktail dress that she wanted to wear the following weekend felt snug. She'd gotten so sick and dehydrated from the diarrhea and vomiting that my dad insisted she go to the hospital. "Not until I change clothes and put on a swipe of lipstick," had been her answer.

It was my father who taught me to appreciate classical music. Plus, the plants love it. Opera less so. The Ficus in my apartment drops his leaves when I play opera. Although, he seems to enjoy Puccini for some reason. The fig tree has a definite preference for Vivaldi, even though (or perhaps because of) the lemon tree's dislike for it. The lemon tree has a thing for Stravinsky. Go figure.

"This vase would be perfect for that arrangement," Tish

says, holding up a vase in a watercolor mix of blues and greens with an artistic heart etched into the side. No words needed.

"I think you're right," I say, transferring the flowers into Tish's vase.

"Gorgeous." Tish reaches out a gentle finger toward a white gardenia.

The mission for this bouquet is simple, open the heart of the recipient. Gardenia for secret love, daffodils for honesty and truth, gladiolus for infatuation, and ivy for affection.

"Who's it for?" Tish wiggles a precisely plucked eyebrow.

"Whoever needs it." My face flushes giving away that I hadn't exactly created it in a random burst of inspiration. I've been preoccupied this morning with thoughts of Nate and Beth and me as the spinster aunt who spends her life talking to cats and plants.

"Who would you give it to?" Tish rests her elbows on the counter, face in palms, looking at me as though I'm about to reveal a big secret.

Who, indeed? No one, truly no one. But that's boring, so I say, "Chris Hemsworth."

Tish suddenly straightens, her playful grin turning slightly devilish. "Or him," she indicates over my shoulder with a twitch of eyebrow.

"What did I do, now?" Nate says from behind.

"Everything."

Tish laughs. "I swear. You two need to just hurry up and get married."

I roll my eyes at the same time Nate makes a gagging face. Yup, we're mature adults.

"It's the perfect love story," Tish says.

"You mean dramady," Nate answers.

"Murder mystery without the mystery if we had to live together," I add.

"I'm serious," Tish says, laughing.

"I never took you for a romantic," I say, surprised at the swoony look on her face.

"I'm full of surprises. I'm good at reading people. You two belong together."

Nate makes a dubious face and shakes his head. "She snores, has no idea how to change a tire, and can't cook anything that requires more than three ingredients."

"Hey," I protest, tossing the clipped end of a daffodil stem at him. "He's not wrong," I say turning back to Tish. "Then again, he's got the romantic tendencies of a tumble weed and hasn't yet figured out how to pull the duvet cover up and plump the pillows when he gets out of bed."

Tish holds up a hand to extract herself from the middle of what could easily turn into a full-on bicker-fest of who does, or doesn't do, what.

We watch as she departs with the tinkle of the bell over the front door. I elbow Nate. "Close your mouth, you're dating someone."

Suddenly self-conscious, I tuck a curl behind my ear, only to have it bounce back and poke me in the eye. My jeans have similar rips in similar places to the ones Tish wears except that mine have a ready-for-the-dumpster look versus Tish's Instagram-ready vibe.

"She's too young for me, anyway."

"She's 23. How old is Beth?" I'm usually a decent judge of age range but I couldn't get a good read on Beth. First thought was our age, then I'd amended that to early twenties but that didn't feel right either. Maybe it was her teen crush expression that threw off my radar.

"She just turned 29."

"Just?"

"Two months ago."

"Hm," I mumble. I want to ask if he bought her something, if they were already "kinda" seeing each other, but when I see the look on his face all the good-will I was nurturing for Beth wilts faster than dehydrated daisies.

"You're ditching me again," I accuse.

"I am. I'm sorry. Beth asked me to come to the school open house with her tonight."

"How romantic." I try for a breezy tone. I fail. It's Wednesday.

"Funny. Her booth is about space programs. She thought it would liven things up if I was there to answer questions."

"Ah," I say.

To his credit, Nate looks apologetic. "I know it's Wednesday and I'm sorry for bailing. I'll make it up to you, I promise. It's just this one time."

"In addition to Valentine's Day and Friday night and ..." I throw my hands up in who-knows-what-else gesture. "Fine." It's not fine but what am I going to say? Then I notice that he's eyeballing the arrangement I've just finished. "Oh for god's sake. Really?"

"It's beautiful."

So that's why the Gardenia insisted on being included. Beth.

I sigh. I'm not sure Nate needs any extra help gaining Beth's affection but who am I to stand between flowers and their mission? I tie a green ribbon around the stems and hand the vase to Nate.

"You're the best. Put it on my account?"

"You don't have an account."

"Then we should start one. That's something I need to talk to you about but I'm late, so it'll have to wait. Tomorrow?"

"Nate?"

"Tomorrow." He kisses me on the cheek and before I can protest, he's off to meet his perfect new girlfriend.

# 8

# THE FAIREST THING IN NATURE, A FLOWER, STILL HAS ITS ROOTS IN EARTH AND MANURE.

## — D.H. LAWRENCE

The food I'd bought this morning for our Wednesday dinner mocks me from the fridge as I break off the end of the baguette and stuff it in my mouth. Is eating an entire baguette from the paper bag akin to drinking an entire bottle of wine from a paper bag?

Wine.

I open the bottle the guy at the store said paired well with the salmon I won't be cooking. Wine in hand, I walk to the wall of windows in the living room and rest my forehead on the cold glass, which serves to both ease the headache I've been battling since Nate broke the news and dull my reflection.

My little feline shadow winds herself between my legs but when I don't respond, she gives me a gentle bite on the calf.

"Fine, I'll open."

She responds with another nibble.

"I'm not your chew toy." I lift my right leg before she can give me yet another love bite as Nate calls them. Personally, I can think of better ways of showing affection.

The moment I open the door, Lulu slips her head between

the wrought iron railing. The balcony is far too narrow for anything more than a few pots and a small cat. It's also, perhaps, the best part of the apartment. Well, this and the fact that it's mostly free and makes my commute as simple as walking down a flight of stairs. There's a quaint Frenchness to the balcony that I adore. I can't count how many hours over the years I've wedged myself between the railing and the French doors and people watched.

During the summer, the pots are full of herbs and cherry tomatoes, a buffet for the neighborhood birds. Now they look like a miniature haunted forest.

I shiver deeper into my favorite chenille throw, and perch on the concrete ledge. It's cold enough that even Lulu steps onto my lap. I wrap the blanket around her and she rewards me by starting to purr.

We don't stay like that for long, it's too cold and the concrete ledge is too uncomfortable. Well, I don't stay like that for long. Lulu could have stayed longer in her comfy, warm spot. She gives me a look of utter disgust before going inside, jumping onto the couch, and positioning herself in my corner.

I refill the wine despite having barely drunk a quarter of my original pour. It's good. The guy at the store was right, but it doesn't taste as good drinking it alone, no offense to Lulu.

I reach for my phone and snap a picture of the glass. I type "pour you one?" then delete it, then type it again, and delete it again. He's busy with Beth.

"What do you think Lou? Should we watch a movie?" I flip on the TV and surf through a dozen channels before turning it off. "Okay, no TV. What should we do then?" She yawns, stretches, rolls onto her back and promptly falls asleep. If only I was a cat.

The unopened voice message on my phone glares at me like a guilt-tripping Jewish grandmother. He called again this after-noon. I'd stared at my phone when the number appeared and counted the number of rings before it went into voicemail. That's four calls in one week.

A sigh, loud enough to disrupt Lulu's slumber, escapes from me as I make the call.

"Hi, Mom," I say when she picks up on the third ring. She's out of breath and someplace with a lot of noise. "Did I catch you at a bad time?" I glance at the clock. It's almost 9:00 p.m. for me which means 7:00 p.m. for her.

"No, no, I'm home. Give me a minute." There's more muffled noise then complete silence. I stare at the phone to see if she's disconnected the call. "Okay, that's better." Now all I can hear is her breathing and the sound of the fountain on her patio.

"Mom, are you having a party and didn't invite me?" I tease.

Mom is an interesting combination of socially needy and social recluse. When I was young she'd get into a mood and declare that it was time to have a party. She'd throw herself into planning the shindig with the focus I saw her channel into her work. Like everything with my mom, her parties were epic. Always a theme, always elaborate, always exhausting—for her and anyone caught in her blast zone.

The day before a party, she'd have a meltdown and want to cancel which is when my father would step in to take care of the final details. The morning after, she'd wake on a cloud of exhilaration until the coffee kicked in and the left-behind mess came into focus. That's when she'd retreat to her room with a migraine until the house was spotless again thanks to my dad.

"I'm not having a party," she huffs. "But since you brought it up, we need to talk about you coming for a visit."

I blink once, twice. "I don't think I brought it up, actually," I hedge, then, before she can weave a magic spell to lure me into her southwestern web, I add, "I was hoping you'd come here next month. Nate and I are going to throw a party for our birthday."

Note to self: get Nate in on this plan now that I've set it in motion.

"It's not a good time for me to be away," mom says, and I can picture the dismissive wave of her hand.

The opera season doesn't start for a few more months. "You could just come for a long weekend." I can count on both hands, and still have fingers left over the number of times we've celebrated my birthday together since I turned 16. Well, 15 if we're being picky. Mom was a bit too preoccupied checking herself into the wellness facility in Santa Fe to remember my Sweet Sixteen which was as close to "sweet" as a cavity.

"Busy getting ready for the season?" I search my brain for any clues from previous conversations about the lineup for the upcoming season. I'm sure she's told me and I'm just as sure that I listened to only an eighth of any of those conversations.

It's not that I don't appreciate what she does, but I still have a smidge (or more) of childhood resentment that Mom chose a job across the country over me.

"There's just a lot happening, and I can't be away. It's too much to explain on the phone. You and Nate need to be here." She says this with a finality that's pure Mom.

"That's a lot of schedules to coordinate, Mom. Why can't you just come here? You haven't come for a visit in years."

"Why must everything be a negotiation, Callie?"

I didn't play my parents off each other intentionally. Mom defaulted to no and dad defaulted to yes. Negotiating got me to the half-way point at which Dad would then tip to yes more often than not.

"Fine," I mutter, not in a *fine I'll come* but in a *fine whatever you say*. "What's new on your end?" I change the subject before it turns into a battle of stubbornness. Why I thought of calling her when I'm already twitchy is a mystery. You'd think after all these years, I'd learn that mom isn't the one to call when I need a comforting pep-talk or sympathetic ear. That's Nate. But he's off playing Space God at the high school with his new girlfriend.

"Too much," she sighs.

I wait for her to continue. She always continues. She thrives on busyness and drama and no conversation is complete until she's relayed every she-said, she-did, I-said.

When she doesn't continue, I'm faced with a dilemma: nudge or move on to the next topic. Normally, I play along and give her the nudge I know she's waiting for. But the unopened voice messages tap at my patience bell.

"Have you heard from Dad?" I blurt.

"Shit," she hisses into the phone.

"Is that a shit about dad or a shit because you stepped on a cactus?"

"Have you talked to him?" Classic Mom non-response.

"I asked first."

Mom does this inhale through her teeth when she's close to boiling over. I don't want to fight with her.

In the background the sound of a car revving vibrates across the line from Santa Fe to Maryland.

"Those damn neighbors. They got some hotrod project car for their teenage son. He spends most of the afternoons and evenings in the garage working on it."

"Mom?" I wait.

"I've asked him to keep the noise down in the evenings. Why he needs to work on it every night is beyond me. I mean really, who needs something that big and noisy anyway? The world would be a better place if people stopped driving those polluting machines. And don't get me started on the volume of his music."

Technically, I hadn't gotten her started on the muscle car either.

"Mom?" I try again.

"Do you know that last weekend there were three of them

in the garage working on that car until almost 11 p.m.? At least there's the city noise ordinance otherwise they would've continued blaring music all night."

"Mom!"

"You don't have to yell, Callie. I heard you the first time."

*And yet you ignored me.*

"What does Dad want?"

"Oh for god's sake, now the dog on the other side is howling. This was such a nice, peaceful neighborhood when I bought the house. Callie, I need to go. Listen, Honey, I really need you to come for a visit. I'll call you tomorrow."

Before I can respond, the call disconnects.

I'm left feeling even more unsettled which I could have predicted if I'd given it half a thought. It's not that I don't get along with my mom, but rather we don't seem to know how to negotiate the mountain of eggshells without causing more damage.

And because the evening already stinks, I open the latest voicemail.

"Hi Callie. I know you're hurt and angry and probably hate me. If only I could reverse time, there are so many things I'd do differently. Leaving you, being away from you is the hardest thing I've done. I want, no, I need to explain. I've talked to your mom, obviously since I have your phone number. I'm rambling, I'm sorry. I'm nervous.

"Please let me explain. Even if you can't forgive me, at least give me the opportunity to apologize.

"I love you, I always have."

# 9

## IF YOU TEND TO A FLOWER, IT WILL BLOOM, NO MATTER HOW MANY WEEDS SURROUND IT.

### — MATSHONA DHLIWAYO

I don't believe in coincidences. I also don't believe, especially don't believe, that some higher power makes decisions about what each of us deserves or can handle or whatever rationale she (he?) uses to throw a giant bramble bush in our path. Case in point: Dad showing up after seventeen years, Mom's insistence yesterday that I need to come to Santa Fe, and Maggie's announcement this morning that she's going to Santa Fe.

"Maggie, it'll be fine," I say for the fourteenth time. It's not like I haven't worked here most of my life.

"Yes, yes, I know. But ..." she begins to protest again. Maggie is twitchier than I've seen her in ages. It's the Rose Ecker effect.

"I'm perfectly capable of running the store for a week." I hold up a hand to stop any further arguments. I can't tell if she's trying to find an excuse not to go or trying to reassure herself that it's okay to go.

She pulls her mouth into a tight line, deepening the creases above her upper lip. It's an uncharacteristically sour expression. Maggie is the most easy-going person I know. Even when it comes to my mother. Most of the time, at least.

"Maggie," I say, lassoing my frustration. Playing conversation dodgeball with these two may very well send me over the edge this time. "Is Mom okay?" The weirder than usual tone in Mom's voice yesterday brought back memories of the day she told me she was checking herself into the wellness "spa" and I'd be moving in with Maggie until further notice.

"She is."

"This has to do with Dad." I'm looking for confirmation even though the answer is obvious.

"Of course it does," she grumbles. The look on Maggie's face snaps me back seventeen years, to the look of betrayal and Mama Bear fury. Had he stayed around to face the fallout of his bombshell, I have no doubt Maggie would have introduced him to the sticky end of a fly swatter.

"Why is he calling, Maggie? What does he want?"

When he left, I'd blamed my mom. I couldn't see any reason for him leaving other than something she must have done to drive him away. It took a few years and more than a few degrees of maturity to realize the depth of what his abandonment had done to her. My anger shifted. And Maggie had been right there, fanning the flames.

Maggie whirls away from me at the sound of a customer.

"Look busy," she commands then turns with a Maggie smile to the customer.

"Hi," the woman says as she steps in and closes her umbrella. "It's really coming down out there."

"You're brave to venture out in it," Maggie says, offering to take the dripping umbrella.

I take the opportunity to escape and, gathering an armful of peonies, ease around Maggie and begin sorting them into buckets.

"Is there anything specific we can help you with?" Maggie asks.

"I'm just looking," the woman answers, then a beat later, "Actually, yes there is."

My ears prick to attention.

"It's my birthday. My mom always sent me flowers on my birthday, but she passed away seven months ago. And my fiancé used to give me flowers, but we broke up last month. So, um, I thought I'd buy some for myself."

"I'm a firm believer that the best flowers are the ones we treat ourselves to," Maggie says.

The Jasmine plant in the window appears to straighten, its rich, sweet smell a reminder that happiness is just a blossom away.

"I have just the thing," I say, surprising the birthday girl and Maggie. "Will you give me a couple of minutes to put something together?"

I remove one of Tish's creations from the shelf, a mug-shaped vase with the word "happy" etched into the side. A waterfall of blues and greens pool into a deep aqua base that matches the handle. Vase this week, mug next week. From the buckets, I pull daffodils for self-love and simple pleasures, crocus for healing and happiness, and a few bamboo stalks for good fortune and wishes. Something is missing though. I close my eyes and wait. Of course. Jasmine.

"These are my favorite," the birthday girl reaches out for a crocus. "My mom always included them in the bouquets she sent me."

"They're my favorite, too. Crocus is often seen as the harbinger of new beginnings." This is the arrangement I would prepare for myself, the perfect combination of comfort and hope, beauty and humbleness.

"Jasmine was my mother's favorite. How did you know?" She blinks back tears. From the corner of my eye, I catch

Maggie swallowing a moment of emotion. "And this vase ..." she trails off, finishing the sentence with her fingers as they trace the word in the ceramic.

"The artist lives right across from us," Maggie supplies, pointing across the courtyard. "Give it a good run through the dishwasher and, voila, you have a mug for a relaxing cup of tea."

"It's perfect," the woman repeats. "Thank you." She catches my eyes and there, in that look is the reason I love what I do.

Because flowers have a magic that can ease whatever hurt or ugliness or just plain nothingness that takes hold of our thoughts and emotions. Flowers remind us to raise our heads and take a breath.

# 10

# LOVE IS FLOWER LIKE. FRIENDSHIP IS LIKE A SHELTERING TREE.

— SAMUEL TAYLOR COLERIDGE

"Is it over yet?" I drop my head onto my arms in exhaustion. Thursdays aren't usually very busy but for some reason today we had non-stop walk-ins. Then there's the minor detail that the only other person working bailed a few hours ago to prepare for her trip to Santa Fe. So, what should have been a manageable load turned into chaos.

Thankfully, Nate stopped by on his way home with a much needed double shot chai latte, and moral support if not actual hands-on support.

Despite turning the sign to closed and locking the front door an hour ago, two people peeked in and knocked with urgent flower needs. I could have sent them on, it's not like the grocery store a block away doesn't have a decent bouquet selection. If it hadn't been for the spontaneous birthday arrangement this morning, I probably would have held my ground. But the glow of happiness on her face had given me that momentary bump of adrenaline each time another request came in.

There was the guy who forgot his anniversary and waded through five days of the silent treatment before figuring it out. For him, I'd prepared a simple arrangement of daffodils for forgiveness. And later I put together a congratulations bouquet for a customer to give her bestie on starting a new job, that included sunflowers for luck and ambition, and amaryllis as a sign of hard-won success.

Nate flips the overhead lights off and says, "Yup, I'm calling it. Want to get something to eat?"

I shake my head and sink into the one comfortable rolling chair with a sigh of relief.

"I can help clean up?" Nate offers. I shake my head again. "We could go upstairs and find something to watch?" When it's clear I'm not going anywhere, he slides over a chair from the other side of the worktable and plops down. "Or we can hang here."

"Ding, ding, we have a winner." I close my eyes to avoid seeing the scattered leaves and stem tips and snipped ends of ribbon littering the floor. I'll clean up later. Or tomorrow morning. Maggie won't be here so what's the harm as long as the store is ready when I unlock the front door?

"Any idea what our moms are up to?" Nate asks. "This trip seems to have come up rather suddenly, even for them."

"Not a clue."

"Something to do with your dad?"

I give him my best "duh" expression. "I just hope they're not planning on getting all Thelma and Louise on him."

Nate's eyebrows link. "That's not the duo you mean."

"I know, but they're the only ones who came to mind who would pull together and cause mayhem to support each other."

"Okay, I see how you got there. But what's so urgent to make my mom drop everything and fly across the country?"

"You should have heard my mom last night. Weirder than usual. She couldn't keep a thread going and the moment I asked about him, she practically pulled a muscle changing the subject. I wonder what he's up to."

"You would know if you returned his calls." Nate states the

obvious with an expression I suspect he picked up from teacher Beth.

"Yeah, but no."

"Don't you think you're taking this too far, Callie? I mean, the guy is your father. Yes, he screwed up but hear him out. Maybe he had a good reason?"

"Like what? He's a spy and spent the last fifteen years in a Canadian prison?"

"Canada?" Nate laughs.

"Don't laugh," I pout.

"Then stop being ridiculous. Call your dad and figure out what the hell is going on."

I soften. We have an unspoken agreement between us regarding our dads: we don't actually discuss them. We have opinions about our own dads but when it comes to each other's dad, we don't offer judgement or advice.

"Now, I have a favor to ask." Bossy, big brother Nate becomes shy best friend Nate.

"As long as it doesn't involve my parents or jumping from a plane, I'm in." I've never been able to resist when Nate asks for a favor.

"I need your help with Beth."

I stare, slack mouthed. When we were kids, I played courier multiple times between Nate and whatever crush he wanted to get closer to. And a couple of times in college he asked for an introduction to someone I was friendly with. But Beth? He seems to be doing just fine without me.

"Help with …? This better not be something weird she's convinced you to do."

"You really are impossible." He exhales, and I brace myself for what's next. "I like her, Callie."

"And she seems to like you. So what's the problem?"

"She's different from anyone I've ever dated. This will sound weird, but when I'm around her, the world just feels calm. I don't feel any pressure when we're together and she has this amazing knack for thoughtful gestures. Like the other day, she showed up at my house just as I was leaving for work with a hazelnut latte because the day before she ordered one and I commented that the smell reminded me of my grandmother, that it never failed to make me smile. She knew I had a big meeting that I was dreading, so brought one by."

I stare, mouth slightly open. Hazelnut lattes? How did I not know this? Of all the details I know about Nate, this one poignant nugget is something he shared with Beth, not me. He's been my best friend our entire lives and this simple, sweet detail is something he shared with someone else.

"That's very thoughtful," I say around a mouthful of cotton. Not only did I not know this about hazelnut, but I also didn't know he'd been stressed about work. That's something else he shared with her instead of me.

I drop my legs to the ground, wincing as feeling shoots back into my left foot.

"What's the favor?"

"Help me woo her."

"Woo?" I snort a laugh. "Who uses the word 'woo'?"

"I'm coming to you for help and all you can do is make fun of me?"

"I'm not making fun, I swear," I say, trying to cover the smile that refuses to be covered. "It's just such an unexpected word."

"What's wrong with it?"

"Old fashioned?"

"It fits her though. She's ... different."

I replay the night at the bar. Old fashioned is not how I would classify Beth. Perky. Perfect. Problematic.

"What exactly does helping you woo her entail?"

"You know me and romance. I suck at it. And I don't want to screw this up."

"Yeah, you are pretty challenged." I wipe the smirk off my face at his puppy dog expression.

There was the time Carmen (or maybe it was Rachel) let it slip she was planning a romantic anniversary dinner (in his defense, who celebrates a seven-month anniversary?). She'd bought him a pen that looked like a rocket (super cute). I'd taken pity on the girl and prompted Nate to buy her something, even offered to go with him (he declined). Bless his cluelessness, the guy showed up with a pair of running shoes because the week before Carmen/Rachel had casually mentioned she needed a new pair to start exercising again. You've got to give the guy props for listening at least.

"Why do you need help? She seemed pretty smitten from what I saw. Okay, okay," I concede, "How exactly am I supposed to help you woo her?"

"Use your magic charms with flowers to help me be romantic?"

I gesture around the store. "Voila, flowers."

"Callie!" He deflates into the chair.

"Yes, Nate, of course I'll help." Best friend me takes over. This is, after all Nate and there's no universe where I wouldn't move mountains to help him. "One problem," I say a minute later. "She knows I work here. She'll know who put the arrangements together."

"Yeah, but your arrangements aren't just groupings of flowers. You know what to combine to make magic happen." He looks like a little kid who's peeked behind the secret curtain. "But if the topic comes up," he starts, stops, looks around at the flowers around us.

"Yeah, yeah, don't worry." I lean forward and pluck a flower out of a bucket by my feet and hand it to Nate. It's a lovely white chrysanthemum for loyalty. "Mum's the word."

Helping people express their thoughts and feelings is part

of the job but this time, I'll be playing Cyrano for my best friend.

68 ORLY KONIG

of the job but this time, I'll be playing Cyrano for my best friend.

# 11

## NO MATTER HOW CHAOTIC IT IS, WILDFLOWERS WILL STILL SPRING UP IN THE MIDDLE OF NOWHERE.

— SHERYL CROW

I never liked the saying "when it rains it pours." Partly because I actually like rain, but, also, it makes zero sense. Except today, I feel like I woke up armpit deep in that cliché. Someone appears to have opened the flood gates and I'm on the wrong side.

Maggie's abrupt departure Thursday afternoon was just the first drop. The real fun started the following morning. Whatever is going on with Maggie, it's also caused a major lapse in her memory. It's not enough that I now have to run the store by myself for who knows how long, but she forgot to schedule weekend help. Worse than that, she failed to schedule (and order for) a charity event happening today. Today!

Twenty centerpieces, four large arrangements for each corner of the ballroom, and a long runner for the silent auction table. Today!

Imagine my surprise when Scott Pearce, the client, called Friday afternoon at 4:26 p.m. to confirm what time I'd arrive on Sunday morning to set up before the luncheon begins.

Oh, and it's pouring outside. Because, yeah, when it rains ...

There'd been a moment (several, way more than several, to be honest) while Scott waited for me to answer his question when the thought had tumbled around in my brain to tell him I couldn't deliver on the order. If it wasn't for Scott, I very well may have.

"Hey, be careful with those," I bark at my last-minute delivery person.

"What you meant to say, is thank you and I owe you," Nate responds with a challenging smile.

"Thank you. I owe you. And be careful." I can't help it.

It had taken more negotiation (begging) than I've ever done to acquire the flowers. And a very long night of work to get everything ready. Not to mention bribing Julia with a free lunch and dinner if she came in to help at the store.

"It'll be worth it," I mumble as I ease out the back door of the store, butt first, holding a glass vase with an oversized arrangement in each hand.

*It'll be worth it. It'll be worth it. It'll be worth it.*

Paws Please holds a special place in my heart (and couch) and I'd do almost anything for Scott and Jeremy. They started Paws Please five years ago when Scott found a puppy on the side of the road on the way to visit his aunt at her nursing home. It was too cold to leave the little puppy in the car, so Scott tucked him into his coat and in they went. The short visit lasted several hours and the puppy visited everyone on the floor. At one point, the puppy conked out in Scott's arms from all the attention and Scott had to promise they'd return later in the week.

That's all it took. Scott quit his job as an advertising exec, convinced his husband Jeremy to buy a house with property, and start a rescue. He began training the rescues to be therapy friends. Some were adopted as service or support animals, others stayed as permanent "employees" of Paws Please and travel to nursing homes and schools and hospitals.

Three years ago, I was helping Maggie at one of the Paws Please charity events when a kitten decided I needed extra help. She spent the whole evening following me, chirping at me, curling up in my lap or my bag at every opportunity. She even hitched a ride on my shoulder at one point. As I was packing up the van at the end of the afternoon, I found the kitten, sound asleep in my bag. Scott proudly announced that I'd been adopted.

"This is the last one." Julia hands me the focal point arrangement for the silent auction table. It's the prettiest of the pieces, if I do say so myself, with snapdragons for protection and Peruvian lilies for prosperity, tucked among roses and orchids.

"Thanks," I say as I set it down in the back of the van. "Sure you'll be okay at the shop until I'm back?"

Julia nods. "Don't worry about me. Just make sure you don't come back with a cat or a dog or a miniature pig."

"Miniature pig?" My curiosity stands at attention.

"My cousin has one. You know you can actually potty train them? Hers goes in the litter box with her cats. And he asks for walks like the dogs do." Julia scrolls through her phone until she finds a picture of a little pig wearing a party hat and bow tie. "That's him on New Year's Eve."

"Oh my god he's adorable," I take the phone from her and stare at the grinning pig.

"Can you please not give her any ideas?" Nate comes up behind Julia, jiggling the keys to the van. I hand Julia her phone and reach for the keys but Nate snaps them into his palm. "I'm driving."

"You don't have to go," I say, reaching again for the keys.

"Of course I do. You're going to need help getting everything inside. Not to mention someone has to keep you out of trouble. I doubt Lulu will be pleased if you bring home a sibling for her."

Last year, Maggie threatened to evict me if I brought home the Basset mix I'd been canoodling with during the charity luncheon. I only half believed her, but that half was deterrent enough. Then I have days like this when I'm thankful I have a pet that uses a litter box instead of needing walks in the rain.

But if Julia is right, a mini pig wouldn't require walks.

"No," Nate says.

"What?" I pretend not to know what he's talking about.

"Just no." He shakes his head and gets into the van. "Although I'd pay good money to watch the shitshow when you break that news to my mom."

"She loves animals."

Nate turns in exaggerated slow-mo and cocks an eyebrow. Even if Maggie wouldn't object, the community association would have a conniption.

"Anyway, I'm not in the market for any new roommates." I slide into the passenger seat.

"Seatbelt."

"We're going three blocks," I protest but do as instructed.

Nate maneuvers the van out of the parking lot and drives the six minutes to what used to be the mansion of the original property owners. It's been beautifully restored, inside and outside, and now hosts weddings and concerts and art exhibits and charity functions.

"Kind of a waste to drive here," Nate grumbles as he backs the van into the spot marked for deliveries.

"Were you going to carry all those vases from the store? And in the rain?"

"No." He emphasizes the O.

"That's what I thought." Teasing aside, I'm just relieved he's here with me. I knew he'd agree to help, well, hoped he would.

The pre-Beth Nate was a slam dunk for helping. The Beth-ified Nate is a bit less reliable.

Case in point, the missed Wednesday dinners, dodging my idea for a trip to Ikea, and, in case anyone can forget bailing on Valentine's Day.

The service door of the mansion opens, and Scott rushes out. "Thank god you're here. I was so worried." He pulls me into a hug that knocks the air out of me.

I catch Nate's eyes over Scott's shoulder and smother a laugh at his expression.

"Scott, relax. We're 20 minutes early. I promised we'd be here before 10 a.m. and it's before ten. The luncheon doesn't start until noon. We've got plenty of time." I give him three we're-all-good-release-me-now taps on the back.

"You didn't sound very convincing when we talked on Friday," Scott insists, tightening his grip before finally releasing me.

"Would I let you down?" I ask, hurrying to grab an arrangement before he decides to give me another hug. Scott wouldn't dream of squashing a flower, not even for a moment of comfort.

"Okay, okay. You're here, that's what matters." With a flourish, Scott waves us to follow him inside.

"No worries, we've got this," Nate mumbles as we each load up. He bends to whisper, "How are your ribs?"

"Bruised." I shimmy trying to loosen my insides compressed by the hug. Scott is one of those amazing humans who can hug any hurt away. Like the time he and Jeremy happened to come into the restaurant where I was sitting at the bar, alone thanks to a failed first date. Scott saw, Scott marched over, Scott hugged until the pieces that had cracked inside me sealed back together. They'd insisted I have dinner with them and, my disastrous date turned into one of the most fun evenings I've had.

Scott waves us forward, anxious to get the charity luncheon

set up before guests arrive. Not that there's any danger of that. We have just a few arrangements to set up. But I'm used to his neurotic energy at these events.

"Oh for piggy-sake, why aren't the tables set? I have to get the caterer off his duff. Love you." He blows kisses at us and hustles off to locate the caterer.

"If we could only bottle that kind of energy," I say.

"You mean mania? No thanks."

"Your mania, my enthusiasm. One on each table, please." I point at the centerpieces Nate holds.

Nate looks from the vases to me. "Really? I would never have guessed."

It's been like this all morning. This is the Nate I grew up with. Playful, sarcastic, easy to be around. Not the guy who was wound tighter than the giant poodle sitting in the corner, his every nerve twitching in anticipation.

"Hi, handsome," I say, and the oversized poof of a dog bounds at me, his entire body vibrating. "You, my friend, need to switch to decaf." Preston is a foster fail. He's too high strung to be a therapy pup and too high strung for most of the people looking to adopt. Which is just as well because Scott and Preston seem to be kindred spirits. I've often thought about adopting a dog just to have someone look at me the way Preston looks at Scott.

Lulu looks at me with the cool detachment of a master to her subject. The only time I get even a remote "you're awesome" glance is when I open a can of tuna, or we're hiding in the closet together during a thunderstorm. Once I adopted her, or she adopted me as Scott insists, she abandoned all pretense. I still adore her though.

For the next hour Nate and I dance around the caterers. The centerpieces get a quick fluff and I trail behind, placing a single Bluebell next to each salad knife.

"Callie," Jeremy's voice booms over the clatter of china on

china as the waiters set the salad plates at each place setting. "You are amazing. Simply amazing. Absolute genius." He picks up the individual flower and studies it. "Absolute genius," he repeats.

I'd chosen the Bluebells, a symbol for kindness, knowing Jeremy would catch the hidden message. Jeremy is an avid gardener. The one requirement he made when he and Scott bought what's become the animal sanctuary, is to reserve a corner of the property for his garden. A plot with an animal-proof fence.

"You're staying for lunch, right?" he asks, setting the flower down and pulling me in for his signature left cheek, right cheek, left cheek kiss.

"I'm afraid not. Maggie is out of town and I need to get back to the store. I'll come back later this afternoon to collect the vases."

"Oh poo. I'll have something wrapped up for you," he says, disappearing before I can protest. Well, I did promise Julia lunch, right?

I walk through three rooms before I finally find Nate sitting by a fireplace, feet stretched out in front of him, eyes on the fake flames in one of the many fireplaces in the mansion.

I stay by the door, watching Nate watch the flames. I want to know what he's thinking, what that faraway look is about. Or who it's about.

"There you are," Jeremy's voice breaks the moment. "I had the kitchen pack a couple of meals and an extra in case. You're the best." We do another round of cheek kisses and Jeremy waves at Nate. With a final blown kiss, he disappears to welcome the early arrivals.

"Ready to go?" Nate asks, pushing up from the chair. He's still staring into the fireplace.

"What's in there?" I nod toward the fireplace.

The corners of Nate's mouth tick up. "Thirty-three years of

friendship." He puts an arm around me and leads me out. "I say we snarf down our luxury lunch in the back of the van, what do you think?"

I bump my hip into his. "You do know how to show a girl a good time."

# 12

## THE FLOWER THAT FOLLOWS THE SUN DOES SO EVEN IN CLOUDY DAYS.

### — ROBERT LEIGHTON

Lulu gets a running start and skates through the mosaic of papers spread out on the living room floor. For the last two hours I've been scouring orders and notes and holy crap I have no idea what's in Maggie's brain. Her ability to keep details of the store in her head always fascinated me. Still does. And for the most part it works.

Until it doesn't.

The more I look, the less I understand. I'd gotten lucky with the Paws Please event. The chances of getting that lucky a second time are slim. Which means I have to find the key code to Maggie's brain.

Lou flops onto her side and bunny kicks at a piece of paper until she's loosened a sticky note attached to it. She chews at the pink sticky then jumps up and shakes her paw to dislodge it.

"Come here, you weirdo," I lean over to remove the offending note from her fur. "What's this about?"

Maggie has written: *Deadline: March 13*

Deadline for what? There are a handful of papers spread

out on the floor and under the couch. A few with corners chewed off, a couple with kitty prints where her highness stepped on them after having shoved her paw into my dinner. I find a reminder for an art exhibit at the gallery down the road, an announcement to local merchants about a special community soft opening for a new restaurant, a flyer about the annual Spring Tour organized by the community, and a request for proposal for a wedding.

My phone lights up with an incoming text. A picture of a hand holding a wine glass at an angle, the dark red liquid shimmering with a fireplace in the background.

> Me: Tease

> Nate: I know

I take a picture of my mug with its murky liquid and send it to Nate.

> Nate: WTH?

> Me: Herbal tea

> Nate: Why?

> Me: Working. Your mom left a mess of orders.

> Nate: Herbal tea won't cut it.

> Me: Now you tell me?

Nate sends a picture of the wine bottle.

> Me: Stop teasing

> Nate: I'll pour you one

> Me: And drink it too?

> Nate: It'd be my pleasure

Me: I hate you

Nate: You love me

Me: I'd love you more if you came over with that bottle

Nate: It's illegal to drive with open alcohol containers

Me: You have others

Nate: It's late

Me: It's not

Nate: Some of us don't start work at noon

Me: Rude. I don't. And especially not with the mess your mom left

Nate: face palm emoji

Me: Not funny

Nate: Wasn't meant to be

Me: What are you doing?

Nate: Drinking

Me: Not funny

Nate: Wasn't meant to be

I lean back against the couch, pushing Lou off a piece of paper that had escaped my attention earlier. Maggie's unruly scribbles about flower choices for, what? Whatever it is, it's happening on Saturday.

Me: I quit

Nate: Quit what?

Me: This job

Nate: You can't

Me: Watch me

Nate: And do what?

Me: Become a cat groomer

Nate: cry laughing emoji

Me: I'm serious

Nate: Fine, you're serious. You're quitting your job. Why?

Me: Your mom is making me crazy.

Nate: Welcome to my world.

Me: I live in your world.

Nate: Voluntarily. Which makes me seriously question your sanity.

Me: Good point.

Nate: Right?!!!!!!

Me: You alone?

Nate: Is that your best pick up line?

Me: What are you wearing?

Nate: Want a pic?

Me: vomiting emoji

Nate sends a picture of his legs clad in green and blue plaid flannel pajamas stretched on the ottoman toward the fireplace.

Me: Jealous

Nate: I bought you a pair like these

Me: Of the fireplace you dork

Nate: Buy a house. You too could have one.

Me: Think cat grooming earns enough to buy a house with a fireplace?

Nate: Doubtful.

Me: Figures. Back to the drawing board.

After a couple of beats, I type:

Alone?

Nate sends a picture of the other side of the couch. Empty.

Me: She could be in the kitchen. Or bathroom.

Nate sends a picture of an empty kitchen, then adds, I'm not getting up to take a picture of the bathroom.

Me: smiling face emoji

It makes me weirdly happy that he's alone and texting me. It's not like we don't do this regularly but somehow tonight feels different. The last few weeks have felt different.

The last few weeks *have* been different.

Nate: So …

I watch the three dots jump and disappear, jump and disappear.

When the dots disappear and don't reappear, I type:

So?

Nate: Any new messages?

My stomach plummets along with my mood. Bad enough

I'm dealing with Maggie's mess, now I also have to think about my father's mess. Whatever that mess is. Because, no, I still haven't called him back and his messages still hover on the casual spectrum. Although the last one from two days ago felt a bit more insistent about us talking.

Me: Define new

Nate: Today

Me: Nothing today

Nate: Yesterday?

Me: Nope

And because the gods have a sick sense of humor, my phone rings.

Me: Dammit, you jinxed me.

Nate: And you just sat there watching the call go into voicemail?

Me: Ah, yeah!

Nate: You have to get over this.

Me: Why?

Nate: Seriously, Callie, you can't ignore his calls forever.

Me: Watch me

Lulu steps onto my lap, purring and kneading my thighs. She puts a dainty paw on my chest and leans up to rub her nose against mine. Whoever said cats don't care never had a cat. Lou may act like she hates me half the time, ignores me other times, but she always seems to know when I'm faltering and could use a bit of tuna-smell affection.

Me: What are you hearing from Maggie?

Nate: Way to change the subject

Me: What can I say, I'm good.

Nate: I'm not done with you yet. But as for
Mom, I'm not hearing much at all. You?

Me: Nada. From either of them.

Which is strange. I mean, Mom, okay. There are plenty of times when I don't hear from her for most of the week. But Maggie, should have at least checked in on the store.

Me: Maybe they're off on one of those fancy
naked sweat lodge retreats.

Nate: laugh crying emoji

Nate: And eww

Me: Or something's wrong …

I wait for him to brush me off, tease me about following in the melodrama path established by our moms. When he doesn't respond, I type:

Are you on your way with the wine? Is that
why you're not typing?

The three dots make their appearance and disappear. I'm about to tap on FaceTime when he finally responds.

Nate: Sorry. I need to go but I'll check on you
later. Callie, you really need to answer
your dad.

# 13

# MINDS ARE LIKE FLOWERS; THEY OPEN ONLY WHEN THE TIME IS RIGHT.

— STEPHEN RICHARDS

Some days you own the world and some days you can't remember why you walked into a room and don't notice that your shirt is on inside out and backwards until you take it off at the end of the day. Mother Nature is having one of *those* days.

This morning had started like a typical early March day in Maryland: cold and blustery with snow flurries. Thankfully, the weather had kept most people home. Thankfully because (a) I wanted to scream each time someone opened the door and brought in a gust of winter with them, and (b) I didn't sleep much last night, having multiple fake conversations in my head with my father, and I'm not feeling peoply as a result.

But Mother Nature forgot what room she was going into, and winter turned into a perfect spring day. So, I followed her lead and came outside with my lunch.

I close my eyes and turn my face to the sun. According to the weather app, it's a balmy 51 degrees. Warm enough to take off my coat but not quite warm enough to untangle myself from my scarf.

According to the same app, it's 78 degrees in Santa Fe. I loosen the scarf and pretend I'm there instead. Although that would mean dealing with whatever family drama is going on, so maybe 51 degrees isn't so bad after all.

"Can I join you?" A voice pulls me back to the park bench. I scoot over and motion for Tish to sit. She hands me a cup of coffee then settles next to me. I look questioningly at her and she shrugs, smiles. "Courtesy of Michael."

My eyes move to the coffee shop across the courtyard, even though I can't see inside from here. "Thanks." I take a sip, the warm liquid pooling on my tongue as the added pop of flavor connects. I turn to Tish for confirmation.

"Yeah, he added lavender to it. Said you looked a bit down earlier and he thought you could use a mood boost." She pokes at my thigh and smirks. "You have an admirer."

I feel my face flush and loosen the scarf a bit more. "He's just being nice," I say, avoiding another glance at the coffee shop. Michael is seriously cute. And nice. And thoughtful. But interested in me? Not a chance.

"He is," Tish agrees. "But he also likes you."

"He's like that with all the regulars," I brush off the comment. I know for a fact that he gives the dance instructor at Two Left Feet a free Chai Latte when she comes in Fridays before her beginner tap class. The lavender shot in my latte isn't a sign of anything other than him being a nice guy.

Tish takes a sip of her drink. "Any man who can fix a latte this amazing is worth his weight in beans."

"Can't argue there. Cheers." We clink paper coffee cups.

I sip the lavender latte which, as always, is perfect and allow my thoughts to drift. Sadly, my thoughts circle back to my mom which counteracts the soothing elements of the lavender.

I've wondered over the years if my relationship with her would have been different if dad had left sooner. Or later. Would we have been closer if she hadn't felt like the third wheel? Or if I'd been more mature when he left and hadn't heaped the blame on her?

"So, is Michael right?" Tish asks.

"About?"

"You being down?"

I shift on the uncomfortable wood bench, inadvertently sitting on the end of the scarf and pulling it taut in the process. I struggle to release myself from myself.

Life as a wallflower has taught me to keep my feelings private. Few people really want to hear about your worries or feelings. Even fewer actually care. It's not that I don't want to open up to Tish. It's more about not wanting to need her friendship. Being vulnerable leads to need. Need leads to disappointment. Disappointment leads to hurt.

"More frazzled than down," I finally say. "With Maggie away, I'm managing more of the store than I normally have to. And you know Maggie." I shrug as though the rest of that thought is obvious to everyone who knows Maggie.

"Maggie has left me a challenging Where's Waldo game with orders," I add.

"Really?" Tish sounds genuinely surprised. "She seems so on top of everything."

"Oh, she is. But her system for staying on top of everything is here." I tap at my temple. "Not very helpful when she's thousands of miles away."

"Vacation?"

I'm not sure anyone would classify a trip to visit my mom as a vacation. Well, maybe Maggie. "In a way. She's visiting family."

Tish gives me a quick sideways look but doesn't push. Not only is she amazing with clay and knows music and books, she reads people with the precision of a profiler.

Thankfully we're both distracted by a large hairy dog barreling for us and launching himself onto the bench next to

Tish. She laughs and rubs at the giant head where I'm assuming his ears are. It's hard to tell in the mass of dreadlocks what she's actually petting.

"Yo, Bob, get down. You insane mutt." The man attached to the gyrating mound grabs for a collar buried somewhere in the midst of the dreads.

"He's fine," Tish says as Bob shoves his huge body onto her petite one. "Ouuff. Bob, buddy, you're a bit big for my lap."

"He's a menace," the owner says but doesn't do anything to keep Bob from smooshing Tish.

"Gary, this is my friend Callie. Callie, this is Gary and, of course, this handsome guy is Bob." Tish does the introductions, her face buried in Bob's fur.

Gary reaches to shake my hand. "It's a pleasure to meet you, Callie." He has a pleasant smile, friendly eyes, and nice hands.

I'm a hands girl. Maybe because mine are rough and cut up, despite my obsession with lotion.

I tuck my hands into the folds of the scarf, self-conscious of my sandpaper skin against his smooth skin. I'm supposed to say something. *Think, Callie. Social interaction.*

"You live in the neighborhood?" Duh. Stellar opening line.

"On the other side of the Green." Gary tilts his head in the direction of the communal gardens. The land the community was built on was once a private farm. The developer kept many of the original buildings, including the old barns which were converted to a neighborhood farm.

The idea is pretty neat actually. Plots are free with the understanding that at least a portion of what you grow will then be sold at the weekly farmer's market. Money from the market then goes back into the communal space for upkeep and supplies.

"Don't you guys have a plot there?" Tish directs the question to me, then as explanation, turns back to Gary and adds, "Callie is the creative muscle behind Fancy Fleur."

Gary looks confused, so I point at the store across from where we sit.

"Maggie thought we could grow some of our own flowers but running the store takes all of our time. She still likes to tinker out there from time to time but I'm a disaster with anything that needs nurturing."

"Really?" Tish asks.

People assume because I'm a florist that I'm also an avid gardener. Outdoor dirt contains worms and bugs. I don't like slithery things.

Gary's watch dings a reminder. "No rest for the wicked. I have a meeting to get to. Tish, always fun seeing you. Callie, I hope I'll see you around."

I smile, nod, mumble an "I hope so," which I don't fully mean.

In silence, Tish and I watch Gary and Bob jog away, Gary looking far more elegant than his dog whose ropy dreads flop from side to side with each step.

"Pure bred or mutt?" I ask.

"Man or dog?" Tish snorts at her joke.

"Funny."

"Pure. That mass of hair is a Bergamasco."

I shouldn't be surprised that she knows that but I am. "I've never heard of that breed."

"They're not that common."

"That's the first time I've seen one."

"They're very loyal to their people and extremely sociable," Tish says.

I laugh. "I got the sociable part the way he crawled right into your lap."

"I find it endlessly fascinating what people's choices say about them. Like choice of pet, what they choose to collect, what their hobbies are, what they drive." Tish is still looking in the direction Gary and Bob jogged off.

"You and Gary?" My curiosity can't stand it any longer.

Tish turns to assess me. "Oh shit no. He's fabulous but he's not my type. You, however, would be perfect for him."

"I don't think so."

If I'd been perfect for every guy someone claimed I was perfect for, I'd be living in a reverse harem. Not that the idea sounds appealing in any way. None of the guys I was "perfect for" felt the same. Plus, there's only one guy I've ever met who's perfect for me.

Perfect except for the minor detail that I've never thought of him as a romantic match. And even now, with the pact deadline looming, there's a petite problem named Beth.

"Are you working on anything new?" I move the subject to safer ground.

"Yeah, but I'm not sure what's going to come of it yet. You know how it is."

I do. It's how I feel when I'm surrounded with flowers. I hear what they have to say, I feel what they want to convey. I don't force them together. No two bouquets are ever identical. Not even the ones that may appear to be (okay, except for Valentine's arrangements when even the roses seem to shrug their leaves in resignation). It's what excites me every day about coming to work.

"Can I ask you a question?" Tish asks.

I sip at my coffee and wait for the question.

"Why don't you date? Is it because of Nate?"

I tilt my face up to the sun and close my eyes at the sudden brightness as the cloud shifts. "I date. I'm just not good at relationships. And Nate doesn't count."

"Why not? He's perfect."

"He's not that perfect. You forget, we grew up together. I know him too well. It would be weird." The cloud returns and I shiver into my scarf. "Want to hear something funny though?

When we were in college, we made a pact that if we were still single at 33, we'd get married."

Tish looks at me out of the corner of her eye. "And aren't you turning 33 next month?"

"Yup. Luckily he's now dating someone great so we're off the hook." I meant to say it as a joke, but as the words come out, I realize it's not entirely a joke.

And apparently it didn't sound like one either because Tish repeats the word, "luckily" with a skeptical tone.

# 14

## IF WE COULD SEE THE MIRACLE OF A SINGLE FLOWER CLEARLY OUR WHOLE LIFE WOULD CHANGE.

### — BUDDHA

It's with a huge sigh of relief that I finally turn the sign around to Closed at the end of the day. Mother Nature did another about face and is now sprinkling the world with a layer of fairy dust. I turn off the lights in the store and lean against the glass of the door, enjoying the cold against my forehead. We keep the store cold but even with the below average indoor temps, I'm feeling flushed.

The culprit for that was the impromptu visit by Gary a few minutes ago. He came in looking for a plant to give as a house-warming gift. Turns out Gary is a history buff with a fascination for how people have used plants, flowers, and herbs for good and not so good. If I was anyone but me, he would be perfect for me.

What I'd told Tish wasn't a lie. I do date. I certainly don't want to stay single my entire life. But relationships require trust and loyalty and while I have an abundance of loyalty, the trust part scares the leaves off my life tree.

I've made an art form of the two-date rule. Only a handful of guys have made it past that. The problem they all have is that they're not Nate. Which is weird because Nate isn't boyfriend material. At least not for me.

At least not until recently. Not until I started thinking about the pact. The pact and Beth to be precise.

A knock on what I consider my secret door startles me. The door opens to the stairwell to my apartment. No one uses it except me and sometimes Nate and the occasional delivery person. From inside the store, it looks like a fun display for seed packets with a mural I'd painted to hide the fact that it's actually a door. In the stairwell, I painted an arrow pointing back outside with, "the store is this way." And on the apartment door I've hung a sign that reads, "This is not the door you're looking for." What can I say, Nate's nerdiness is contagious. But in truth, I may actually like Star Wars movies more than he does.

"Hi." I let Nate in.

"Hi yourself. I thought you'd be upstairs by now." He gives me a kiss on the cheek the way he usually does. And for the first time, my cheek tingles.

I brush off the feeling and take a step forward, ready to call the day done. "I was going over some orders and lost track of time. Perfect timing though, I was just going to head upstairs."

Nate steps past me into the store. "You didn't see my text?"

"I've been busy. When did you send it?" I pull my phone out of my back pocket. I hadn't received any texts from Nate all day.

"An hour-ish ago?"

I scroll to messages but find nothing from Nate. I turn the phone so he can see.

He frowns and pulls out his own phone. The frown deepens and suddenly my phone pings with an incoming text.

"I forgot to hit send," he explains. "Now you have it."

"You're standing in front of me, why not just tell me?"

"Because I'd meant to send the text. Now I've sent it."

I glance at the text.

> Hey. Sorry but need to cancel on tonight. Can I
> swing by for flowers?

I type a response.

> Help yourself.

"I'm standing right here," Nate says when the text lights up his screen.

"But if you'd sent it an hour-ish ago, I would have responded with that text."

"Touché."

"So, why are you ditching me this time?" Not that I don't have a good guess. But I've been looking forward to a relaxed evening with someone who actually wants to spend time with me and not just because I have fingers that can pop open a can of tuna.

So much for that.

"Beth and I are going to hang out."

"Duh. I figured that. But tonight was supposed to be you making it up to me for missing last time."

Nate turns to me, his face a poster of contrition. "I'm sorry. I'm the absolute worst."

"You are."

"Are you mad at me?"

And because he really does look sorry, I answer, "Very," even though I'm only moderately mad.

There've only been a handful of times in our entire lives that I was very mad at Nate. Once when we were six or seven and he told Mattie Hennesy that he needed to invite me to his birthday party or else Nate wouldn't go. Mattie had invited me with the clarification, in front of the entire class I should add, that he thought I was weird but I was Nate's friend so I could come. Not entirely an invitation.

My palms get sweaty remembering that moment, all eyes on me, except for Mattie who had already forgotten about me. I'd barely spoken to Nate the rest of that day and had, of course, refused to go to the party. Then Nate did a Nate thing and showed up at my house instead of going to the party.

"I didn't know how to say no," Nate says.

There's no way I can stay mad when he gives me those eyes. Not that I'm going to let him off that easily. "And yet, you can say bugger off to me without any hesitation."

For a blink, he looks genuinely wounded. I sigh and soften the next blow. "What's the plan for tonight? And how do you intend on making this up to me?"

"Dinner?"

"Is that what Beth has planned or what you're planning?"

"Both?" He gives me a cheeky grin.

"Lame." I roll my eyes at him.

Nate stretches his back, wincing.

"Did you hurt yourself contorting through the excuses of why you're ditching me?" I tease.

"Ha, ha. Beth got me to try hot yoga with her and I'm still sore."

This time I don't have to fake shock. "You? Yoga?"

"Yup. Hot yoga no less."

I shake my head. "I don't even know who you are anymore. Although any girl who can get you into a downward dog pose is worth an armful of lilies."

And just like that, I can feel the flowers. White lilies for sweetness, lilac for first emotions of love, white roses for worthiness, and a few sprigs of fern for sincerity. A hopeful, sweet arrangement with potential.

Because isn't it all about potential? The potential for happiness. The potential for someone who will share the moments of your days. The potential for not becoming a lonely person talking to plants and cats.

The potential of a budding relationship.

I wrap the arrangement in silver tissue paper and tie a green ribbon around it.

"It's beautiful. You really do have a magic touch." Nate says from behind me.

"Thank you but the magic is in the flowers."

"No, the magic is in you." Nate gives me a side hug and a kiss on the top of my head. Warmth floods through me.

"Before I forget," Nate says, "I was thinking we could all have dinner on Sunday."

The hitch in his tone when he said "all" and the need-to-be breezy attempt with "before I forget" gives him away.

"What have you done?"

"Nothing."

"Then what did Beth do?"

"It's not her."

"So it *is* you."

"No. Well, kinda. There's a new guy who just started, engineer, super nice. He relocated from California and doesn't know anyone except for a few of us at the office. I thought it would be fun to invite him over."

"Let me get this straight, you and Beth, me and this new-to-the-area super nice guy?"

Nate nods, his mouth stuck between a hopeful semi-smile and a please-don't-throw-something grimace. Set-ups are not in our friendship agreement. The one and only time he set me up with someone ended in disaster.

Well, disaster for me because I was naïve enough to get my hopes up. Disaster for Nate because I'd gotten my hopes up. That was the second time I'd been really, really, angry at him. You're seeing the common denominator here, right?

"Before you say anything, it's not a set up. I swear. Just dinner." We both learned the no-set-up lesson.

"On one condition." I hold up a finger, to make the point and as a warning. "You go to Ikea with me Sunday morning."

Nate groans. "Anything but that."

"Nope, that's the give."

My love for Ikea is about as rabid as my love for farmers markets and Nate's love for the Air and Space Museum. Secretly, we both enjoy all of the above, but the fun is in teasing each other.

"Fine. But then dinner is at your house."

I hold out my hand to shake. We'll be ordering in anyway so who cares. And then I'll have two engineers to assemble the furniture.

"I really do need to go now." He picks up the arrangement I just prepared. "You truly are the best," Nate says, giving me another hug.

I watch as he walks out, cradling the flowers in his arms. Potential, hope, love.

If I allow myself to think about it, the irony of what I do for a living is a giant thorn bush in the middle of my life path. I help people express their thoughts, emotions. I help people connect. I create beauty and joy and love.

I do for others what I can't do for myself.

# 15

## DON'T WAIT FOR SOMEONE TO BRING YOU FLOWERS. PLANT YOUR OWN GARDEN AND DECORATE YOUR OWN SOUL.

— LUTHER BURBANK

"You do know this is the mark of insanity, right?" Nate asks. He takes a sip from the cardboard coffee cup and angles in the driver's seat waiting for me to respond.

We've been sitting in the Ikea parking lot for fifteen minutes.

"What's crazy is how many other people are also waiting for the store to open." I flash a grin at Nate. "Who knew there were this many people up and ready to shop before 10 a.m. on a Sunday morning."

"How did I let you talk me into this?"

It's not a question and he's not expecting an answer, but I do anyway. "Because you feel guilty about roping me into meeting your new colleague. And for all the evenings ditched me for that new girlfriend of yours."

"I have nothing to feel guilty about. A, he's a nice guy. And it's not like I'm setting you up on a blind date. Not that it would hurt you to date once in a while."

"I do date." Nate gives me the eyebrow raise of doubt. "Sometimes," I add. "And I have a coffee date on Friday." It's not completely true but it's also not *not* true. I mean, Gary had suggested coffee when he stopped by the shop for the housewarming plant, we'd just never taken it to the date and time stage.

"Ohhhhhh?" Nate drawls the word suggestively.

"No. Go away. It's just coffee."

"How'd you meet him?"

"Hey, the doors are open, let's go." I launch myself from Nate's SUV, not waiting for him to turn off the ignition and follow or get to the B explanation of what he isn't feeling guilty about.

"Damn, girl," Nate huffs when he catches up to me. "You could have at least given me a chance to finish my coffee."

"No time to waste." I ignore his comment, pointing in the direction of a family room display.

I had an idea to reorganize the store and add a cozy place to sit in the bay window. Not that folks come to hang out at a flower shop, but it will create a showcase for some of the plants and special arrangements. And if I move a couple of pieces from my apartment downstairs to accomplish that, I then have space for something new and fun upstairs. What, I don't know yet. But like the saying goes, I'll know it when I see it.

"I like this." I run my fingers over the back of a faux suede chair.

Nate plops into the chair and wiggles about under the protest of its wood frame. "It's okay. Not the most comfortable though." He pops up and moves to another chair in a fake living room display. "This one is better."

I frown. "I don't like the color. Or the shape of the arms."

"What's wrong with the shape?" He strokes the arms of the chair as though soothing it from my criticism.

I shrug. "It's not *the one*."

We continue our walk through the cavernous showroom with its tiny display rooms, each inviting in its perfect simplicity.

"Would this work in my apartment?" I'm standing in the middle of a room with tall bookshelves along one fake wall, a black couch in front of them with a handful of colorful throw pillows, a fluffy shag rug in an interesting teal color underfoot, a white swivel bucket chair on one side of a coffee table that pretends to be reclaimed wood, and an entertainment stand on the opposite wall from the bookshelves. Floating shelves surround a window that looks onto a fake balcony.

"Which part?" Nate surveys the furnishings and knick-knacks surrounding us.

"All of it."

"Have you lost your mind?"

"This room is amazing." I sit on the couch and pat the cushion next to me. Nate sits down and I lean into him, resting my head on his shoulder as we stare ahead at the black screen of the pretend TV.

"This is so weird," he whispers.

"Come on," I jump up suddenly, grabbing his hand and pulling him deeper into the bowels of the store.

A couple with a stroller steers around us and I suddenly realize we're still holding hands. I bump my shoulder into Nate's. "Look at us, just like a regular couple."

Nate smiles down at me and for a few minutes we walk through the store, hands clasped. The perfect couple.

"Do you and Beth shop together?" I try to picture him doing this with her.

"Nope."

"What do you guys do together then?"

Nate looks down at me again, the smile turning into a smirk.

"You're gross." I drop his hand and weave my way around a handful of people to an open space with various coffee tables.

"Has it really been that long since you've been out on a date?" Nate teases.

"No." *Yes.* "I'm just curious what you guys do, that isn't that. I mean, how serious is it getting between you."

I know Nate and I've seen him with plenty of his dates. But the little time I've spent with him and Beth and the little he's said about her is sending up all sorts of warning bells that this relationship is different.

Nate bends to inspect the tag on a particularly hideous excuse of a table.

"Back away," I say, putting a hand on his bicep and nudging him back.

"It's not that bad."

"It's that bad. This one though ..." I lead him to another table with glass in the center showcasing the contents of a display drawer.

"Why would you want anyone to see what you're stashing in the drawer?"

"It's a display. For pretty things." I affect an upper-class tone that comes out sounding like I'm holding in a burp, which is then promptly followed by a real burp.

Nate starts laughing. "You're ridiculous."

"Yeah," I agree. He's the only one who ever sees this side of me. I don't know how to be ridiculous with anyone else.

My mom didn't do ridiculous. Dad did, though, and it was yet one more of the things we used to tease her about. When he left, he took the silly with him. Nate never gave up hope that I'd find my ridiculous side again. Eventually I did. But it came back more cautious, like a skittish cat that'll only play with their one person.

I snap a picture of the tag for the table I like then retrace my steps to the living room and snap a few more pictures for quick reference when we go to the warehouse of credit card death.

"How many things are you planning on buying?" Nate sounds concerned.

"All of those, assuming they have them in stock."

"You do realize not everything will fit in my car. And where are you going to put all of this? Your apartment is already full."

By the time we finish our tour of the showrooms and make our way to the warehouse, I've laid out my plan for Nate and he's laid out a counter plan and we've negotiated a compromise.

An hour and a small fortune later, I'm appreciating the size of Nate's SUV as we arrange boxes and argue over what should go where.

"What?" Nate asks, stopping mid slide of a box into the car.

"What what?" I reach for the box, assuming he'd stopped to rearrange the space.

"You were staring at me with that weird face."

"It's my face, don't call it weird."

"Your expression, you goober."

"No weird expression. Mirroring your face maybe?"

Nate rolls his eyes.

"You know what they say," I continue, on a roll now, "the longer a couple is together, the more they start to look alike."

"We're not a couple."

"We kind of are." I toss that out with a dollop of sticky hope. Because being around Nate is easy and comfortable and I know who I am with him. He's the only one who doesn't make me self-conscious and self-critical.

I stare at Nate, turning over an unfamiliar tingle that's not attraction but not *not* attraction.

# FLOWERS ARE LIKE FRIENDS, THEY BRING COLOR TO YOUR WORLD.

## — UNKNOWN

"This place is adorable. I've always wondered what these units are like," Beth says, surveying my apartment. "Is it noisy with all the businesses though?"

"Not really. Weekends sometimes. But the restaurants close at 10 p.m. and since it's not really a singles-come-to-mingle type of destination, there isn't much commotion at closing time. Mornings can get loud with deliveries. Luckily, I'm a morning person."

"Me too," Beth says. "Nate on the other hand ..." she raises her hands in a whatchya gonna do gesture.

We both look to where Nate and his new colleague, Eric, are turning a simple bookcase into a project worthy of the International Space Station.

"He likes his sleepy mornings," I add, a weird need to establish my history with Nate creeping into my gut.

"That he does. What's the trick to getting him up early on a weekend?" she asks.

"Bribes." We'd spend at least thirty minutes negotiating any early morning activity. And by early, I'm talking pre-11 a.m.

"Where does this go?" Nate asks Eric, looking suspiciously at a small strip of laminated wood.

"I think at the top?" Eric sits back, surveying the pieces of the bookshelf spread around them.

"Do you think they know what they're doing?" I loud whisper.

"Heard that," Nate yells without looking up from where he's hunched over a shelf.

"I know," I yell back.

Eric looks up from the instructions and smiles at the exchange.

I was slightly dreading this evening but so far, I'm having a surprisingly good time. Granted, since they arrived an hour ago, it's been mostly poking fun at the rocket scientists and their inability to put together a bookshelf that has picture instructions, and clinking beer glasses with Beth each time the boys say "wait."

"Wait, it's that one next." Eric points at a different piece of the bookshelf puzzle.

"Sip," I say and tap the rim of my glass to Beth's.

We drink as Nate glares at us.

"Maybe we should take over the hard labor and let the boys deal with dinner," Beth suggests. The more I'm around her, the harder it is to find flaws. Not that I'm trying. Okay, I'm kinda trying.

"You two suck." Nate sits back on his heels. "But you know what," he turns to Eric, "I think they're on to something."

"I think we're being challenged," I say to Beth.

"I think you're right," she says. I notice the exchange of a look between her and Nate.

Nate catches me watching them and winks at me. My brain tiptoes through the flower patch, thinking what the next Woo-Beth arrangement should include. Maybe it's the way she looks at him, or the way he talks about her, or the recent times he's ditched me, or the fun from our morning shopping trip, but I'm starting to wonder if a world where Nate and I aren't just best friends isn't such a crazy idea.

I give my head a slight shake to knock that thought back into place. Because Nate and I are just best friends.

"What do you say we show these boys how it's done?" I suggest.

"Brilliant idea," Beth agrees.

Nate stands and walks the handful of steps from the living room to the kitchen. He hands me the Allen wrench that conveniently comes with the furniture. "Okay, smarty pants get to it."

He opens the fridge and extracts two beers, handing one to Eric.

"What about us?" Beth asks, holding up her mostly empty glass.

"No drinking and operating power tools," Eric answers.

I stare at the L-shaped tool. "Power tool?"

"It's all in the wrist," Eric says with a grin.

"Dude." Nate barks a laugh and fist bumps Eric.

Beth turns to me. "Did he just 'dude' him?"

"I'm sorry, Beth. I've clearly failed in raising him properly." For the briefest of seconds, Nate and I lock eyes before he winks and it's just another Nate and Callie moment.

"Think there's hope for him?" She plays along.

We stare at the boys while they watch us in a who's-got-the-last-quip standoff.

"Maybe, but it won't be easy," I say.

Nate rolls his eyes. "I should have known better than suggesting this."

"You should have. You didn't. You deserve every bit of it." I smirk at him.

Eric laughs, a deep, relaxed sound that fills the apartment with ease. Whatever Nate's motives were, I'm glad I agreed. The evening is a nice end to a fun morning.

Beth and I take up where the guys left off. Unlike them, we actually follow the instructions, pointing and passing, and assembling the different size boards without chatter, and in half an hour we've finished one of the units.

"Hey, you two, make yourselves useful and take those two chairs and that side table down to the store," I say, snapping the guys out of a conversation about an upcoming mission they're working on.

"Yes, boss," Nate says, setting his glass down. "Any place special you want them?"

"By the window. I'll rearrange tomorrow. Are you ordering dinner or should we?"

"You pick," Eric says. He picks up the second chair and follows Nate down the stairs.

"Preference?" I ask Beth.

"Not Thai," we say at the same time.

"What is it with Nate and Thai?" she asks in a whisper.

"It's a phase. He does this. Last year he went through a Mexican phase. I don't think I've eaten as many enchiladas my entire life as during those few months." Come to think of it that phase isn't over. My stomach flops at the memory of the Valentine's Day enchilada.

"Okay, so no Thai and no Mexican," I sum up the options.

An hour later we're all sitting on the floor around the coffee table, two pizza boxes open between us.

Nate leans to Beth and says something I can't hear. She smiles at him and, once again, I feel my stomach do a sidestep-shuffle move.

I turn my attention to the pizza. And to Eric. "So, Eric, did you always want to work in the space industry?"

He sets the slice of pizza on the plate and indicates one minute while he finishes the bite. "Nope. I wanted to be a professional rock climber." My eyebrow shoots up and he chuckles. "That's what my parents said as well. My mom delicately reminded me that she can still take me out of the will if I do anything stupid and living in a van going from crag to crag was indeed stupid. She wasn't more enthusiastic about my compromise to work at a climbing gym full time and climb outdoors when I can. Luckily for both of us, that dream died quickly during college. I still worked at the gym through grad school and went out once in a while with my buddies, but the reality was I enjoy nice things and nice things require a bigger salary than I could make as a climber."

I take in his cashmere sweater draped over the back of the couch, the crisp jeans that look casual and fancy at the same time, and the watch that's too subtle to be anything but expensive.

"I'm impressed." I laser focus my attention on Eric to avoid seeing Beth pick a pepperoni from Nate's pizza then lean into him and pop it into her mouth. Nate hates when anyone takes food from his plate. Residual of growing up with two older brothers I suppose.

He notices my look and winks at me. We have a moment when it's us, Nate and Callie, a moment that reminds me that this is who we are. It's who we've always been. It's how the world makes sense.

"With my climbing aspirations?" Eric asks, his tone easy and playful.

"That you listened to your mother."

"Ah. Well, she can be pretty scary when she puts her foot down. In all seriousness though, I've always been a space nerd. Of course, when I was little, I wanted to be an astronaut. At least until I learned how they go to the bathroom in space."

"Way to impress the ladies," Nate says, laughing.

"What can I say, I'm just cool like that," Eric plays along.

"Cool? Did you really say cool?" Beth teases. "My high schoolers would tease you mercilessly for using that word."

"It's been a long time since I was even remotely cool." Eric flashes a smile directed at Beth. And just like that, I'm back in school, watching the pretty girl get all the attention.

"Why high school?" Eric asks Beth.

"I always thought I'd teach elementary school, but it turns out I'm intimidated by little kids," Beth says. She looks to Nate as though for corroboration. He gives her the I-get-it eyebrow lift. I want to call him out. Nate loves kids. He's always wanted kids. I've never seen anyone so natural around them.

"My first student teaching job was first grade, and it was a disaster," Beth continues. "Those kids had my number after the first ten minutes I was in the class, and they didn't let up. I was seriously considering abandoning the idea of a teaching career. Luckily for me, the principal at the school took a liking to me and after a bit of tough love, she frog-marched me to the high school for an interview."

"And your interest in space?" I ask her. I study Eric's face as he studies Beth's, the curiosity in the shared connection.

"My father worked for NASA. I grew up in that world."

It strikes me again how little I know about her and just how perfect she is for Nate.

Then comes another flash. What if she's not the only one who's perfect for Nate?

And just like that, I know what needs to be done. The next arrangement will include a single Iris for uncertainty. Not necessarily to break them up but just slow things down, just enough to give our pact a chance.

# 17

## IT'S THE TIME THAT YOU SPENT ON YOUR ROSE THAT MAKES YOUR ROSE SO IMPORTANT.

### — ANTOINE DE SAINT-EXUPERY

"I grabbed the mail," Julia says, walking into the store on Monday morning. "Can I switch the sign to open?"

I look up from the pile of papers on the table then glance at the clock. "Oh crap, yes. Thank you. I completely lost track of time." After Nate, Beth, and Eric left last night, my brain spun itself into overdrive. I'd rearranged the family room, finished the second bookshelf that we hadn't gotten to thanks to the arrival of dinner, and then somewhere around 3 a.m., had the "I'm missing something" lightbulb about the Spring Tour.

For the last eight years, the neighborhood committee has organized a Spring Tour in early April. It's a "fun filled day of community" according to the flyers in the window of every restaurant and store. The main streets are closed to cars, and restaurants and shops set up tents and tables showcasing their goods. But beyond the extra foot traffic that the tour brings, the big prize has always been the contract to decorate the Mansion.

The mansion was, once upon a time, the expansive home of the Roth family who owned the property. When they sold to the developers, the mansion was turned into a showcase for special events. For the Spring Tour, the committee decks out the mansion and features work by local artists of various mediums with proceeds from sales going to charity.

Since that first year, Fancy Fleur has had the privilege of being the featured florist.

"Hey, Julia, have you seen anything from the Spring Tour committee about this year's event? I've gone through every pile Maggie left on the desk, in desk drawers, notes on the calendar, even emails and can't find a thing on it. Usually by this time we're already meeting with them to discuss details."

Julia shakes her head in surprise. "Nothing?"

"Nothing." I leaf through the pile of papers one more time, you know, just in case.

"That's not like Maggie."

It's not. But then Maggie hasn't been like Maggie lately either. Exhibit number one, this sudden trip to Santa Fe. Exhibit number two, the group text this morning to me and Nate from Mom and Maggie saying they've bought us tickets to come visit—in two days.

Before I managed to get to the count of four, Nate was lighting up my phone.

Nate: WTF?!!!!

Me: Don't yell at me. I have no idea.

Nate: I'M NOT YELLING

Me: raised eyebrow emoji

Nate: Okay, I'm yelling. But WTF?!!!!!

Me: shrugging emoji

Nate: SAY SOMETHING

Me: I've got nothing

Nate: Not helping

Me: Neither is yelling

Nate: Those two are up to something

Me: Ya think?

Nate: Not helping

Me: I haven't had enough coffee for this

Nate: coffee emoji

Me: Not helping

Nate: I'm coming over after work. We're calling them together.

Me: K

Nate: K ????

Me: Okay ????

Nate: face palm emoji

Me: Don't you have a rocket to launch or something?

Nate: To be continued

Me: Yup

Nate: Yup ????

Me: Go work!!!!!!

His phone had developed an interesting case of Tourette's since that exchange and every thirty minutes or so, I'd get another "WTF?!!!!!" text. I've ignored them. Because truly, there's nothing to add.

So now, in addition to having to scramble for coverage for the store, I have to figure out where things stand with the Spring Tour contract. And that makes me twitchy.

"While we're on the subject of Maggie not doing Maggie-like things," I say, "what's the likelihood that you can be here full time starting, oh, tomorrow?"

That stops Julia in her tracks. "For how long?"

"Long weekend. I'll be back on Tuesday."

Julia raises an eyebrow, waiting for more of an explanation. I don't think Maggie and I have ever both been away from the store at the same time. At least not for more than an hour or two.

"You want to leave me in charge? Of everything?"

I nod. "Including Lulu if that's okay."

"I've never opened or closed the store." Julia worries her lower lip and, though I trust her completely, the worry spreads to me. It would be irresponsible of me to leave while Maggie's away.

Yet Mom and Maggie hadn't asked us to come, they'd arranged for us to come. That simple-ish fact is more than unsettling.

"It's easy," I assure Julia. "I'll walk you through it today and tomorrow. Assuming you're available?" Because she hasn't actually said yes. And if Julia doesn't say yes, I'm out of options. The only other people who work for us are very part time, no one I would trust the way I do Julia.

"You can even stay in my apartment," I offer, hoping to sweeten the deal. Julia shares a townhouse with two roommates, an on-again-off-again couple who are presently in the off-again mode making for a rather uncomfortable vibe.

"You could have started with that and saved us minutes of agony," Julia says. "If I have to listen to Max and Emily bicker over the yogurt or toilet paper or thermostat for much longer, I may lose my mind."

"So you'll do it?"

"I'll do it." Julia flashes a smile.

"Any chance you want to do me one more favor? Grovel to the Spring Tour Committee?"

"I can," Julia says, and I almost drop the vase I'd just picked up to give her a hug.

"Wait, seriously?" I know it's wrong to dump that responsibility on someone else but Julia has a way with people. I've watched her sweet talk customers and suppliers, a skill Maggie possesses, but one I do not.

"Seriously. Jeff is a great guy. I don't mind reaching out to him."

I exhale, the first wave of relief I've felt all day.

Coverage for the store—check.

Someone to feed and love on Lulu—check.

Uncovering the mystery of the spring tour contract—in progress.

My phone flashes with yet another WTF?!!!!! from Nate. I turn off my phone and attempt to focus on shoveling through a few more surprises in the disorganization that is Maggie's process.

THE WORKDAY DIDN'T DO much to calm Nate's frustration with our moms. Didn't do much to calm mine either but at least I had Julia to help ease some of the load. At least until she reached Jeff Barnet.

"Before you launch into Mom and Maggie, I need to talk to Maggie about shop business," I say, hoping to preempt Nate's eruption.

"It's all part of the same problem. I don't understand how she can just up and leave like she did. She'd never do anything to jeopardize the store." I can practically see the smoke coming from Nate's ears as he paces. Even Lulu gave up trying to keep up with him and now sits on the counter watching him suspiciously.

"You're stressing out the cat." I reach to pet Lou but she slaps me away, her attention solely on Nate.

"How are you not furious?" Nate whirls on me.

I hold my hands up, earning another swipe from Lou. I glare at her, then at Nate. "Who said I'm not? Unless I can turn this cactus of a mess into a work of art, we're going to lose one of our most important events."

The conversation with Jeff had been the fresh poop on a compost heap of a day. When the deadline came and he still hadn't heard from us, Jeff had called. And called. Even stopped by the store. Whatever conversation he'd had with Maggie, stayed with Maggie.

"I don't get it, Nate. I mean, how, why, oh hell." I let my head drop into my hands. Nothing about this makes sense.

"Call," Nate says, pointing at my phone.

"Why me?"

"It was your mom who bought the fucking plane tickets without discussing it with us first."

I've heard more f-bombs from Nate today than I usually hear in a year.

"Fine," I say and initiate a call to my mom on speaker.

"Hello?" Mom answers.

"Hi, Mom."

"Callie?"

Nate rolls his eyes and I swallow a groan. Who else would call her "mom"? And hello caller ID?

"Yes?" I make eye contact with Nate who's now rolling his eyes at me for apparently not being sure if it really is me.

"Mom, is Maggie there? I need to talk to her about something with the store first."

"Then why didn't you call her phone?" Mom says, irritated.

"Because we want to talk to both of you. But I have a question for Maggie first."

"Move over," Maggie orders my mom. "You got the email with the tickets?" she sounds as agitated as my mom. Normally Maggie is the laid back one, nothing ruffles her leaves, so hearing her worked up sends both Nate and me into heightened alert.

"Maggie," I take a deep breath trying to compose myself. "We missed the deadline on the spring tour application. I think I can still get us included in the running but it's going to take work."

"Mom," Nate leans over my shoulder to talk at the phone, "we can't just take time off with such short notice." I push him away. I was supposed to have first crack at her.

"Listen to me, you two. I understand work commitments, but family is more important," Maggie says and in the background I hear my mom grumbling, "For god's sake, why is this so difficult."

While the two of them bicker over why we're having this discussion, Nate taps the mute button and says, "What the living hell." It's not a question and it doesn't require an answer.

"Mom?" I ask, taking us off mute. "What is going on?"

A pot slams into the sink. Nate and I both lean back as though the danger could reach us through the phone. We gape at each other and I'm so thankful that I chose to call instead of FaceTime.

"Just be on that plane," Mom says, and the phone goes dead.

Weird we know, weird we've lived through. This isn't normal weird.

# 18

# FLOWERS DON'T TELL, THEY SHOW.
### — STEPHANIE SKEEM

I grip the armrest and push my head into the headrest. Inhale, one, two, three. Hold, one, two, three. Exhale, one, two, this is insane.

"Will you stop it. You're stressing me out," Nate mutters next to me.

I turn my head and glare at him. The plane jolts with a bang that sounds like the wing is being ripped off. I squeeze my eyes shut and tighten my stranglehold on the armrests.

"They finished loading the suitcases and closed the cargo door," Nate says, prying my fingers from the vinyl and metal armrest. I transfer my grip to his hand, making him wince. "This is going to be a long ass flight if you don't chill."

I wasn't always this neurotic about flying. Not true, I've always been this neurotic. I just haven't flown in a few years so everything feels new and scary. Bonus stress: I have zero idea what's waiting for us on the other end. Santa Fe, sure. My mom and Maggie, okay. But why the command appearance, complete with purchased tickets? And how does my long lost dad fit into the equation?

"I'm chill."

Nate flexes the fingers of the hand I've been gripping.

"Distract me." I ignore the look he's giving me. I suck in a breath when the plane begins to move. "Shit, shit, shit."

"Will you stop?" Nate growls as the flight attendant walks down the aisle doing a seatbelt check. She stops her forward momentum to assess my panicked face and death grip on Nate's hand.

"I'm fine," I say, giving her a tight smile. "Just haven't flown in a while."

Nate extracts his hand and pats me on the leg. "She'll be fine once we're in the air," he assures the flight attendant.

"Have you heard from your dad again?" Nate turns his attention back to me after the flight attendant moves on, closing the overhead bins as she continues her walk toward the back of the plane. *Clack, clack, clack.*

Come to think of it, no. Then again anyone in their right mind will get the hint after five—seven?—unanswered messages.

"I said distract me not feed my anxiety." I turn to the window to watch the world crawl by. "Is the pilot driving us there? I can drive faster in my car."

Nate exhales, sounding like a frustrated horse. "This is going to be a long ass trip," he says again. "You will, at some point, stop complaining, right?"

"I'm not complaining." I pout into the small, dirty window. "Maybe we'll crash and I won't have to deal with our moms. Or why Maggie is trying to run the shop into the ground. Or why my father has resurfaced."

"Oh for gods sake, Callie. We are not crashing," Nate says, flashing an all-will-be-fine smile at the woman in the seat in front of me who's twisted around, eyes large with concern. He leans closer to me and whispers, "Get a grip before they throw us off this plane. Don't even think about it," he adds at the flash in my eyes at the momentary thought of a potential escape route.

"Fine, we're going and it'll be awesome." I jazz hands the awesome which gets a twitch of a smile from Nate.

"Maybe not awesome but hopefully not a disaster. Anyway, it's been a long time since we had an adventure together."

"Hmm," I say, trying to wrap my braincells around the idea of this being an adventure. Nope, I can't get past nightmare.

The pilot announces that we've been cleared for takeoff. Nate threads his fingers through mine and gives a gentle squeeze and I instantly feel a tenth of a degree better.

He's always had this effect on me. As kids, as teenagers, as young adults, as not as young adults. I can always count on Nate to have my back (and occasionally to give my back a gentle push like he did getting me onto this plane).

"What do you want to do while we're there?" Nate asks, refocusing on his task to distract me.

My turn for the side eye. "Not be there."

Nate shakes his head then slaps his palm to his forehead. "Why do I try."

*Okay, Callie, pull yourself together,* I give myself a little pep talk.

"I guess that depends on the parental units. They're up to something so most likely they have every minute of our stay mapped out. And even if not, they know I'm a flight risk and will keep us under house arrest."

"Maybe. But I'm sure we can sneak off for an hour or so at some point. We're good at that." He winks conspiratorially.

"You forget how good they are at anticipating our rebellions."

As the youngest of three, Nate learned from his older brothers how to spin an almost truth that was just on the brilliant side of getting him out of a grounding. Then again, by the time he started pulling those stunts, Maggie was so worn down by the other two, that Nate's creativity was wasted on her. My parents, on the other hand, almost lost their shit every time Nate pulled me into one of his stunts (which was every time). And unlike Maggie, they adjusted to our rebellion with sharpened senses.

When we were twelve, Nate convinced me to sneak out one night because he'd read the conditions would be ideal for seeing the space station (yeah, he was a nerd even back then). The plan had been perfect. Nate would spend the night (nothing unusual there) and at 1 a.m., we'd sneak out my bedroom window, crawl along the roof of the sunroom, then drop down with an assist from the tree at the edge of the house. Nate had just cleared the skylight and I was plastered against it like a starfish in an aquarium, trying to get my footing on the edge of the roof when the light came on in the room below me and there, looking up at my smushed underside, stood my father.

My parents grounded me for a week but then reduced it to a day when Maggie dismissed our shenanigans as harmless.

"How about the Very Large Arrays?" Nate suggests. Ever since watching the movie *Contact* he's wanted to go.

I love his passion. I understand the fascination. But driving three hours to look at large white disks pointed at the sky is not my idea of a fun adventure. His child-like enthusiasm softens me, though.

"Maybe. But can we not sneak out via the roof?" I smile and he laughs. The plane bumps through a lining of clouds. Nate tightens his hold on my hand.

"Hey, do you remember meeting Kyle Harrington?" Nate takes a sharp detour in our conversation path.

The name rings a distant bell, but I can't pull a face from memory to join it. "Maybe?"

"He works with me. He's in the marketing department. You met him at one of the company parties. Picnic maybe? Anyway, he's a super nice guy. His divorce was finalized a few months ago. He's been dating a bit, but the dating scene isn't really rocking his rocket."

"Really? Gross." I grimace.

Nate drops his chin to his chest and laughs. "I didn't mean it like that. We work with rockets. In my head it sounded funnier than the cliched boat."

"Filter next time. And no. You are not setting us up."

"Why?"

"Because I'm not interested."

"What if it wasn't a setup?"

I twist in the seat to look at him. "Let me see if I have this right, the Eric mission was an underperformance that failed to land me in dating orbit, so now you want to try again with Kyle?" Yes, Eric and I had hit it off. Yes, he's attractive. Yes, I would've maybe, probably, entertained the idea of a date if he'd asked. But he hadn't.

"Look at you getting all fancy with terminology. You forgot the mating and erection portions of the mission though."

I groan and drop my head into my hands. "What's with the sudden urgency to hook me up with someone?" Like I don't have an idea but I want to hear him say it, especially since he normally respects my queasiness with dating. He's often quick to state the benefits of coupledom but he doesn't set me up unless I've specifically asked, which I've done only once.

Thirty-three always seemed so far away. We had all the time in the world to find our perfect others. Yet here I am, clinging to a relationship with an indifferent cat and a shedding Ficus while Nate seems to have found his perfect other.

"What makes Beth so perfect?" I'm talking to the window and between the engine and sudden announcement over the loudspeaker, I'm not sure Nate even heard me.

"There's no such thing as perfect. But someone can still be

perfect for us. Beth is surprising and fresh and she brings out a side of me I rarely let out."

A twinge of something weirdly resembling jealousy twists at my stomach.

"How can you be sure she's the one though?"

Nate shrugs. "I guess by the butterflies in my stomach when we're together."

"That's probably just heartburn. You need to lay off the spicy food."

He laughs. "Maybe."

"I sometimes wonder if I know how to be with anyone but you."

Nate's expression clouds and he twists to look at me. "Yes, you do," he protests.

My head starts a slow shake. "Not really. Not completely. Talk about screwed up trust issues. The moment someone wants to go out with me, I immediately question what's wrong with him." No surprise where that insecurity comes from but damn, my father left a lifetime ago. Shouldn't I have gotten over it by now?

"There's someone out there who will be your perfect. And we'll always have each other. That won't change."

"It already is." The weight of that realization forces me deeper into the seat. Then again, that could also be the plane changing altitude.

"To some extent, I guess, it's inevitable. But you're not getting rid of me. Ever."

It's not that I worry about us not being in each other's life, we're too connected. We've seen each other through every life event, every up and down. We know everything about each other. There's nothing I wouldn't confide in Nate about and nothing I wouldn't do for him. I know it's the same for him.

This is the first time, though, that a relationship has

impacted our friendship. We've spent less time together, had fewer late-night text and FaceTime sessions. And the last time we fell asleep on my couch together, there was an undeniably awkward moment when we woke up, spooning with his arm around me.

"What?" Nate challenges me. "You've got a weird look on your face."

"Why didn't we ever..." I don't finish the thought out loud.

Nate leans his head closer to mine and whispers, "Ever have sex?"

I feel my face flush even though that's exactly what I was going to ask. Another piece of evidence bagged and tagged ... I've never felt uncomfortable joking with Nate about sex.

"Yeah. No. Not just that." I can feel Nate's nearness and if I turn my head a smidge more, we'll be kissing distance. I look down the aisle at where the flight attendants have started with the beverage carts then open my tray even though there's still fifteen rows before they'll get to us.

"Because we're family." Nate settles back into his seat, and I feel a whoosh of cold air fill the space his body had just occupied.

"But we're not actually family." What exactly am I trying to prove?

Nate is the only one who's ever seen past the plain facade to the real me. He sees a side of me most guys never cared to learn about. I don't have the pretty to draw the initial want-to-know-you or the looks to move beyond the I-like-you-as-a-friend. But even seeing the real me, he's never seen me as anything but his best friend.

We're quiet as the flight attendant hands out drinks and a snack. I fight the miniature bag of pretzels wishing I could smash that last comment as easily as I'm killing the pretzels. This is Nate. Nate and I will never be more than best friends. I don't want us to be more than best friends. Don't I? It doesn't matter anyway because he doesn't see me as anything other than a sisterly best friend.

"Wasn't there a time when in-flight snacks were actual snacks? Like a sandwich and chips?" Nate complains, popping a pretzel into his mouth.

"And a cookie," I add, staring into the small bag of what's become pretzel crumbs after I manhandled it open.

Nate leans down and pulls something from his carry-on bag. He dangles a ziplock between us. "Voila. Cookies."

I push his hand down and hold a finger to my lips. "Keep your voice down. Are you nuts? We could get mugged for those."

The woman in the seat in front of me twists and peers between the seats again. I flash a smile and Nate whispers, "Nothing to see here." She chuckles and turns back to the front.

Nate opens the bag and I take out two Oreos, stuffing one in my mouth, whole. "Oh my god, that's amazing." Between the seats, I catch the woman looking sideways again. Nate reaches the bag through the open spot and offers her one. She turns again and whispers thanks, then runs her fingers along her mouth in a zipped-shut motion.

We finish the bag of Oreos in record time, all conversation shelved.

My head droops against the window, suddenly heavy.

"Geez, if I'd known the Oreos would calm you down, I would have pulled the bag out earlier."

"Smartass." I love, though, that he knows me well enough to have packed Oreos. I'm not much for desserts or sweets in general but there are three things I can't resist: Oreos, lavender lattes, and Nutella.

The plane jolts and my heart leaps into the overhead bin. Nate reaches for my hand and I lean into him. With my head on his shoulder and my hand in his, my heartbeat slows, and I feel myself relax.

As my eyes flutter shut, I catch a glimpse of Nate scribbling a note on a napkin with the airline logo on it.

# 19

# FLOWERS ARE A PROUD ASSERTION THAT A RAY OF BEAUTY OUT VALUES ALL THE UTILITIES IN THE WORLD.

— RALPH WALDO EMERSON

"Scoot," Nate swats at me until I've rolled to one side of the bed. He crawls in next to me and pulls the blanket over our heads. It's far too early for a wakeup call considering how late it was when we finally got to bed last night after getting into Santa Fe.

Mom and Maggie had played a brilliant game of distraction, refusing to give even the slightest clue as to why it was so desperately urgent that we come for this visit with a two-day notice. I'm amazed neither of them got hurt with the insane hoops they were tripping over not to tell us anything of importance.

I giggle as Nate settles under the duvet next to me. We're eight years old again. Sleepovers were nothing special when we were growing up. Nate defaulted to staying at our house to avoid the commotion caused by his brothers. At first, we slept in the living room in sleeping bags and makeshift forts. But being downstairs interfered with my mom's morning routine so we started sleeping upstairs.

At some point, my parents caved and bought bunk beds for

my room. The night almost always started with us in the lower bunk talking until my father shushed us. Nate would then get into the top bunk, and we'd continue whispering until someone fell asleep mid-sentence (usually me). But always in the morning, Nate would command "scoot" and crawl into the lower bunk.

I can't remember the last time we did this though. Falling asleep on the couch together isn't the same. And I'm suddenly, acutely aware of every inch of the man under the blanket with me.

The sofa bed in Mom's den squeaks and Nate and I dissolve into silent giggles. He holds a finger to his lips which doesn't help sober us.

"Be vewy, vewy quiet," I whisper. "I heard someone in the kitchen. My mom I assume?"

"Yeah. I was careful not to be spotted but I think she heard me. Her hearing is scary."

"Seriously. My mom has the hearing of a moth." I never understood how my mom knew exactly what I was mumbling when she wasn't looking at me or even in the same room.

From down the hall, I can hear the banging of pans. "Why is she fixing breakfast already? It's too early," I complain.

"It's 7 a.m."

"It can't be. It's still dark outside." I peek out from under the heavy blanket to confirm my suspicion.

"I smell pancakes," Nate says and attempts to push the duvet off.

I yank it back up. "If I'm not mistaken, and I rarely am in these cases, she's making Nutella pancakes."

"Oh shit," Nate says and yanks the blanket over our heads.

Two things that will forever be bound together with mental duct tape: Nutella pancakes and unwelcome news. Which makes it odd that I still have a weakness for Nutella but sometimes the stomach overrules common sense.

"We got to bed at 2 a.m., Nate. That's not enough sleep. What time is it really?" I attempt to roll over which isn't easy considering the weight of the blanket and Nate holding it down over us.

"It's 5:33," says a voice from the other side of the comforter. "And breakfast is ready."

Nate's eyes bug and he mouths, "She's in the room." I swallow a laugh.

"Come on, before the pancakes get cold." There's a pause and I can picture her staring at the two lumps in the bed, mouth tight, eyes narrowed. Lounging in bed is not something she approves of. Not that anyone in their right mind would consider being in bed at 5 a.m. lounging.

"Nice to see some things haven't changed," Maggie says when Nate and I come into the kitchen.

"Meaning?" Nate asks without breaking stride toward the coffee pot.

"That you two still think we can't hear you when you're whispering under the blankets." Maggie smiles into her mug, blatantly avoiding a pointed look from my mom.

There's so much about this visit that's already causing me heartburn and we haven't started with the spicy New Mexico food yet. Or the reason our mothers commanded us to come. I pinch the bridge of my nose, hoping to stave off the headache knocking at my temple.

Nate winks at me, sending a flash of heat up my chest and neck. I'm instantly aware that what we did at eight, is a bit (understatement) suspect at 33. Even if there's nothing between us other than sibling-like love and friendship. Thirty-three year old Nate doesn't look (or feel) like eight-year old Nate.

I refocus, trying to get my cheeks back to their nonchalant pink. "So, Mom, why the special pancakes?"

Mom looks up from the cast iron griddle covering half of her stove, the look of surprise surprising. There's no way she doesn't remember the connection between this choice of breakfast food and bad news.

When my pet goldfish, Sparky, floated to the top of the bowl and she flushed him before I woke up, we had Nutella pancakes. When our long-anticipated trip to Disney World was cancelled because she had the opportunity to work on a production of Carmen for the Lyric Opera in Baltimore, Mom softened the blow with Nutella pancakes. And when she broke the news that she was checking herself into a wellness center in Santa Fe after my father left, it was over Nutella pancakes.

Nate slices his fork through a pancake allowing a river of brown hazelnut goo to escape onto the plate. How can something as simple as a pancake bring on both hunger pangs and an anxiety attack?

I stack three onto a plate and dive in before my mom can ruin the first bite. Enjoyment then heartburn. It's how we do breakfasts.

Mom places another plate of pancakes on the table and slumps into a chair. Nate kicks me under the table, eyes wide. Mom never slumps. Maggie leans across the table and squeezes my mom's hand. Air leaves my lungs.

"Mom?" I ask when I've finally managed to swallow the bite of pancake.

"I know you have a lot of questions. We'll answer all of them, but I need you to promise something first. Promise you'll keep an open mind and don't be hasty with judgement."

"That's two things," Nate says. The three women at the table glare at him. "Geez, tough crowd." He stuffs a large bite into his mouth.

Maggie clears her throat and, apropos nothing related to the Nutella pancakes, says "It's supposed to be clear tonight. Good viewing for the meteor shower."

"Jack told me about a spot folks go to for celestial shows. You two should go tonight," my mom adds as though this is a completely normal conversation for us to be having at 5:30 in the morning after she's just laid the foundation for what I suspect will be a teeth-rattling revelation.

"Who's Jack?" Is he one of the things I need to keep an open mind about? Mom has had a few gentlemen friends, as she refers to them, in the years since my father left but none were serious as far as I know. Walt lasted a couple of years, but Mom insisted he was just a "fun partner for trips." Barry was a "fun partner for hanging out." And Jim kept her feeling young. The less I knew about any of them, the happier I am.

"Jack is the lighting director at the opera house," she says as though, duh, I should know everyone she does. I shake my head because Mom rarely talks about anyone in her life. I only discovered that she was halfway around the world with Walt when I called her cell and he answered with a fake Australian accent because they were in Australia. "Anyway, he's an astronomy enthusiast. You could go with him if you want." She perks up as though this is the missing piece to a perfect plan.

"We'll consider it, thanks," Nate says and gives me a what's-that-about expression.

"So, Mom," I start to redirect. Before I have time to finish, she jumps up as though electrocuted and refills coffee mugs. Because caffeinating us will absolutely help with the "no hasty decision and judgement" request.

"David is in town." The words drop in rapid slow motion.

My brain slams to a stop and it feels like all of my organs are scattered throughout my body. "What? What do you mean he's in town?" I catch myself looking down the hall as though he'll pop out of one of the bedrooms.

"We'll visit with him this morning and then go for lunch," she continues without acknowledging my question. "There's a nice little restaurant in town with a charming patio. Their chicken tortilla soup is the best. Everything on the menu is excellent."

"The bison tacos are to die for," Maggie chimes in.

I gape. Soup? Bison tacos? Seriously?

I hold my hands up to stop the chow wagon. "Dad?" I prompt.

Forget chow wagon, this is a manure tractor. We've gone from meteor showers to bison tacos with a helping of an estranged father.

"This is not making any sense. Why is he in town? And why are we going to visit with him?" I have a sudden, ridiculous vision of us sitting around a small table with tea and cookies. This trip just got so much worse than I imagined.

My dad. Here. Now. The words crash about in my head. Nate takes my hand under the table and squeezes.

"Where is he?" Nate asks, which seems like a ridiculous question because Mom just said he's in town, but that's just my brain refusing to hear what it doesn't want to believe.

"David is in the hospital. He's sick."

Mom jumps up as though whatever my father has is contagious and she could catch it by sitting where she just dropped the word. She clears her plate even though she hasn't touched a thing on it.

"Sick how?" Nate asks, leaning forward. Under the table, he places a hand on my knee.

"He has a brain tumor," Maggie fills in when mom doesn't respond.

"Operable?" Nate asks.

Mom shakes her head.

I want to tell them they're wrong. My father was—is—a bear-hug of a guy. He's the kind of person who lights up a room the moment he walks in. He's the person who always knows what to say at the right moment. I may still be smarting from unresolved issues after his departure and I may have stubbornly held onto those issues when he reached out, but my father is not the type of person who gets an inoperable disease.

# 20

# LOVE HAS ITS OWN INSTINCT, FINDING THE WAY TO THE HEART, AS THE FEEBLEST INSECT FINDS THE WAY TO ITS FLOWER, WITH A WILL WHICH NOTHING CAN DISMAY NOR TURN ASIDE.

— HONORE DE BALZAC

I'd be lying if I didn't admit to having a few fantasies over the years about seeing my dad again. In some of the scenarios, he calls to me on the street as I'm walking somewhere. Sometimes I'll look up while I'm in the store and imagine him standing there, a look of love and hope and regret on his face. In one fantasy I tracked him down, I don't remember where I found him, probably one of the locations from the postcards he sent that first year he was gone.

The common theme in every one of these visions, is that he looks exactly the way he did the day he left. He sounds the same. He's even wearing the same clothes—jeans with a distressed patch on the left thigh; a grey cashmere sweater over a peach button-down shirt, the crisp triangles of the collar and rounded hem exposed; and his black Converse. Always his black Converse.

Today, though, the man in the wheelchair looking out the

window looks nothing like the man in any of the fantasies or any of my memories.

"David," Mom says, marching past me. I wince at the sharp tone of her voice, far too loud in the stale air of the room.

The visiting room, as the nurse referred to it, is overly cheerful with soft yellow walls, upholstered chairs in light blue, wicker chairs with red and white cushions, and serene paintings of the ocean. It all feels like a cruel joke when we're in the middle of a world in shades of brown (no offense, Santa Fe).

The optimism of the sunny morning is smothered by the fake brilliance of the overhead lights. It takes every ounce of willpower not to turn and run back outside.

A puzzle is spread out on a table in the middle of the room. Someone has completed the border and a couple clusters of matches sit in the middle. To the left, people talk soundlessly on a large screen TV. I don't recognize the program. Then again, I can't remember when I last watched daytime TV.

"David," Mom says again, squatting next to the wheelchair and placing her hand on his forearm. There's a tenderness to her tone this time that forces the breath from my lungs. He turns to her and smiles, a smile so genuine that if I was a stranger watching, I'd think they were a loving couple.

I close my eyes to block the image in front of me and cycle through memories.

Dad used to surprise her with little gifts. A jar of her favorite bubble bath, the purple tulips she liked, a scarf. Scarves were, still are, her signature piece. Today, she wears a red scarf with black hearts on it. Not the one I would have chosen. Mom would buy the green tea ice cream Dad loved and she'd have a bottle of wine ready when he got home. Small things but, now that I look back, meaningful to the two of them.

Dad pushes against the floor, moving the wheelchair so he's facing mom. My eyes slide down to his feet. He's wearing shiny white sneakers with grippy rubber soles.

I feel his eyes on me and I force myself to look up. He lifts a hand as though waiting for someone to take it and help him up. Mom stands and pats the top of his hand gently. His eyes are locked on me, his hand moving in mid-air like when we went on road trips and we'd stick our hands out the car window, letting the waves of the wind take control.

"I'm going to get us something to drink," Mom says, giving me a nudge toward my father. "Give you two a chance to catch up."

Catch up? Catch up is something you do with someone you haven't seen in a few months or a year, not with the father you haven't heard from in sixteen years. Where do we even start? *Hi Dad, how've you been? How's life?*

I glare at my mom's back but she's already halfway down the hall. This was a total ambush. She should have prepared me better. She should have stayed with me. I should have insisted that Nate come. At least he wouldn't abandon me to face this alone.

*This.* My father.

"Callie, come," Dad says, nodding toward a grouping of wicker chairs. He uses his white sneakers to walk his wheelchair in the direction of the chairs, his hands resting in his lap. Not resting exactly. The right one hasn't stopped moving. He catches me looking and places his left hand over the right, anchoring it.

"It's so good to see you," he says, once I've perched on a chair across from him.

I nod. I'm supposed to say, "it's good to see you, too," or some such. But it's not good to see him. Not like this. Not after so many years of wondering where he was, what he was doing, why he didn't reach out.

"You have questions," he continues. It's a statement. The quiet that settles between us is the invitation for me to ask whatever question I want.

"You're not wearing your black Converse." *Wow, Callie. That was brilliant.* Let's just pretend the giant purple elephant in the room is wearing an invisibility cloak.

He looks down as though surprised. "Ah. Yes. These have more traction. They're hideous, aren't they?" He whispers, leaning toward me as though the admission will land him in trouble.

I nod. They're what we used to call Tourist Beacons. "I still always picture you in your black Converse."

I wasn't expecting to admit that I think about him. I was expecting even less the rush of gratitude on his face.

We both fall silent again and pretend to watch the people around us. A natural in social situations I've never been but even for me this is ridiculous. He is, after all, my father, not a stranger. Except he is a stranger. I don't know anything about his life since the day he walked out. Come to think of it, I'm not sure I knew anything about his life before he left. How else to explain the absolute gut-punch of surprise at his departure?

"Why did you leave?" The appropriate place to start would probably have been asking about his health or maybe apologizing for not returning any of his messages. But no, turns out I have enough of my mom in me after all.

He nods but I'm not sure if it's acknowledgement of the question or an involuntary movement as a result of his disease. The tumor, Maggie explained, had invaded adjacent bone and was putting pressure on nerve tissue.

"I fell in love. My," he hesitates and when he finally continues, he's looking out the window again, "friend had a rare form of leukemia. The doctors said he had six months if we were lucky. He had a bucket list of places he wanted to see, and I made a vow to him that we'd get to as many as we could."

*He.*

"The postcards," I say.

"The postcards." Dad turns back to me. I can see the bright, mischievous glint I remember trapped behind a curtain of emotion.

"But ..." But what? But the postcards came for a year, not six months? But why didn't you just tell me? But how did you fall in love with a man? But why did you choose him over me?

I finally settle on a question. "Mom knew?"

"Your mom knew. I loved your mom. You and your mom were my life, don't ever doubt that." He swallows and I bite my lip to keep the snarky response at bay. This isn't the time. "Steven and I were friends. He was a therapist. Not mine," Dad adds quickly. "I met him through your mom, actually. He loved the opera. They had mutual friends and would get together before or after performances. You know opera wasn't really my thing."

I remember. Dad would say, "Why don't you and Maggie go, have a fun night out. Give me a chance to hang out with my girl." We'd go out to eat or bring in food and eat on the couch while watching a movie (something my mom never allowed). I loved those nights.

"I was thrilled that she had someone to share her passion with. Maggie was a fun date, but Maggie could only take so much opera as well. Steven and your mom were the perfect pair.

"Then one day, your mom asked me to join her at a fancy charity gala in support of the opera company. Not something I could say no to. That's when I met Steven. He was funny, smart, we had a lot of things in common, except opera. He was going through a divorce and your mom and I were, I don't really know how to describe it. We just weren't. Steven and I became friends. I was someone he could confide in and he understood what I was struggling with."

Dad pauses, taking in a deep breath and blinking as though attempting to sharpen the focus on the next scene of the story.

*We just weren't.* But they were. My parents had a language

between them, a silent understanding of what the other needed. I used to watch them, mesmerized by the choreography of the life they shared. How he knew to take her hand and lead her to the back patio when she was at the point of overwhelm. Or how she'd straighten his collar even though it never needed it and whisper something into his ear.

But with his confession, I allow the details I'd long pushed aside to come to the forefront. The way Mom would come home some nights and go straight upstairs to take a bath and go to bed. Or the times Dad would claim a craving and we'd go out, the two of us, not even bringing home a take-out order for Mom.

"Did you try to fix the marriage?" I want to know that he'd cared enough to try. That she'd cared enough to try.

Dad nods. "Not therapy, your mom didn't want to do that. But we tried."

"You said Steven was a therapist." I wince at the thought of them talking about Mom behind her back. About this Steven person turning my dad against her, against us.

"He was but he wasn't my therapist. We just talked. About dreams, experiences, what we wanted, what we regretted."

I stand and walk to a water cooler by a table with pads of paper and pens. If Nate was here, he'd probably jot down something soothing and sweet. Nate would know immediately how angry I am. Not at Dad for once, but at Steven. At the man who confided in my father and became his confidant.

I gulp two paper cups of tepid water and force my heartbeat to slow. I fill the cup a third time then fill a second one for my father even though he didn't ask.

"Thank you," he says when I hand him the cone-shaped cup. His hand trembles, spilling some of the water on his pants.

"How did it, when did, what happened?" I finally say when none of the other question attempts come together.

"Steven got sick. His ex-wife couldn't be bothered and I

couldn't bear to see him go through that hell alone. I drove him to his appointments, sat with him during treatments, helped him when he could barely lift his head from the toilet. We'd watch stupid sitcoms and eat ice cream and talk. Lots of talking. Neither one of us expected our relationship to develop the way it did. There was a trust that developed, seeing each other through the rough patches."

"But you loved Mom."

"I did. I still do. There are different kinds of love. And sometimes the person we need isn't the person we're with."

I can't look at him. I can't stomach the idea that Mom wasn't who he needed, that I wasn't who he needed.

"Did Mom know you were having an affair?" I meant it to sound mean and yet the moment the words are out, I regret my tone.

"It wasn't like that. The connection I had with Steven was emotional. Your mother is an amazing woman but she's also hard to penetrate. She loved me in her own way and for a long time that was enough. Until someone showed me what it felt like to be cared about completely."

Suddenly I see myself in his words. Isn't that exactly what I do as well?

"What about me? You didn't just leave her." Tears push their way up but I swallow, blink, force them back. I will not cry, not here, not now.

"I never meant to be gone forever. I wanted to give Steven his bucket list trip. I always intended on returning to you ..." There's no period at the end of his thought.

"After he ..." I prompt but can't finish the sentence either.

"After he died," Dad finally says. "Thirteen days short of a year after his diagnosis."

I'm struck at the specificity. "Why didn't you tell me any of this when you left?" I wasn't a little kid, I would have understood. At least I want to think I would have.

"Your mom asked me not to. And to be honest, I didn't know how to tell you. I'm not sure even I really understood it at the time. I don't expect you to forgive me or even understand what I did. But I hope you'll give me a chance to prove how much I love you. How much I've always loved you." He reaches for my hand. I stare at it, hanging in the air between us, shaking with the effort it must take to ask for something he doesn't feel he deserves.

My body tenses with the need to bypass the outstretched hand and fling my arms around him. I force air out of my lungs and with it, push myself deeper into my seat. Dad folds his outstretched hand into the palm of the other on his lap.

"Why didn't you come back then?'

"I didn't know how." He's looking at his hands as though they're the reason he couldn't figure it out.

"And now?"

He finally looks up, locks eyes with me.

"I'm out of time."

# 21

# TO PLANT A GARDEN IS TO BELIEVE IN TOMORROW.

## — AUDREY HEPBURN

After half an hour of stilted conversation with my dad, the nurse came to wheel him back to his room. I'd been equally panicked and relieved to see him go. Thirty minutes after seventeen years wasn't nearly enough. But it was also more than either of us had the energy for on a first visit. Thankfully, for once, my mom had kept her opinions to herself on the drive home. And thankfully, for once, my brain overruled my mouth. Whatever argument she and I need to have about her role in Dad leaving, in Dad not coming back, in the ambush, will just have to wait until my thoughts and emotions slot themselves into something semi-coherent.

Double thanks that she hadn't insisted on the lunch date. Tortilla soup and bison tacos aside, the thought of enduring an uncomfortable lunch with Mom and Maggie talking about asteroids or coyotes was beyond what I could stomach.

The moment Mom and I walked in the house, Nate whisked me back out. And directly to the delightfully touristy Plaza with its boutiques and restaurants and flowerpots and people. There's an earthiness to Santa Fe that catches me off guard every time I visit. It's the seductive traditions of a world so different from the one I know. Santa Fe insists you slow down to enjoy the world around you. I'm endlessly fascinated by the adobe buildings with their thick wood beams and I'm charmed by the sunsets that are more brilliant than any painting I've ever seen.

"Can we get ice cream?" I gravitate to an ice cream shop like a magnet to the side of a car.

"It's freezing," Nate complains.

"It's freezing in Maryland. It's nippy here."

"Either way, it's cold. And you want ice cream?" But he's already opening the door for me.

It's a total cliché, but ice cream is my attitude adjustment. Especially if it includes Nutella. I order vanilla with Nutella and banana pieces swirled into it.

"Nutella?" Nate asks with obvious, and justified, suspicion.

"Don't judge." I'm still reeling from talking to Dad. It didn't come close to any of the reunions I'd imagine throughout the years.

Nate orders coffee ice cream with fudge and mini marshmallows.

We walk a block, looking into the stores and galleries, eating the ice cream Nate had poo pooed and now devours. I hip check him when he attempts to put his spoon into my bowl.

"Wow. Way to be a friend."

"You've got your own."

"But I like your choice better."

"You always do this."

"So?"

"So next time just say, 'I'll have what she's having'."

"We're not in your favorite rom com."

"And you're not getting my favorite ice cream." I shift my body to shield my bowl as Nate attempts another dip.

We cross the street and start down another block of

galleries. "I'm sorry I wasn't there with you," Nate says. I can't imagine how hard it was."

I stop to get a better look at a wood bowl that would be perfect in my apartment. I gasp at the price. Maybe not so perfect. Nate hasn't stopped though and I have to take a couple of jog steps to catch up to him.

"It's probably good that you didn't come. That whole visit was surreal."

"How?" he asks around the spoon in his mouth.

I stare, stopping mid-stride. Nate takes the opportunity to get a scoop of my ice cream. He grins as he slides it into his mouth.

"Rude. And what do you mean how? How could it be anything but surreal? For one, a long-lost dad who resurfaces after seventeen years. Then there's the way my mom kept touching his arm. The conversation, if you can call it that, was painful. Want me to keep going?"

"Let's start with the last one. There's a lot of emotional baggage that needs to be unpacked."

"Can't we just throw that bag over a bridge instead?" For seventeen years, I've carried around hurt and anger and disappointment. Hearing my dad's voice in those messages had spurred a host of feelings, none of them charitable. Seeing him today, looking nothing like the man I'd tucked away in my memories, brought up more hurt and anger and utter despair.

"Would it help to visit him again today? Without your mom this time?"

"No. The nurse said to come back tomorrow." I toss the now empty bowl into a trash can but keep the spoon in my mouth. Nate sees me eyeing his bowl which is still almost half full and holds it out for me.

"I like mine better," I say after the third bite.

"Then stop eating it." Nate lifts the bowl out of my reach. He stops in front of a jewelry shop and grabs at my arm before I have a chance to escape. I did not inherit the shopping gene from my mom.

"Come on," he takes my hand. "I want to go in."

The moment we're inside, a tall, lanky blonde approaches Nate. "Welcome. Is there anything I can help you find? For your, um, friend?" She eyeballs me, then, accurately summing me up, dismisses the idea that we're a couple and flashes a smile at Nate.

"There's a bracelet in the window I wanted to get a closer look at, please." He points at whatever caught his eye.

With Nate and the salesgirl busy discussing the bracelet, I turn my attention to a table-top display in the center of the store.

I touch the tip of a pendant, a silver leaf on a lariat necklace. It's delicate without being dainty, intricate without being fussy, modern without being abstract. A leaf, the symbol for hope, growth, rebirth. And death. It's a reminder that life is momentary, that we need to cherish the time we have, enjoy the beauty, and accept the changes.

"Do you want to try it on?" A voice asks from behind me. I jump in surprise, almost knocking over the necklace display and capsizing another with three bracelets slung on it.

Nate grabs at the bracelets before they can tumble off the table. "I'm sorry about that. Can't take her anywhere." He flashes a smile at the salesperson then a cheeky grin at me.

He lifts the necklace from the display and steps behind me. With his free hand, he moves my hair over my left shoulder and clasps the necklace around my neck. My skin tingles at the soft brush of his fingers on the exposed skin at the base of my neck. His eyes drop to the pendant, the tip of the leaf perfectly positioned between my breasts, then back until our eyes meet in the mirror in front of us. I'm trapped between the heat of his eyes in our reflection in the mirror and the heat of his body behind me.

"It's beautiful," he says.

My fingers linger on the cold metal of the pendant. My dad's words swirl around us. *Sometimes the person we need isn't the person we're with.*

What if the person you're with is the person you need but you're not the person he needs?

I blink and Nate quickly steps back, returning to the counter and a bracelet laid out on a black felt pad.

I remove the necklace and hand it gently back to the sales-person who hovers, unsure if the future of the sale is with me or Nate. She, rightly so, chooses Nate.

I take my time, pretending to look at rings and earrings and bracelets in the various cases along the perimeter of the store.

My body hums with the nervous energy of an impending storm. Nate says something to the sales lady. She picks up the bracelet and the necklace I just tried on and walks to the register.

As he walks by me, Nate puts his arm around my waist. That same tingle sends a shiver through me. Nate tightens his hold and looks at me, concerned.

"Air conditioning," I say, rubbing my arm. Not the most plausible of explanations but he doesn't call me on it.

"Can you please remove the tag," Nate says, picking up the necklace.

"Nate," I protest but he's already slipping it around my neck.

"It's perfect, like you." Our eyes meet and in that moment I see the promise of feelings we've never explored.

I touch the leaf. "Thank you," I whisper.

"Shall I put the bracelet in a box?" the sales lady asks.

"Please," Nate answers.

I turn to look just in time to see a silver bangle with a moon pendant being tucked into the black velvet of a gift box.

# 22

# AND THEN MY HEART WITH PLEASURE FILLS, AND DANCES WITH THE DAFFODILS.

— WILLIAM WORDSWORTH

"Where are you taking me?" I grip the handle on the passenger door as the jeep bumps over uneven ground. The browns of the landscape have taken on a golden hue from the last flames of the setting sun. If I wasn't so unnerved by being in the middle of nowhere, I'd probably appreciate the beauty. But I'm a city girl and I find these wide-open nothings terrifying.

"You'll see," Nate answers, the playfulness in his voice is a stark contrast to our location and the events of the day.

"In the movies, this is where the bad guy kidnaps the stupidly naive woman to murder her."

Nate laughs. "I'm not the bad guy."

"Am I stupidly naive?" I chance a look at him.

Nate returns the look. "Far from it."

"You have to say that, you're my best friend. And keep your eyes on the road."

"Get over yourself. There's no road." He motions around us. I resist pointing out that that's part of the problem. "As your best friend, I know you better than anyone so I'm pretty confident with that assessment. And there are no bad guys out here. Relax," he adds.

"No bad guys but what about wild animals?"

"Reeee lax," he pulls the word apart as though that'll make all the difference.

Relax. Sure. I force my body to become one with the seat and breathe out as much stress as my lungs are willing to part with.

"I'll protect you." Nate reaches for my hand, giving it a gentle squeeze. He's teasing me, sort of, but it's comforting anyway, and I weave my fingers through his.

"Is this about that insane idea my mom was talking about?" I twist to look at the nothingness around us.

"Maybe." He's having far too much fun. "You'll thank me. I promise."

"I'll thank you to take me to a cozy restaurant instead."

"This will be so much better. Trust me."

If it was anyone else behind the wheel, I'd probably be leaping from the car, reminding myself to tuck and roll. "Fine," I answer and ease back into the seat. "There is an odd beauty out here, isn't there?"

Nate laughs. "I knew it."

"Shut up."

"This is why you rented a jeep instead of a normal car?"

"Busted. I've always wanted to do this, but we've never had time on previous visits. And after this morning, it seemed like the perfect opportunity.

My hand automatically goes to my neck. The feeling of the pendant on my skin sends another wave of anticipation up my spine. I shush it, reminding myself that this is Nate. And he also bought a lovely, meaningful bracelet for his girlfriend.

"It's my fault we're here," I say, watching the dirt swirl around the jeep as Nates takes us deeper to nowhere.

"What are you talking about?"

"If I'd returned his calls, we wouldn't have been summoned."

"That's ridiculous. Do you really think this is a conversation your dad would have had over the phone?"

"I don't know." I turn my attention back to the dirt outside. Despite the fact that my father has dominated most of my thoughts and I just brought him up, I don't actually want to talk about him. The necklace glints in the reflection in the window. Had I imagined the way Nate looked at me? The shock of his touch on my neck?

"Helloo?"

I realize we've reached a parking lot in the middle of nowhere. There are a handful of cars, all spaced far apart for privacy.

"Good thing we came when we did or we wouldn't have found a parking spot," I quip.

"Funny. Come on." Nate hops out of the jeep and walks around to my side. I grip the handle and we play a half-hearted game of wills against the passenger-side door. I don't do wide open spaces and wild nature. I can handle squirrels, deer, an occasional fox, as long as it's not too close. I'm fine with lakes, trees, and the whooshing sound of cars on the unseen but never too-distant highway.

Why my mom chose to move here is a mystery. The opera house, fine, but there are opera houses in cities as well.

I finally relent and step out. Nate pulls a blanket and pillow from the back seat then motions for me to join him on the hood.

"Now that you've dragged me out to the middle of nowhere, want to tell me what we're doing here?"

Nate leans into me, our shoulders bumping. "Patience, dear girl. All will be revealed soon."

"Dear girl? And how long from now is soon?" Sitting here, our arms touching, reality far away, I silently hope that soon won't actually be that soon. This is a different Nate and one I'm liking.

I shift my weight, putting a bit of space between us. I can't *like* like this Nate.

Nate slaps his forehead. "Why do I try with you?"

I shrug and he pulls me back the couple of inches toward him.

"It was awful seeing him," I say into the void of the fading day.

Next to me, Nate's body tightens and relaxes with the inhale and exhale.

"I know how much this sucks."

"I'm so angry at him, Nate. I'm angry that he left, I'm angry that he didn't come back, and I'm angry that he finally came back only to leave again." Nate is the only person I can say this to. I feel like the worst person in the world. Yet oddly relieved to have admitted my feelings,

Nate wraps an arm around my shoulder, pulling me into him. Above us, stars twinkle, tiny lights turned on by an invisible being. I'm not the only one who likes the lights on everywhere I go.

The sky darkens into a deep charcoal with a million pinpricks of light. I shiver, partly from the drop in temperature now that the sun has abandoned us, and partly from the sudden sense of the insignificant role I inhabit within the vastness of the universe. The darkness of the desert night spreads over us like a blanket, surprisingly comforting, like the weighted blanket that at first I was so sure would suffocate me and that I now can't sleep without. In the distance comes a yip from an animal, a coyote maybe? I pull my legs up on the hood just in case.

Nate leans back and, somewhat awkwardly, I do the same. It seems foolhardy not to remain vigilant to our surroundings, to become potential dinner for whatever wild beasts roam these parts, but the heat radiating from the engine and the fairy lights above us soothe my anxiety.

From the darkness, someone from a neighboring car yells, "There." My body constricts the same moment Nate points at something in the sky.

A flash of light zooms across the darkness. Another burst chases the first. Then a third.

"Wow," I exhale the word.

"Beautiful, isn't it?" Nate whispers.

My eyes follow the path of another shooting star, then another. "I've never seen this many."

"Shooting stars?"

"Stars." Awe takes my breath away. Maybe I should reassess being such a city snob. "What's that?" I point at a bright object moving steadily but without the ferocity of the shooting stars.

"The space station," Nate answers.

"Seriously?"

Nate opens an app on his phone and holds it up to the sky, positioning it between us. A circle appears over the bright spot, "International Space Station" written in tiny letters next to it.

"That is so cool. Can you imagine being up there?"

"It would be pretty amazing," Nate answers. "Although I couldn't be up there for a long mission. I can't imagine having to live cooped up for months or years when you can't step outside and take a breath of fresh air or smell the soil after a rain or just, I don't know, go for a run."

"I guess," I stretch out the word. "But I bet life is predictable up there. There'd be little risk of someone you haven't heard from for half your life suddenly reappearing. Or of having yet another crappy first or second or third date. Although I suppose it would give a fresh perspective on long-distance relationships."

"I wouldn't necessarily qualify hurtling through space then

having to ride a fireball home, predictable. And dating isn't such a bad thing with the right person."

"I guess." I give him the win. "Then again, ..." I stall and Nate nudges me with his elbow. "Never mind." It's too beautiful here to sully the moment with thoughts of my dad. Or my pathetic excuse for a love life. Or, I turn to look at Nate, that weird something that happened between us at the jewelry store.

"Hey." Nate turns to look at me. "This is me. We don't do this with each other."

He's right, we don't.

I sit up, wincing at the give of the metal under my bottom. *Please don't dent, please don't dent.*

"Talk to me." Nate sits up as well and leans forward to look me in the face. Sometimes I really do hate that he knows me so well. And I really love that he can read me so perfectly.

A shiver takes over my body. The temperature has dropped more. At this rate, I won't have to worry about being eaten by a wild animal or abducted by aliens, I'll freeze to death first.

Nate pulls me into him, wrapping his arms around me. His body feels different against mine. The hug is questioning, as though asking permission to hold me. I lean into him, a silent agreement.

I force air into my lungs and a smell of something impossible envelopes me. "Lilies," I say.

"What?" Nate pulls back to look at me, probably to see if I'm having heat stroke from the warmth of his body.

"Lilies. That's the most common flower used in funeral arrangements. Do you know he has his death all planned out?"

"Oh, Callie," Nate whispers into the night.

I nod. It's just like my dad to have every detail nailed down so as not to burden anyone else. Tears burn my eyes. With the pad of his thumb, Nate wipes them away. I blink him into focus. He's so close I can feel his breath in the space between us.

And then there's no space between us.

**23**

---

## WE DON'T ASK A FLOWER ANY SPECIAL REASON FOR ITS EXISTENCE. WE JUST LOOK AT IT AND ARE ABLE TO ACCEPT IT AS BEING SOMETHING DIFFERENT FROM OURSELVES.

— GWENDOLYN BROOKS

"**A**re you okay?" My father asks for the fifteenth time since we settled into the visitor room at the hospital. He'd insisted we sit out here, not in his room despite the fact that he seems to have lost half his weight and energy since I saw him yesterday.

No, I want to say, nothing is okay. Or maybe it is. I don't know anything right now. Instead, I nod and mumble, "Yeah." I can't erase the years of silence like a wrong answer on a chalk board. That hurt is written on my heart with permanent marker, thick, black permanent ink.

I barely slept last night. Because, holy space station, Nate and I kissed. Not the chaste hello/good-bye/congratulations kisses we've historically planted on each other without a second thought. This was a stomach-melting, swoony-type of kiss. The kind of kiss that changes the laws of gravity. I'd half expected the space station above us to be yanked back to earth.

I would almost chalk that up to a vivid fantasy if there

hadn't been more kissing when we pulled up to Mom's house. We'd been quiet on the ride back, fingers intertwined on the gearshift between us. There was so much to say and nothing we were ready to talk about. In the darkness of the jeep outside of my mother's house, Nate traced the outline of the leaf pendant, lingering on the point that rested just above the dip between my breasts. I held my breath.

He did too until he leaned forward and kissed me again. If the first kiss was amazing, the second was life changing, the kind you scoff at in novels.

"Nate," I'd said breathlessly, the only word spoken since he said my name before that first kiss.

He shook his head and kissed me again, softer this time. "Not yet," he'd said. We walked to the front door hand-in-hand and then Nate delivered me to my room, parting with a kiss on the cheek and a whispered good-night.

My cheeks flush at the feelings and the thoughts that had kept my awake all night. I clear my throat and shift in the uncomfortable vinyl chair.

David, as I've come to call him in my head, waits expectantly.

"How are you feeling?" I ask, wanting my brain to stay focused on something other than the kiss. Because, seriously?!

The guy sitting in front of me is not my father. He resembles him in some ways—the same line of the nose, the same way he fiddles with the cuff of whatever long sleeve shirt he has on, the same way his left eye opens a bit wider than the right when he's weighing what you've just said. But where the father I knew had an invisible bubble of happiness around him, this man reeks of regret. Even the hands I once adored, strong and gentle, are now brittle and rough.

"I've had better days," he says with a wry smile. "But I'm here with you and that's a gift I never imagined I'd have."

He waits a breath, but I can't bring myself to say what I

know he's waiting to hear. It's not good to see him again. Not like this.

"Maggie says you're pretty much running the shop these days," Dad says after an awkward pause.

"With Maggie. Can you imagine her ever giving up control of the store?"

He chuckles. "Nope. I expected you to continue at the store though. You were a natural. But there's also a part of me that thought you'd find your niche elsewhere." After another moment of silence, he blurts out, "Seattle."

"Seattle what?"

"I pictured you living in Seattle."

"Why?" I've never been to Seattle. I don't know much about it except that it's artsy and lovely and rainy and has great food and coffee. Okay, maybe that does sound like a place I'd enjoy.

"This will sound weird, but when Steven and I arrived in Seattle the first time, I felt your presence there with me. Everywhere we went, I expected to see you."

"Interesting," I say. What are you supposed to say to something like that? I have so many questions like why was Seattle on the bucket list of places? What did they do there, how long were they there? Where did they live between trips? If he was always thinking about me, why didn't he ever call or write more than just those few little words on a postcard?

But I don't ask because asking means being pulled back into caring and caring means it'll hurt so much more when he leaves again. If I'm still nurturing the hurt, then maybe, just maybe I'll be able to shield my heart better when the inevitable happens.

"You're happy?" he asks, forcing me to refocus on the now.

"Yeah," I answer.

In every reunion scenario, we'd volleyed questions at each other, answers flowing like an opened canal lock. Not in a million mental rehearsals for this moment did I imagine how impossible it would be to ignite an actual conversation.

I notice that Dad's attention has moved to the door behind me and a sudden itch of caterpillars crawling up my spine makes me sit straighter.

"David, it's good to see you," Nate's voice hovers above me as one hand rests on my back and the other reaches to shake my dad's hand.

I force the caterpillars and the butterflies to settle down before they embarrass me.

"Nate. What a wonderful surprise." Dad grips Nate's hand. "I wasn't sure you'd come."

"Of course, I was going to come. I wouldn't miss the opportunity to see you." Nate pulls a chair closer to me and sits. He's so natural, so genuine. So unlike how I am with my own father.

Our knees touch and there it is, that tingle of something unexpected and new and thrilling and terrifying. I shift, just enough to turn and smile at Nate, the move subtle enough to give our bodies breathing space without being obvious. Every fiber of my being wants to scoot as close as decently possible. And from the tilt of his head when I moved, he feels it, too.

"Maggie has been catching me up on your life. You've done well for yourself. I always knew you'd be a rocket scientist." Dad smiles, no doubt remembering that he was the first to predict that Nate would be a rocket scientist.

After Nate's father died, David stepped in to help Nate build and launch his model rockets. After one of their rockets had "underperformed" and crashed into Maggie's carefully cultivated herb garden, singing the parsley and rosemary, she'd banished them to the open field at the end of our neighborhood. They'd be out there every weekend testing another rocket design.

"You called it," Nate agrees. "I get to geek out every day and no one there thinks I'm odd." He throws out an elbow to nudge mine.

They continue talking about rockets and the latest mission Nate is working on and I ease into spectator mode. My dad had adored Nate like a son. And in many ways, he was a son. Nate hated the commotion of his older brothers, and our house provided the escape he needed. I, on the other hand, loved the chaos of the older Cameron boys. But I adored my quiet companionship with Nate.

The ease of their conversation feels like a thorny reminder of what I lost when my dad left. I never struggled with what I could share with him. Everything. Just like with Nate.

As a kid, I accepted my place as their backup crew. I found a comfort and strength knowing that I was, at least in part, helping those I love. I felt like their secret weapon and that made me special, even if only a couple of people recognized my part.

Like when Nate was chosen to speak at our high school graduation and the day before he finally admitted that he had absolutely no idea what to say. We stayed up all night working on a speech that ended up bringing the audience to tears—in a good way.

Sensing my shifting mood, Nate reaches over and takes my hand. I notice David's gaze drift down then immediately look away. Would he approve of me and Nate as a couple or would he think it's a mistake? What would Maggie and my mom think if they knew we'd been in the jeep kissing like teenagers?

Does it matter what they think?

No.

Yes.

It shouldn't matter what others think, only what I think. And what Nate thinks. Except I have no idea what he thinks because we haven't talked. Mom and Maggie hovered over us this morning like two overcaffeinated hens.

I pull back and observe while my father and Nate talk as though it was just a month ago since they'd last caught up. I say a silent thanks for having Nate in my life. Nate, the one person who can make the most awful situation feel almost normal.

# 24

# THE BUTTERFLY IS A FLYING FLOWER, THE FLOWER IS A TETHERED BUTTERFLY.

## — ECOUCHARD LEBRUN

The 155-acre property that makes up the Santa Fe Opera is, in a word, magical. The Ranch, as it's called, is part of the lower grounds of the property and, despite being off-season and a Saturday afternoon, today it's a lively combination of musicians practicing in unseen studios, staff and artists relaxing on benches among the shrubbery, and the grind of construction as technicians prepare the sets for the upcoming season.

When Mom suggested we grab a coffee and go "to campus" after the visit with my father, it hadn't registered that this is where we'd end up. In all the years she's lived here, worked here, this is the first time she's brought me. She'd boycotted my request to stop at a flower shop, saying she had a better idea. Not that I'll publicly admit it, but she may be right.

There's always been a level of mystery around mom's work. For as passionate as she is about opera, she doesn't talk about what she does. Once when our teachers asked for parent volunteers for career day, I'd asked, no, begged, my mom to come. I mean, how cool is it to make gorgeous costumes that thousands of people will see?

I received an adamant no. No explanation, just no.

"Hey, Mom, why don't you ever want to talk about what you do?" I ask as we weave our way around the grounds.

She nods a hello at two people walking our direction, then points for me to take a left.

"It doesn't seem important."

"How can you say that? What you do is amazing." I remember once finding sketches and notes about fabrics and props. There had been drawings of the sets and creative vision for the production. She'd made the kitchen table a canvas for a whole new world. I'd been mesmerized.

But when mom found me sifting through the papers and swatches, she'd all but lost her mind. It was the first time I remember her bringing work home, and the last. Any questions I had were mowed down and buried like incriminating evidence.

"I didn't say it wasn't." She points at a building, and we follow the path toward it.

"Are you a spy?" I stop walking and narrow my eyes at her.

She guffaws and I'm oddly proud at having gotten a reaction that isn't a dismissive huff.

My relationship with my mother, I realize, has so many levels of insecurity. At almost 33, you'd think I would have gotten over them.

On any given day, if you asked what kind of relationship we had, I'd reply with an emphatic "good, very good." It is good. Although, I think it's good because it's what I've decided I want it to be.

Look, I know the truth. I know my mom didn't really want kids. She wanted a career in the opera. She wanted to work in the great opera houses around the world. She wanted to become *the* costume designer, to collaborate on productions that will go down in history.

I'd asked Maggie once if I was an accident.

"Heavens no," she'd answered, "Your mom just needed to see that kids didn't mean the end of everything she wanted. After Lucas and Mark came along, she started to get it. She loved those hooligans, especially Lucas."

I'd joked that Mom probably had hoped for a boy and would have been happier if she and Maggie had switched us at the hospital.

I'm not sure it's fair to say she resented me or my father for the life she ended up leading, but I'm not sure it's completely wrong either. Not that she ever said anything or made it obvious, but there was always a piece of her missing. Mom was happiest when she was working.

"A spy? That's what you came up with?" Mom says, amused.

"That's the only explanation I can come up with for why you refuse to talk about your work." My mouth quirks into a smile at her expression.

And just as quickly as the easy smile came, it's gone. Mom does an about face and moves us in the direction of a bench tucked back on the lawn, protected by bushes and the canopy of an oak tree.

We sit and I wait. And wait.

A woman carrying an armload of sketch pads, fabric swatches spilling from top and bottom and sides, walk-trots past, tossing a, "Hey, Rose," as she passes us. Mom lifts a hand in response. A couple of young men wander by, deep in discussion about adding more trumpets to the penultimate scene. The cuter of the two with long floppy blond hair winks at my mom. His eyes hop to me and he gives me a quick nod hello.

I melt into the wood of the bench, scootching an inch or three away from my mom. As though putting distance between us will make my plainness less obvious. It's around her that I feel most self-conscious. Like how is it possible that *I* came from her? It's around her that I feel most invisible.

When I was little, she tried dressing me in cute clothes, and did my hair in pigtails or braids. But I couldn't play with Nate and his brothers in cute dresses. After a few expensive rips and stains, Mom gave up. When I hit my teens, she tried again, this time with makeup and fashion choices that made the popular girls bug-eyed with envy. But I'd rub the makeup off within minutes and end up with sad raccoon eyes. And the fashionable clothes never felt like me. Again, she gave up.

And no, Mom clearly doesn't subscribe to the third time is a charm idea because she never tried again.

"The reason I never wanted to talk about my career," Mom says, and it takes me a second to quiet the excited pounding in my ears. I'm finally going to learn the secret to my mother. "It's the only thing I have that's completely mine. It's where I found myself before your dad and I got married. It's the place I'd escape to when I didn't recognize who I was becoming. Then after your dad left, that person, that other me, was all I recognized."

The sting of her confession burrows deeper than any splinter. Being a mom, *my* mom, wasn't enough for her.

As though she immediately realizes what she's said, Mom reaches over and lays her hand on mine. "I love being your mother. You are the best thing that ever happened to me."

I snort a laugh before common sense can step in to protect me.

"That's not fair," she says, flattening an invisible seam on her linen slacks.

I hear the hurt in her voice and instantly feel bad. I know she loves me. Maybe not in the conventional Mama Bear way, not the way Maggie envelopes me into the fold of her affection, but Mom has never been conventional. And isn't that what makes her so amazing?

"When I needed you most, you left." It's not until I've allowed the thought into the wild that I realize how deep I've buried it. I went to my father when I needed a hug or an encouraging word. Without him, Mom should have stepped in. But it had been Maggie and Nate.

Mom turns to stare at me. "That's not how it was."

"How was it then, Mom?" I brace myself to hear her say that I didn't need her, that I was better off with Maggie. She's tossed those answers at me for most of my life.

Mom stares off into the distance, at the range of mountains and the gathering storm clouds. About the time I'm ready to give up on us having a meaningful mother-daughter conversation, Mom says, "I wasn't the mother you needed, the mother you deserved. But I suppose I assumed my shortcomings didn't impact you because you had Maggie."

I want to protest that Maggie wasn't my mom but she's not wrong. I turned to Maggie because we shared a connection, we had our flowers. Maggie let me find myself among the blossoms, no nudging, no lessons-to-be-learned.

My mom had tried but she'd tried to bring me into her world of fashion and glamour, a place I was never going to fit. Mom didn't know how to let me be me, especially since *me* had nothing she could recognize in herself.

We fall silent, listening to unseen squirrels and birds in the trees around us. More people walk by. A warm breeze flutters through the trees and I close my eyes, allowing my thoughts to swirl un-tamed with the leaves and the clouds. I breathe in air that's so different from home. Here I feel my lungs expand and fill. Maybe this is why she chose to stay here. Maybe this is the only place she could breathe deeply, completely.

"Every production I've been involved with is an opportunity to escape into a new world. A world that I have some control over. I never felt that in my life," Mom breaks into my thoughts.

The admission knocks me off balance and I'm glad we're

not walking. I always saw her as the most confident person I know.

"I never regretted marrying your dad, well not most of the time." She gives a wry smile and a twitch of her shoulder. "And I certainly don't regret having you. But my work was the one place I could be myself. I was terrified of the pressure to be a perfect wife, to be the perfect mom. I didn't know how and the harder I tried, the less I succeeded."

I'm suddenly back in fourth grade, staring in horror at the mess in the kitchen. Mom had signed up to provide the snacks for that Friday's movie hour in our class. The week before, Evan Scott's mom had made individual cheese pizzas and mini chocolate chip muffins. Not only had she waved photos of her delectables in front of all the mothers in the neighborhood, but it had been all Nate and I talked about the entire weekend.

So, of course, Mom had to outdo Evan Scott's mom. For all of my mom's talents, baking isn't one of them. After Dad cleaned up the kitchen and calmed her down, orders had been placed. The following day, we had cute little tea sandwiches and mini apple tarts for movie hour. I'd kept my mouth shut when Mrs. Oakley gushed about how amazing my mom was to make those.

On the flip side, when Mom stepped in to help with the school production of The Addams Family, the production went from meh to packed house, and not just by family members obligated to attend. Kids who never had an interest in theater clamored for roles. For the first time in school history, the theater teacher turned away volunteers because everyone wanted to be involved. Everyone wanted an opportunity to be near my mom.

"That's not true," I say, although even to me it doesn't sound as believable as I'd hoped.

Mom raises an eyebrow, looking at me from the corner of her eye. "Not every woman is cut out to be a mom. Or at least a typical mom. I don't know how to say this." She smiles, a smile that's sadder than anything I've seen in even the most tragic of operas.

"I failed you in so many ways, Callie. I'm not really apologizing because I don't think I could have done differently. It just wasn't in me. I'm not asking for forgiveness. I loved you with more of my heart than I ever thought possible. And that scared me. The more I loved you, the more I needed you. But you didn't need me back."

"How can you say that?"

Mom takes my hand to stop me. "You refused to nurse. The only way you'd eat those first days was if your dad gave you the bottle. You wouldn't even take a bottle from me. Talk about rejection." Her mouth quirks into a sad half smile.

"Sorry?" I offer with my own half smile. No one has ever told me that story.

"David was a natural with you. He's the warm, fuzzy one. I'm, well, I'm not. For every failure as a mother, there was a success at work. The universe reminding me what my strengths were. So yes, when David left, I panicked and ran. I didn't know what else to do."

There's something I'm supposed to say here, something I'm supposed to feel. There are plenty of feels and plenty of words but none that I can turn into anything that makes sense.

"You were happy with Maggie and the boys," she says as though it answers all the questions.

"I was safe with Maggie and the boys." Safe isn't the same as happy. Yes, I was happy but I was happier with my parents.

I have memories of us sitting around the dinner table laughing at a story Dad was telling or at the neighborhood pool when dad pretended to be a shark and swam under the float Mom was snoozing on, then flipped her into the water.

No, it hadn't all been fun and laughter. We had our share of drama.

Mom tightens her lips into a line and I catch my breath. Whatever she's about to say is going to sting.

"Callie, your dad called after Steven passed away. He wanted to come home. Of course, by then there wasn't a home to return to. I was living here, and you were living with Maggie. He wanted to return to Maryland and buy a house, that you two could live in together." Mom releases a long breath, her body sinking as though her spine had been inflated by that very air. "I told him not to come back. Maggie backed me up. We thought you were better off not having to deal with that mess."

I wait for the words to settle, hoping that when they do, they'll be in a different order, a less damning order.

"You let me live with the belief that my father didn't want me in his life, that he didn't love me. You let me live with the belief that I didn't matter enough to my own parents."

Mom wipes at her face, then looks at her fingertips as though she, too, is stunned by what she's seeing. I have never seen my mom cry. Not once.

A man walking on the other side of the path looks over and smiles. He waves at my mom. I can't help but notice the way she tucks a strand of hair behind her ear and ducks her head as she waves back at him. At 56, my mom may be more beautiful than she's ever been. I resented her for moving to Santa Fe, for leaving. But now I see it, she's thrived here. She turned into a butterfly here.

And me? I'm still the discarded chrysalis.

# 25

# HAPPINESS HELD IS THE SEED; HAPPINESS SHARED IS THE FLOWER.

## — JOHN HARRIGAN

Everyone has a sound that immediately transports them to their childhood. For some, it's an ice cream truck. For others, it may be the sound of sprinklers *phoot phooting* in the early morning. For me, it's pots being slammed onto the stove or into the sink. Pots being slammed means mama drama. No yelling. My mother never raised her voice. But boy did she relish the sound of stainless steel on hard surfaces.

My father would let her fume, get out whatever had worked its way under her skin, and then he'd calmly walk into the kitchen once she was done, and clean up the mess. He was good at erasing the evidence. Except for the tomato sauce stain on the ceiling from one particularly cranky evening. I still remember watching, mouth wide, eyes wider, as the spaghetti peeled itself from the ceiling, strand by strand, and splattered to the floor. I suspect Dad left the stain there on purpose. It became the "higher being" we'd all say a silent prayer to when things went sideways.

But back to slamming pots.

"Do we need to intercede?" Nate asks.

"Do *you* want to go in there?"

"Not particularly." He looks appropriately cautious as another metal-on-metal clang breaks the silence of the morning. Our knees touch and both of us look at the line that blurs him and me.

Yesterday afternoon had been like every other we've spent together. Except for one teensy weensy detail … the unmistakable current of change. I thought we were doing a bang-up job of being discreet. There had been a handful of shy smiles and inadvertent touches that, pre-kiss would have seemed completely normal. But we must have been emitting some shift in dynamic because Mom's left eyebrow got a workout watching us. And I caught her and Maggie exchanging knowing, curious looks.

"Nate." I want to talk about the kiss, the kisses. I want to talk about how he'd held my hand leaving the hospital yesterday and the way we sat for hours last night by the firepit in Mom's yard listening to the crackle of the wood and not talking about the one thing that needed to be talked about. But talking makes it real. Talking puts the act into the world and as much as I want to know what it means for future us, I don't want it to change the us we've always been.

"Callie," he answers without looking up from his phone.

"Problems?" I ask, nodding at his phone. Talking about something else is safer than talking about what happened, what I'm feeling. Because what if he doesn't feel the same?

"Hm?" he asks, finally turning to look at me.

"Problems with work?" I ask again, this time with the clarifier.

"No." He stands and walks to the fountain that looks as desolate as the three pots on Mom's back patio.

Our backyard when I was a kid had beautifully maintained flowerbeds and raised boxes with herbs. Dad spent hours out there taking care of the lawn, weeding the flowerbeds, trimming the herbs.

There are no herbs or flowers here. No lawn. The only greenery are the two trees and even they look more brown than alive. I wonder how much of this is due to the location or as a defiant indictment of the life she left.

"You okay?" I ask when Nate begins to rearrange the loose stones at the base of the fountain. I mean, cleaning and organizing at home is one thing, cleaning and organizing an outside fountain is fishy.

"Yeah, just thinking," he says, and my stomach does a drop and roll.

"About?"

Before he can answer, Maggie opens the sliding door and scoots out, closing it quickly behind her. She lowers herself into the chair that Nate vacated. "Damn she's in a mood."

I pull my attention from Nate and the conversation we're not going to have. "What triggered her this time?" I ask.

Maggie gives me her *seriously* look. "That's a silly question."

Okay, maybe it is, but it's also not.

The door opens and Mom calls out, "Who wants coffee?" All three of us shoot a hand up.

"Caffeine should help this situation," Nate mumbles, pulling a chair over. This time, however, he sits across from me.

Mom emerges with a tray and four cups of coffee. It's still cool enough that I welcome the hot coffee. "When are you going to the hospital?" she asks me.

"Soon. You're not going with me?" I'm partially relieved, partially freaked out.

"No."

Nate catches my eye and mouths, "I'll go with you."

I respond with a slight shake of my head. This time I need to talk to my father without distractions. But first, I need answers. "Mom, why are we all here?"

She studies me as though pondering to what depth my question dips. "I told David to come to Santa Fe."

I assumed she had but to hear her say it catches me off guard. "How long has he been here?"

Mom and Maggie make eye contact and Maggie gives her a go-on nod. "Almost three months."

Math may not be my strength, but I count a handful of weeks between when he got to Santa Fe and when he first tried to call me. "And when did he call you to tell you he was sick?"

"October."

"October?"

"October."

"October," Nate says with a verbal exclamation mark. "And yes, that's five months ago."

"You were in touch with him for all that time before anyone saw fit to clue me in?" I glare from Mom to Maggie to Nate.

Nate lifts his hands. "I didn't know until now either."

"Why?" I challenge the moms.

"Don't blame Maggie. When he got the diagnosis, he reached out. He was "putting his affairs in order" he said. It was hard talking to him at first. I wanted to hate him." She stops to take a sip of her coffee. Her hands shake as she lowers the mug to the table,

"I couldn't let him go through this alone." Mom looks to me and whatever anger she's been holding onto, floods out in a rush of emotional release. She loved him, really loved him. All the feels I've been lugging around are nothing compared to the boulder she's carrying.

"Oh, Mom. I'm sorry." I reach for her hand, and she lets me take it.

"Obviously this isn't how I wanted him back but it's nice having him around again. Strange but nice." I see it now. The way she touched his arm, the glances they shared, the unspoken understanding between them. Not unlike how it once was.

Not unlike the way Nate and I are.

There's a tap on my foot and I glance up. Nate is watching me. His eyebrows lift in a "You okay?" I answer with the slightest of nods.

"You two have something you'd like to share with us?" Mom asks.

"No," Nate says at the same time I sputter a "What?"

Mom and Maggie roll their eyes.

"You forget we've known you both your entire lives. We know when you're up to something," Mom says. Maggie smirks from behind her mug.

"There's nothing to share," Nate says, doing a very obvious job of looking uncomfortable.

"You don't lie well. Either of you." Maggie wags a finger at us.

"Oh fine," Nate says. "We may as well tell them. They're clearly on to us anyway."

I feel my body prickle with anticipation, anxiety, and dear god, something suspiciously close to lust. Except that *we* haven't talked about what's happening between us so how can he tell them?

Nate takes my hand and announces that we were chosen as one of three couples to live in a moon base which will be deployed next year. Before anyone can call him on his bullshit, Nate launches into a detailed explanation of the mission, the timing, and the logistics of the deployment and why it's been kept under media blackout.

I stare, open mouthed, when he's done. He picked me to live on the moon with him. Me, not Beth.

My mom laughs, a genuine, trill of a laugh, the laugh I remember from my childhood.

"This one can barely fly across the country, and you want to take her to the moon. Good luck," Mom plays along.

"Good point." Nate releases my hand and sits back in his chair. "It's a long trip which would require a hefty supply of Oreo cookies which will require more fuel than the current design can handle." He exhales dramatically and plummets us back to earth. "I guess we'll just have to scrub the mission."

I palm my forehead as Maggie and Mom bust out laughing again. The sound is foreign and welcome and I add another feeling to the Nate list: gratitude.

I push my chair back and stand. "I'm going to get Oreos," I announce.

"And go see your dad," Mom says, waving me off.

"Want company?" Nate is already halfway to his feet.

"Not this time. Is that okay? I think we have a few things we need to talk about on our own."

Nate sinks back into the chair with a nod of understanding. I feel his eyes rest momentarily on the silver leaf pendant. One more feeling for the list: Hope.

# 26

## THERE ARE AWAYS FLOWERS FOR THOSE WHO WANT TO SEE THEM.

— HENRI MATISSE

The previous two visits were excruciating for so many reasons. But this morning, sitting next to my father in his hospital room as he sleeps, machines beeping and hissing around us, every feeling I've refused to feel for the last 17 years pushes its way to the surface.

The anger I've been nurturing all these years has given way to sadness. Sadness for the years we could have had and the years we won't have.

Tomorrow, Nate and I return to Maryland, to our lives. Two days ago, it was all I could think of. Home, where everything is safe and known. Now, I wish I could stop time and stay here. I have so many questions for my dad. So many unresolved topics with my mom, and lest we forget, the moon colony.

The blood pressure cuff puffs to life and one of the machines connected to my father beeps.

A nurse steps into the room and hands me a can of soda before turning to check on David's vitals. "You look like you could use that."

"Thank you." Ginger Ale, the magic elixir for all ailments. While I seriously doubt it works on broken hearts, I'm willing to give anything a try. I pop the can and take a long sip, then close my eyes and focus on the pop of bubbles in my mouth.

When I open my eyes, my father is watching me. "What a nice surprise to wake up and see you here."

I answer with a tight smile while a fist tightens around my heart.

When I don't say anything, Dad asks, "Is Rose with you?"

I shake my head. "No, I came alone."

Dad nods then points at a cup of ice on the side table. I help scoop a shaving into his mouth.

I sit back after three ice chips and attempt to collect my thoughts. Where do you start when so much is on the line? "Is the Parterre Fountain and the Chihuly glass sculpture as magnificent in person?" So much for unpacking deep seated emotions.

Dad narrows his eyes in confusion. "Georgia?"

I nod.

He nods.

We're off to a fabulous meeting of the minds.

"It is. I kept hoping to go back with you one day."

I have no words.

"I'm sorry, Callie." His voice is so low I have to look up from where I've been focusing my attention on bending the tab off the soda can. It snaps loose and falls straight into the drink, just like my heart when I see the look on Dad's face.

I know he's not talking about the trip to the botanical garden but admitting it would be too painful. "Maybe someday," I say.

"Tell me about Steven," I prompt, wanting to move the conversation away from trips that will never happen.

Dad looks surprised then pleased. "What do you want to know?"

"Everything. Anything." All I know about the man my

father left us for is that he was a therapist, that he loved opera, and had a bucket list of places to visit.

Dad closes his eyes and sinks into the pillow, his features relaxing. Without opening his eyes, he says, "You would have liked him. He could read people, which sounds obvious considering his profession, but it was more than that. He had a funny habit of watching people and making predictions about them. One time we were at a diner in Colorado, some small town off of I-70. A family walked in and Steven said, "New Yorkers, first vacation out west, and the father's idea." They ended up sitting at the table next to us. The moment they sat down, the older of the kids started complaining about the endless drive and why couldn't they have just vacationed in the Hamptons like they do every year. The mom never said a word, just sat there glaring at her husband."

I think back on all the guessing games Nate and I play whenever we're out. What does the guy in the dark suit do for a living? Is the couple at the far table on a first or second date? What kind of car does the guy in the Balenciaga sneakers drive?

"He loved craft beer and was forever on the hunt for unique brewpubs anywhere we went. His dream was to open his own." Dad gets quiet. I wish I could read his mind because asking what he's thinking feels like an intrusion.

"Callie, why haven't you settled down yet?" He turns the conversation on me.

"That's easy, I haven't found anyone as perfect as Nate." I flash a fake, trust-me grin. It's the truth. So horribly true.

"So maybe ..." Dad hedges, his eyebrows doing a weird worm dance above eyes that are grasping for hope.

I shake my head, practically giving myself whiplash. "Nate and I are best friends. Nothing has changed there." *Liar, liar, pants on fire.*

"Pity. I always did think you guys would be a great pairing."

He winces and sinks into the pillow, eyes closed, breathing shallow.

"Do you want me to call the nurse?" I ask, half standing before I've finished the question.

Eyes still closed, my dad shakes his head and reaches for my hand. For the count of four rapid heartbeats, I stare at his hand, unsure what to do next. Seventeen years don't slip away without some residual sediment affecting your ability to move forward.

I ease back into the chair and take Dad's hand. It's cold and brittle. I close his hand in mine, gently and fiercely. "We need to look at a hospital that specializes in ..." I let the rest drift into the white noise of the hospital room. Then I send a silent, "no offense," into the stale hospital universe, just in case.

"I've seen plenty of doctors. Specialists and more specialists. This is it for me, Callie."

"But maybe at Hopkins," I start to protest. Dad shakes his head, the movement causing a coughing fit.

"Not even Hopkins," he says once the coughing subsides. He fusses with the IV line and the blood pressure cuff, straightens the blanket and tugs at the pillow. I stand and help reposition the pillow behind his head and offer him more ice chips. He goes through another round of fussing before he finally looks me in the eye.

"Sit. I need to tell you something."

My legs give out and I sink into the creaky vinyl seat. Now what? He's not my dad? What he has is hereditary? Mom's personality is hereditary? I have a sibling out there somewhere?

"I realize I don't have much sway in the advice-giving department, but just hear me out. I want you to really think about who you are, who you want to be. You have so much to give—personally and professionally—but you've convinced yourself otherwise."

I chafe at his assessment. He has no right to see what I've

spent years burying. "I love working with Maggie." Which is the truth. I haven't settled in my professional life. On the contrary. Maggie has given me opportunities to express my creative freedom in ways other jobs probably wouldn't have.

As for my personal life, we'll just pretend that's all roses and lilies.

"That's not what I mean. I know you love working with Maggie, you always did. And I know you're good at it. Maggie brags about you a lot," he says, then preempts what he knows will be a deflection of praise. "What I'm questioning is why you're hiding."

"I'm not hiding," I protest, a bit too loudly and a bit too quickly. "And what do you know about my life? You haven't been around for half of it." The hurt sediment scrapes against the open wound of the last seventeen years.

"I'm sorry," I add but Dad waves off the apology.

"Don't be. You're right. But so am I." He raises the head of the bed so he's more upright. "Callie, when you look at your world, do you see flowers or do you see weeds?"

Flowers, of course I mean, hello. I'm a florist. But I don't answer, because the answer isn't that obvious.

Truth, I've never been able to see the beauty within me. I'm a loyal, generous friend. Nate never lets me forget that. And I'm a talented, dedicated employee. Something Maggie is quick to remind me if I'm having a bad day. I do see flowers everywhere. I just don't see myself as one of them.

# 27

# TAKE TIME TO SMELL THE ROSES.
## — PROVERB

I glower at the glass vase and uncooperative flowers. "Will you please just behave yourselves? I need you to cooperate. We're out of time," I say, putting the plea out for the floral gods to take notice.

It's been all of one day since Nate and I returned from Santa Fe and I, apparently, left my creative mojo there along with my favorite sweatshirt and a not very favorite but comfortable bra.

"I'm no expert but sassing the flowers doesn't strike me as the most effective technique," Alex, one of our delivery guys, says, setting down two more buckets of daffodils.

"Meow," Lulu agrees with him.

"See," Alex says with a laugh and strokes Lou's head. She rewards him by launching into a loud purr and bumping her head into his hand.

Since the moment I walked into the apartment Sunday evening she's been lovingly dismissive. If she's not in my lap, she's got an eye on me. We've shared my coffees, fought over the tuna salad I had for lunch yesterday, and she got the better half of the rotisserie chicken I picked up for dinner. She sat on the edge of the tub and slapped at the bubbles last night when I took a bath and, this morning, I woke up with her sitting on my chest staring at me.

Then there's the bite mark from when she decided she'd had enough petting even though she was still curled up in my lap. And the gash on my leg from when I attempted to leave the apartment to come down to the shop this morning. Let's not forget my favorite mug that I set down on the counter just long enough to reach for the milk and which is now in a thousand pieces in the bottom of my trashcan. She'd been very pleased with herself until the coffee from the flying mug splashed her. Needless to say, I'm paying for that as well.

"I've tried several combinations, and nothing feels right," I say, taking a perky daffodil from the bucket Alex just brought. I hold it next to the square glass vase, but the delicate purple flowers of the dendrobium appear to recoil at the idea. "Not helpful," I mumble at the orchid.

"What are you trying to convey?" Alex asks.

I tilt my head, focusing on the vase and the four dendrobium stems. "It's a take-a-chance bouquet."

What happened in Santa Fe was apparently staying in Santa Fe. Despite having spent four days riding a current of emotions together, the moment the plane landed at the DC airport, we reverted to being best friends. We've yet to talk about the kiss or whatever feelings are blooming. Or wilting. I've been looking for hints in the moments and looks between me and Nate. I've been reading and re-reading between the lines of every conversation. I want to know the very thing I'm afraid of knowing. What does post-kiss Nate and Callie look like?

There was one time when we almost kissed in college and had a brief, and embarrassing, should-we-shouldn't-we conversation. We decided on shouldn't, obviously. Because despite that moment of beer-inspired what-if, the idea of acting on it was terrifying. We filed that moment in the very back corner of the things-we-don't-discuss closet of our friendship.

But this time wasn't an almost kiss. It was a full on, knee-buckling kiss. Kisses. Except this time, when there actually is something to discuss, we've avoided the topic like you'd avoid a heaping pile of poop on the sidewalk. I know I'm not imagining the change between us and while I'm dying to hash it out with Nate, talking could also expose whatever happened as a mistake. Or worse, that he regrets what happened.

Yet, last night after work, Nate and I spent almost two hours on the phone. It's the first time we've done that since the early days of Beth entering the picture. We talked about my dad and the odd craving I had for a Nutella and banana crepe. We talked about Nate's dilemma over what car to get next, and how quiet it was in our own homes all of a sudden and how easily we'd adjusted to the strange but not completely unpleasant four days under one roof with Mom and Maggie.

It feels new, like the early days of a relationship when you're getting to know each other. And it feels like it always has, how we've been our entire lives. If anyone forced me to pick one of these Nate and Callie's, I'd run the other direction with my hands over my ears. Because I want both.

"Is the arrangement for someone specific?" Alex pulls me back to the problem at hand.

"Not really." It sort of is. It's a floral pep-talk for me. But even the flowers are at a loss with what to tell me about my Nate dilemma.

On the table, my phone flashes with a notification.

Nate: Eric asked for your number.

"Well, I know you'll find the perfect combination. You always do," Alex says.

"I love your optimism." I manage a smile, dragging my eyes from my phone.

"It's not optimism. I've been around long enough, and I've seen what you can do." He turns away to study the various blooms in the storage cooler. "I see beauty, but you see so much more in them. Has it always been like that?"

"Nope. They just used to be pretty."

"That's BS." Alex grins.

Another text pops up from Nate:

> I gave him your number. Can I come by later?
> Need to talk. And I could use one of your
> magic flower arrangements.

Disappointment pops inside, leaving a sour burning. I force my attention back to the arrangement and Alex.

"Even before I knew much about the meaning of flowers, I had a tingly sense for combinations of blooms." I keep the one tiny detail that I feel what the flowers want to say to myself. It's not something I've told anyone other than Nate. "The fascination with hidden meanings came in college. I was mesmerized by the Victorian era, how they used flowers to convey messages. The more I dug into the myths and the symbols, the sharper my tingly senses became. And, voila, here we are." I spread my arms and force a smile.

"I knew it," Alex says. I'm oddly proud to share that bit of myself with him. "Well, I'd better get going. I have one more delivery today. And you have a customer to take care of."

Sure enough, someone clears their throat, a not very subtle, subtle attempt at getting my attention.

"Hi," I say, pulling on a smile and turning from Alex to see the one person I'm not yet prepared to face.

"Hi," Beth says, and I'm surprised at the blush of unease that spreads across her cheeks.

I acknowledge another customer who's just entered the

store, grateful for the reprieve from a private conversation with Beth. And from the look of relief on her face, I suspect she is as well which only heightens my unease.

"Can I ask for your advice when you have a minute?" the newcomer asks.

"Of course. What are you looking for?" I flash Beth a duty-first smile and walk to the front of the store where my savior is looking at the arrangement of vases Tish brought in a week ago.

I've become pretty adept at reading customers the moment they walk in. From her white puffy Canada Goose coat with its fur-lined hood and the oversized Louis Vuitton bag, I immediately pegged this one as someone who knows exactly what she wants. Amaryllis. The amaryllis symbolizes self-confidence and pride.

"I honestly don't know," she answers.

Hm, maybe not an amaryllis then.

"Is it a special occasion?"

She shakes her head, takes a deep breath. She nods at one of the ceramic vases, a yellow one with a sunflower engraved on it. I've placed three bamboo stalks in it for the display. Next to it is a pale green glass vase with five bamboo stalks. And behind both of them is a clear, square vase with nine stalks.

"Bamboo is for luck, right?"

"Luck, happiness. Bamboo is always a good choice. A grouping of nine stalks invites fortune, three invites happiness, and five is for health," I explain, not that the question required more than a yes or no but Beth hovering nearby makes me nervous.

"That's interesting. I didn't realize the number of stalks makes a difference," she says.

"Flowers and plants have many meanings. It's one of the things that's always fascinated me about them."

"Do you really think it matters? I mean, if you combine the

wrong flowers or the wrong number of bamboo stalks together?" Her mouth pinches tight.

I'm starting to see where this is going. "I think it depends on what you believe. For some, it's just woo. But in my experience, there's nothing wrong with placing a bit of faith in what we don't necessarily understand."

She shrinks into her coat. "I made a terrible mistake, and I could use some of that woo to redeem myself."

"Tell me," I say.

"My boyfriend of ten months invited me to meet his mother. I was so anxious about meeting her. I mean, ten months isn't that long but it's long and we get along so well, and I don't know. I just wanted to make a good impression." She stalls and I wait. I learned from Maggie how to read the flow of a flower-needing confession. The woman inhales, then drops the punchline. "I brought her a beautiful chrysanthemum plant. She made me leave it in the car."

"Old Italian family," she answers my questioning look.

"Oh," I say. While the rest of the world considers chrysanthemums a flower of happiness, optimism, and prosperity, the Italians consider them the flower of mourning. "We can fix this. How about a bouquet of yellow lilies? They symbolize thankfulness and the desire for enjoyment. And lilies are the national flower of Italy. She'll appreciate that."

"Yellow?" She has her eyes on the stunning orange tiger lilies that came in yesterday.

"Those are beautiful. We can certainly do those, but I wouldn't do an entire arrangement with them. The orange ones symbolize confidence and pride. A little of that goes a long way, especially if you're trying to make amends with his mom."

"Yellow it is." She smiles, gratefully.

I prepare an arrangement of 13 perfect yellow lilies. "Unlike us, the Italians view the number 13 as a lucky number that brings prosperity and life," I explain.

"Perfect," my maybe-not-an-amaryllis customer says with a smile that is every bit the splendid beauty of an amaryllis.

And then it's me and Beth in the store.

"I never realized the nuances of flowers," Beth says.

"Most people don't. And most people don't care as long as the arrangement is pretty."

"Does every arrangement you make have a special meaning?" She's eyeing the vase I was working on earlier with suspicion and interest.

Is she wondering what hidden message I stashed in the flowers Nate gave her?

"Not every bouquet, no."

Another customer walks in and Beth tightens her coat around herself.

"I should let you work," she says.

"Beth, was there something specific you wanted?" I venture. I'm intrigued that she'd come here. She wasn't just walking by. She had a reason to get in her car and drive across town.

Beth shakes her head. "Not really. We can talk another time when you're not busy."

I make a mental note to grill Nate when he comes by later for the flowers. Nate may not have said anything, but Beth's appearance is evidence enough. Something went down and I am, somehow, the centerpiece.

Through the window I catch a glimpse of Beth crossing the road. And I suddenly know exactly what flowers need to go in the arrangement: gardenia for secret love, and dahlia for affection and its double meaning as a warning of change.

# 28

# STRETCHING HIS HAND UP TO REACH THE STARS, TOO OFTEN MAN FORGETS THE FLOWERS AT HIS FEET.

— JEREMY BENTHAM

I settle onto the couch, which Lulu takes as an invitation to hop into my lap. Note to self: take more trips.

"How are you feeling?" I always ask and Dad always brushes the question aside.

"Fine, fine. You know," he says. It's what he always says. "But I want to hear about you. What's new?"

I laugh. "It's only been a couple of days. That's not enough time for anything new to happen."

"It's plenty of time." I can hear the smile in his voice.

Yesterday, after a gentle nudge from him, I confessed to mixed feelings about helping Nate with Beth. Not a full confession, that would require owning up to the confusion brought on by the kiss. But Dad is right. It hadn't even taken a couple of days for the world to shift on its axis in Santa Fe.

"Hey, Dad," I stop, surprised at how natural it felt to call him that. Until now, I've avoided calling him anything except for David and that only in my head. "Where've you been living since you left Maryland?" In my mind, he's been either here or in Santa Fe. The years in between don't exist.

"For the first year, I wasn't living anywhere. Steven and I were on the road more than in any one place. He had a cabin in Vermont that we used as home base but mostly we just went through his bucket list. Some places we road tripped, some we flew to."

"Sounds exhausting." I mentally kick myself. Of course it was exhausting but when the clock is ticking, I can only assume exhaustion wasn't an option.

"But I wouldn't change any of it," Dad says.

"Do you have pictures?" I'm insanely curious about the man my father found a soulmate in. Truth is, I admire him for following his heart. I'm still hurt but I'm also intrigued by the two Davids. The one who loved and married my mom, and the one who loved another man and left my mom for him.

"Would you believe not one?"

"No," I answer because I can't imagine him not taking pictures. My dad documented everything. It used to drive my mom nuts.

Dad chuckles into the phone. "Yeah, surprised me at the time, too. But making the memories was more important than documenting them. Don't tell your mom I said that, please. She'll never let me hear the end of it."

"But haven't you ever wanted to look back at those memories? Don't you regret that now?" That was his argument when Mom would grouse at him to "put that damn thing away already."

"I do, all the time. But those memories are in my heart. Just like my memories of you and your mom. And in my mind, Steven's full of life and fun, not the way the pictures would have shown him."

I close my eyes and imagine myself, a year from now, five years, sixteen years, would I want to look back at pictures of my father in the hospital or would the memories of him I've tucked away from my childhood be the comfort I need?

"I'm sending you a couple of photos from the last few years, though," Dad says, snapping me back to the present.

"Last few years?"

"From work travel. These are a few of my favorites that didn't get into the magazines."

"Magazines? Wait, you skipped something."

"After Steven passed away, I realized that I couldn't go back to a corporate job. He'd encouraged me to follow my passion for photography, and yes, you can laugh at the irony after I said I don't have photos from that period of my life."

I'm glad he said it first, because the words were right there ready to jump out. My phone vibrates with the text from him and I pull it from my ear to look. Which is when I see the time.

"Oh crap, I didn't realize how late it is. Can I call you later or in the morning?" I now have five minutes to make myself presentable. Which is ridiculous because (a) I can't do anything with this mess of me in five minutes, and (b) why is it that Nate coming over is causing this level of anticipation?

The moment I have my shirt half off, there's a knock on the door of my apartment. "Shit. Shit, shit, shit," I mumble, pulling down my T-shirt, that now clings to me like a sausage casing.

"I heard that," comes Nate's voice from the other side of the door.

"Shit." I exhale, attempting to pull myself together. This is just another Wednesday dinner. No big deal.

"Again, I can hear you. Open the door already."

I open the door and wave him in. "Give me a sec to change," I say and walk to the bedroom. From the pile of clothes on the bed, I extract a brown cowl-neck sweater. It's oversized and has ties in a pseudo sweatshirt style. It had been an impulse buy a few months ago and has already paid for itself. I don't think it's seen the inside of my closet since I bought it.

I yank off the T-shirt and come eye-to-reflection-in-the-mirror with Nate. It's not, of course, the first time he's seen me in a bra, but it is the first time since whatever transpired in Santa Fe. And everything we haven't yet addressed.

In the reflection, I see Nate's Adams apple move with a hard swallow. A shiver ripples through me and I lunge for the sweater, severing the current that has the potential to destroy everything.

I finally emerge from the bedroom, fully dressed and having given myself a pep-talk that this is Nate and I'm being ridiculous.

Nate is leaning into the fridge, inspecting the few items in there. "I thought we were having dinner? There's nothing here?"

"We've been out of town, remember?"

"We've been back for three days," Nate complains.

"Your point?"

"That you haven't been to the store in three days?"

I hip check him away and close the fridge. "You don't live here. You have no right to complain about my domestic skills."

"Skills?" He cocks an eyebrow at me.

"I haz skills," I sass back.

"Not in the kitchen."

"Not that you know of." My face flushes, another reminder that all the easy moments between us now have the but-the-kiss Asterix.

Nate's left eyebrow ticks up and he smirks. He takes the beer I offer him and slumps onto the couch. Lulu doesn't wait for an invitation to leap into his lap.

"Ouuf. Watch those little paws, Missy," he says, repositioning her.

"She missed you." Weirdly enough, I did too. Weirdly because it's only been a couple of days without seeing him and we've talked every day since coming back. But it's not the same as being together most of the day, every day in Santa Fe. That was nice. Really nice. Nicer than it should have been.

"I missed her. Although not enough to have my private parts punctured by her claws." He shifts her a second time which only inspires Lulu to hunker down on her desired spot yet again.

"You know you won't win this, right?"

"Yeah," he concedes and moves his arms to allow the cat to settle onto his lap in whatever position she pleases.

"So, did Beth tell you she stopped by the store yesterday?" I ask. I'd meant to confront Nate when he came for the flowers, but he showed up while I was helping a customer who knew exactly what he didn't want, which was everything in the store, and by the time I broke free, Nate was blowing me a kiss and disappearing out the back door.

Nate looks surprised. "No, she didn't. What did she want?"

"I don't know. I was busy. She stuck around a few minutes then said we'd talk another time and left." The more I think about it, the more off it feels. I mean, sure, I've hung out with her a couple of times now with Nate, but we haven't crossed the paved path to solo friendship.

"Weird," Nate says.

I wait for him to expand, to fill me in on their date. He doesn't. I shift on the couch, aware of the quiet in the apartment. The only sounds are breathing from two humans and one cat. And the ice maker dropping cubes into the tray.

"Nate?" He turns his head in my direction, keeping his eyes on the cat still curled up in his lap. "Nate." I repeat.

"Callie?"

"Oh for god sake." The frustration of tiptoeing around the hot-air balloon of feelings takes over.

While my balloon of emotions is expanding, his appears to deflate. "We had an argument during our trip." It takes me a beat to connect the *we* to him and Beth and the *our* to him and me.

"You didn't say anything." I snap my mouth shut. Say

anything to Beth about the kiss, about our feelings changing for each other? Or say anything to me about the fact that they had an argument? D, all of the above.

When Nate doesn't respond, I continue. "What was the fight about?"

"You."

Thump goes my stomach, followed by my heart.

"Why me?"

I stare at Nate, at the person I've known my entire life. He's the same person as the one who sat on this very couch exactly a week ago. He's also the person I had the most insanely awesome kiss with less than a week ago. And the person I've dreamt about countless times in the last few days despite forbidding my brain to go there. Brains, like cats, always do what you tell them not to.

"She knows we're just friends." Nate is looking at Lulu, scratching her chin and I swallow the urge to tease him and ask if he's referring to the cat or me.

*Just friends.* We're not just friends. We're best friends. We're best friends who shared something that's far beyond best friend status.

Nate squirms and Lulu jumps off then saunters away with a twitch of her tail.

Oh god. Ohgodohgodohgod. He thinks Santa Fe was a mistake. The look on his face when he saw me changing wasn't desire. How could I have been so stupid?

I shove aside whatever feelings and needs have clouded my thoughts and default to the Callie I've always been. The role I know best. "You reassured her, of course, that I'm no-one to worry about."

Despite myself, I catch my breath hoping he'll correct me, assure me that I am someone to worry about.

His nod is not the answer I was waiting for. I pull on the strings of the cowl neck trying to ignore the wave of heat building inside the sweater. "I've been talking to my dad," I say attempting to distract both of us from the uncomfortable turn of the conversation.

"I'm glad."

I huff at Nate's uncooperativeness. "Look at these," I pull up the photos Dad texted earlier. "He took these. He's been earning a living as a photographer?"

Nate looks as surprised as I felt when Dad told me. He'd always had a talent for photography and, being Daddy's girl, I thought he was amazing. But to make a living on it, that's another level of amazing.

"Wow."

"Right? They're amazing."

We study a photo of a woman washing a shirt in a river, the top line of a hippo visible in the water downstream. After Steven died, my father switched from domestic exploration to overseas travel. He went from Bosnia to Zimbabwe, Papua New Guinea to Norway.

"Can you imagine traveling around the world like that?" I ask.

"I'd love to hear some of the stories from his trips." Nate scrolls through the photos again.

"Next time we go," I say without hesitation.

"Yeah," Nate answers, handing me back my phone. The heaviness I hear in his voice reminds me that next time we go, it could very well be for a good-bye rather than story-time.

I dip my head to hide the sudden mist in my eyes. Not that I have to pretend with Nate. At least not that I've ever felt like I had to pretend with Nate.

"Hey," he says, tucking a curl behind my ear. His fingers linger along my jawline and his eyes drop to my lips.

I catch my breath as the distance between us tightens. He exhales and I feel the frustration, the need, the confusion.

"Callie," he says, pulling away, his voice as raspy as my insides.

"Nate," I respond, breathless from the almost moment that shouldn't be but should absolutely happen.

"Oh, wow." He runs his hands through his hair, forcing his breathing to slow. Before I can catch my bearings, Nate stands and says, "I need to go."

"Um, okay," I say, unsure if I should go after him. I don't move. There's no need because he's already gone.

# 29

# DON'T LET THE TALL WEEDS CAST A SHADOW ON THE BEAUTIFUL FLOWERS IN YOUR GARDEN.
## — STEVE MARABOLI

"Hey, Callie, there's a Mr. Moran on the phone. He's wondering if he can pick up the order a bit earlier today?" Julia interrupts my staring contest with a purple hyacinth that's shedding its flowers.

I let the hyacinth win this round and turn to Julia. "What order is he coming to pick up?" I've completed two special orders, one for a Jason Bauer and another for Sheila Williams. Nothing for a Mr. Moran.

"He called over the weekend." She says this as though it should all make sense now which it kind of does.

"Shit." I look at the pile of notes from the weekend that I haven't finished sorting. Although I thought I'd caught all the orders and bills and urgent notes. I shuffle to the desk and flip through the "to deal with" pile. A request for proposal for an anniversary dinner in two months, due tomorrow; a call from Jeff Barnet from the spring tour committee; a reminder from Mr. Stiles about the anniversary party he's throwing for his wife; and there it is, a sticky note with a name and a phone number.

I hold up the sticky. "This?"

Julia blanches. "Um, yeah?"

"Julia, this is not an order. There's nothing on here that even hints that he wants to place an order. Did you speak to him or did he leave a message?" I fight back the urge to cry. This just may be the proverbial straw—scrap of paper—that breaks this camel's will to live.

Because if last night hadn't been soul-crushing enough, Nate's text this morning asking if he could swing by later to pick up another arrangement was a brutal reminder of my role as woo co-conspirator.

She pinches the bridge of her nose and closes her eyes tight. She looks more constipated than thoughtful. Finally she says, "I spoke to him?" The uptick in her voice makes it sound like a question, not a statement and I raise an eyebrow.

"And what did he say when you spoke to him?"

Julia's face crumples into panic. "I don't remember. Oh god, Callie, I totally screwed up. The store was busy, and I was so sure I would remember what he wanted. It was an easy order."

"Well, easy or not, this doesn't give me much to work with. I'll call him and sort this out." I bite back frustration, partially directed at Julia, partially at Maggie, partially at my phone blinking that I have six new messages all received within the last two hours and all from my mom.

Julia returns to helping customers and I dial the number on the sticky note.

"Mr. Moran? Hi, this is Callie at Fancy Fleur. I understand you're wanting to come in a bit earlier to pick up the arrangement. What time are you thinking?"

"Can it be ready by 4 p.m. That gets me home with a bit of time to spare."

I glance at the clock. 2:12 p.m. "I think that can be arranged. Let's talk quickly about what you have in mind, and I'll get right on it."

Turns out that what Mr. Moran needs really is easy—seven sunflowers, one for each year he and his wife have been married. I slip in a creamy white Dahlia for eternal love and wrap the bouquet with our signature green ribbon.

One crisis averted.

My phone rings and I snatch an anxious look at the caller ID. I let it go into voicemail. I've never ignored a call from Nate. I didn't answer his earlier text about the flowers, either.

I tap at a number and listen to the ringing before he answers.

"Callie. What a wonderful surprise. I didn't think I'd hear from you until tonight."

"Hi, Dad." The relief in hearing his voice takes my breath away. Every conversation with him is a reminder of the time we lost and the time we won't have. It's like the beginning of a new relationship and yet also like sliding seamlessly into a comfortable old one. "Am I catching you at a bad time?"

"It's never a bad time for you. Hey," he lowers his voice, "are you okay?"

I nod, not that he can see me. But when I try to open my mouth to answer, the words can't get past the cotton ball of emotion and I'm suddenly shaking my head as tears stream down my face. Thankfully, he still can't see me.

"Yeah," I finally say.

"What happened?" Dad presses.

"Nothing, I'm just tired." Which, of course, doesn't fool either of us.

"Okay," he says, leaving the invitation to talk when I'm ready out there.

"What have you been up to?" I ask, wanting the distraction.

"Well, I beat Ed Morris in checkers this morning. And I just took a stroll to the vending machine with Nurse Megan."

I laugh, despite the lump in my heart. "Wow. You have a busier social schedule than I do."

My cat has a busier social schedule than I do. Julia spent her lunch break in my apartment hanging with Lulu because she missed her. Both of them would have been perfectly content if I'd stayed in Santa Fe. Maybe I should have. Maybe if we'd never come back, Nate wouldn't have run out of my apartment like he'd almost locked lips with a venus fly trap.

"What's new with you?" Dad asks cautiously.

"Usual work stuff."

"How about play stuff?"

"I don't have an Ed or a Nurse Megan to get in trouble with."

"Good point. But you have a Nate." Dad waits for a beat, then adds, "I could send you Ed but you have to keep an eye on him. He cheats. I'm keeping Nurse Megan. She has an in with the Vending Machine Gods. It always drops a second bag of M&Ms when she's with me."

Dad and his M&Ms. He'd buy the large bag and put a piece of masking tape over the words "Sharing Size" and write "Individual Size" on it. He still shared with me though.

"Have you seen Mom and Maggie today?" I ask.

"They've been busy," he answers. There's a hitch in his voice that I don't like. It could be due to the tumor or the medication or disappointment.

"Too busy to come visit?" It's not fair for me to be annoyed at them. Mom does have a job and life continues to march forward. But the thought of him alone in that hospital makes me sad.

"Don't be angry with her, Callie. She didn't choose this."

I stop myself from stating the obvious. He didn't choose the brain tumor either.

"Question," Dad starts, his voice suddenly strong and playful. "If you could do anything, be anywhere, what would you choose?"

I close my eyes and I'm back in my childhood home. My

favorite place to hide was on the window seat behind the curtains on the landing between the first and second floors of our house. Tucked behind the curtains, I could watch Nate and his brothers in the backyard. It never took long for Nate to notice me sitting there and in minutes he'd come join me.

It was also the spot where dad and I had some of our best talks. That's where we played our "what would you do and where would you choose" game. In recent conversations, we've resurrected this little trip to fantasy land.

Tucked between the large windows and the thick curtains that looked like they belonged in a medieval castle, I could be anyone I wanted. And I loved sharing those dreams with my father.

"I'd move to Amsterdam and be a tulip farmer."

Dad laughs. "You hate gardening."

I shrug. "I'll learn. Tulips stand for true love. And since they're a spring flower, they've also become a symbol of new life."

"Tulips for the win," dad says.

I close my eyes and imagine myself in a field of tulips. Yellow for hope. Pink for luck. Red for love. Orange for friendship. And a sea of Parrot tulips for their frilly perfection that makes me happy whenever I see them.

"And Amsterdam?" Dad prompts.

"Because I've never been there."

"That's as good a reason as any," he responds.

## 30

# IN A FOREST OF A HUNDRED THOUSAND TREES, NO TWO LEAVES ARE ALIKE.

— PAULO COELHO

"Red or white?" Nate calls from the kitchen.

Beth looks at me for my answer. "White?" I ask.

Beth nods approval and yells back to Nate, "White, please."

Before I'd managed to roll myself out of bed this morning, Nate had already texted about plans for the evening—homemade pizza and a movie.

It wasn't until I pulled into his driveway that the reality of the invite slammed into me. Beth's white Volkswagen Jetta was already there. I should have known. I didn't.

It's not unpleasant with her here. But it's not the evening I was hoping for. Then again, the way he bolted the other night, it's exactly what I should have expected.

The doorbell rings and Beth and I both shoot a questioning look at Nate.

"Did you order backup pizza?" I tease. When Nate said "homemade," I'd assumed it would be the store-bought cheese pizza we usually get with whatever toppings we can scrounge from his fridge. I hadn't taken into account the secret ingredient —Beth. So tonight, homemade is indeed from scratch.

"You better not have," Beth wags a finger at him although she looks far more adorable than menacing. I hate her.

"Give me some credit. Callie, open the door? It's Eric."

I glare at him. "Eric?" I hate him, too (Nate, not Eric).

Nate flashes a sorry-not-sorry grin but he's uneasy, I can see it in the way he's looking just past my left ear.

Wine glass in hand, I open the front door. It's hard to tell what's more disconcerting—how amazing Eric looks in jeans and the gray, long sleeve henley that somehow makes the green of his eyes greener or the kiss he plants on my cheek as though we've known each other forever.

Eric follows me to the kitchen where Nate and Beth have set out bowls of pizza toppings and four balls of dough.

An odd exchange of greetings and teasing and coupling takes place and I find myself on the side of the island with Eric, watching Nate and Beth in domestic togetherness as they step around each other, a hand on the back, a hip nudge, a smile.

This certainly isn't the first time I've seen Nate chummy with a girlfriend and it's certainly not the first time I've seen him and Beth together. But it is the first time since my feelings for him hopped the friendship fence. And the fact that he's avoiding any direct interaction with me tells me he's avoiding that same fence with the caution you'd give a live electric fence.

"So, Callie, I heard you had quite an experience in Santa Fe," Beth says.

The wine glass shakes in my hand, mid-way to my mouth. Nate wouldn't have told her about the kiss. And I wouldn't be standing here if he had. I sneak a look at Nate who is busy rolling one of the dough balls into something resembling a pie crust.

I choose which of the experiences to comment on and say,

"I wasn't so sure when Nate drove us into the middle of nowhere, but yeah, it ended up being amazing." *And the kiss was spectacular.* I take a long sip of my wine, letting the liquid wash those last words back down.

Beth gets a swoony look in her eyes. "That's one of my bucket list items."

"Almost being eaten by coyotes?" Not that we were ever in danger of being eaten by coyotes, I think.

Beth laughs, elbows Nate. "You didn't tell me that part."

*That's not the only part he didn't tell you about.*

"She's exaggerating. We were in far greater danger of being crushed by orbital debris re-entering the atmosphere."

Eric laughs and fist bumps Nate.

"You guys are *so* funny," I sass.

"Fix your pizzas however you like," Beth redirects. "I'm hungry."

The kitchen erupts into a flurry of pizza preparation as everyone reaches for their favorite toppings. Veggies for Eric, prosciutto with mozzarella balls for Nate. Beth follows Nate's lead, adding spinach to hers.

Nate pops a mozzarella ball into his mouth, then feeds one to Beth. There's a moment between them, a look that turns the wine in my stomach to vinegar. I can't remember ever looking at someone the way she gazes up at him. Except for Nate. Nate returns her look, and the vinegar burns through me. No one has ever looked at me like that. Except for Nate.

I pick a few olives from the dish and shove them into my misshapen dough. I don't want to see the wooing happening on the other side of the island. It's what he asked me to help with. It's what he wants. It's even what I want for him, if it makes him happy. And yet, seeing it stings far worse than a flu shot.

Nate pops another mozzarella ball into his mouth and says, "Finally someone else who appreciates my taste in pizzas. This one," he thumbs at me, "comes up with the strangest combinations." He shakes his head in mock-horror.

"That is so not true," I defend my pizza, adding a handful of onions.

Eric looks at my odd shaped pie. "Cheese, olives, and onions? I fear my buddy Nate may be right."

With deliberate precision, I crumble goat cheese into the open space between the toppings.

Nate slaps his forehead. "Baffles me how we can be best friends. You have the strangest taste." Despite the ribbing, he reaches out and picks an olive from my pie. Nate is as much of an olive fan as I am. I glower at him and replace the missing olive before slipping my pizza into the oven along with the other three.

"We're best friends because I put up with you and your weirdness. And I know things." I wave my pointer finger in a don't-mess-with-me.

Beth laughs. "I think it's time for me and Callie to have some girl time. You two get out," she flips the dishtowel dismissively at Nate and Eric.

"Uh oh," Eric says.

"Yeah, not happening." Nate crosses his arms and leans against the counter. "I know where this is heading."

Beth sidles up next to me, shoulder to shoulder. "Ahh, come on. We're trustworthy."

Nate shakes his head. "This one knows far too much about me."

"That's the point," Beth coos and I watch with dismay and awe as Nate's expression transforms into adoration.

A shocking wave of jealousy and need engulfs me. I'm the one who's gone through 33 years of life with him. I'm the one who knows everything about him. We have a connection she'll never have with him.

And yet, there's no denying the chemistry he has with Beth.

Was what sparked between us a fluke? A quick blaze that passed with the speed of a shooting star? At least for him. Because no matter how much I want to push these new feelings I've developed aside, I can't.

I turn to refill my wine glass, anything to erase the image of how he's looking at her. "Listen to the lady," I say. "Before I start spilling all your dirty secrets. Like the time you fell asleep on the neighbor's lounge chairs and they found you there in the morning."

"Continue," Eric prompts with a mischievous glint.

Nate slaps his forehead with his palm, knowing I won't let this one go. The twitch at the corner of his mouth also reveals that he knows I chose the tamest of stories I have on him.

"He was naked and the sprinklers were going." I grin at Nate who groans. "He was trying to drink the water in his sleep."

"Not my finest moment." He winks and for a fraction of a second, our eyes meet. And there, right there, is proof that it wasn't a fluke. Maybe it's not meant to be, but it sure as hell wasn't a mistake. "But not my worst, either," he adds, looking away quickly.

I swallow. "That's for sure."

Beth, I notice, is following the current between me and Nate. Nate notices it too and sidesteps the potential relationship sinkhole by directing Eric to the family room under pretense of finding a movie for us to watch.

"Do we trust them to choose?" I ask Beth.

"No but us making fun of their choice beats them making fun of our choice."

"Touché." I clink my glass to hers. It's not the first time I wish there was something easy to dislike about Beth. Well, other than the fact that she's captured something in Nate. That same something that I desperately want.

"Before they come back for their pizzas, I want to ask your

advice," Beth says in a low voice, not that the guys would hear us over the TV.

I steel myself for what I suspect will no doubt be an uncomfortable conversation and wonder why I didn't opt for a quiet evening with my cat.

"Okay?" I prompt even though I really, really don't want to give her advice on Nate.

She fusses with the leftover toppings, sliding the cheese back into the original bag, shaking olives into their container. Watching Beth move around Nate's kitchen with ease makes me feel like an intruder. A slightly resentful, jealous intruder.

This is what he asked me to help with. This is what he wanted. What he wants.

But instead of winning *the* girl, he won both of us. Now the question is, which one of us will win the guy? And more than that, is the best friend code stronger than whatever is potentially developing between me and Nate?

For a long minute Beth and I watch Nate and Eric discussing the lineup of movies. I groan when they switch to live TV and stop on a basketball game.

"We're doomed," I say.

Beth studies me. "Not a fan?" If she is, then Nate may indeed have found his perfect match which means I'm on the wrong side of March Madness.

"I can fake it."

Beth folds and refolds the kitchen towel and I wait for the ask. As long as it doesn't mean betraying Nate's plan, I can fake this, too.

"So, it's about Nate."

Best friend Callie nods for her to continue while inside, hopeful Callie dreads what's coming my way.

"I was thinking of booking a B&B for his birthday weekend but I'm not sure it's a good idea."

I chafe. It's not *his* birthday weekend, it's *our* birthday weekend. And she can't take him away. We've spent every one of our 32 birthdays together. This birthday is supposed to be ours.

"Why not sure?" I manage to ask.

"I really like Nate. I mean, really, like him." She's still fussing with cleaning the kitchen which is making me twitchy. I resist the urge to grab the sponge. She's already wiped the island four times.

"And that's not good?"

"It's scary. He's doing everything right. And those flowers are gorgeous and perfect and I know I have you to thank."

"All his doing." I brush off the compliment. I'm just interpreting what he wants to say, that's all. Well, what he thinks he wants to say.

A smidge of regret nudges at me for adding the lily of the valley to the latest bouquet. While often associated with love, the lily of the valley can also signify heartbreak. It was a slightly passive-aggressive nod to the universe to do the right thing, whatever that may be.

But despite whatever feelings I'm harboring, my instinct to protect Nate overrules all else. "He really likes you, Beth. I've never seen him like this with anyone."

She turns, all big brown eyes and parted lips and could she really be any more perfect? "Really?"

I nod. "Really."

"It just feels like we're moving so fast."

I can't disagree with that. I'd like nothing more than for time to slow down.

The timer on the oven dings and, looking relieved, Beth busies herself with taking the pizzas out.

Like cats who hear the tuna can being opened, Nate and Eric appear behind us before either Beth or I can think to call them. Without skipping a beat in their analysis of the basketball game and their March Madness brackets, they retreat back to the family room, a plate in one hand and a fresh beer in the other.

"Do you think they even saw us?" I whisper to Beth, just loud enough to get a twitch of a smile and wink from Eric.

Beth giggles and my insides feel like an ice cream pint left too close to a burning candle. And then, because I can't think of anything worse, I say, "I think you should book the B&B."

# 31

A WEED IS NO MORE THAN A
FLOWER IN DISGUISE, WHICH IS
SEEN THROUGH AT ONCE, IF LOVE
GIVE A MAN EYES.A WEED IS NO
MORE THAN A FLOWER IN DISGUISE,
WHICH IS SEEN THROUGH AT ONCE,
IF LOVE GIVE A MAN EYES.

— JAMES RUSSELL LOWELL

"Why are you being so cagey?" Nate asks. It's after hours and we're sitting on the floor of the shop, Lulu curled up in Nate's lap as usual, open containers of Chinese food spread around us. We ordered enough for three meals for some reason.

"I'm not being cagey."

"You so are."

"So not." I wonder sometimes if it's like this for all siblings, couples, I have no idea what to label us. Whenever we disagree, we turn into little kids, relying on the same inane arguments that got us nowhere back then either. Even back then I was the first to cave.

"Then why won't you go out with him?" I can't read his expression, whether he's genuinely in favor of me dating Eric or baiting me to answer a question he's not ready to ask.

"I didn't say I wouldn't." Eric and I had left at the same time last night. He'd been a gentleman, opening my car door and giving me a kiss on the cheek. He'd also asked me out. Or at least he asked me if I was up for coffee or lunch this coming week. Coffee or lunch, or even both, is one of those hedging invites that means "You're pleasant to be around" without the expectation of it being an actual date. While I hadn't said yes, I hadn't said no either.

Guys like Eric don't go for girls like me. They date the pretty girls, the stylish girls, the girls who know how to be flirty and fun. Then again, guys like Nate don't go for girls like me either. But Nate isn't "guys like," he's Nate.

And Nate is dating Beth.

Nate picks up the last egg roll and offers it to me. "Half?" I ask. He nods and breaks it in two, handing me the slightly larger piece. Typical Nate.

"So?" Nate nudges once he's finished his half of the egg roll.

"So nothing. He's nice."

"But?"

"No but." We already went through this when the conversation was about Beth. It's far less fun being on this end of the "but" question.

His left eyebrow pops up.

"Geez, you're not going to let this go, are you?"

"Nope. I want you to be happy."

"Who says I'm not?"

"Are you?"

"Yeah. At least when you're not ditching me for someone else."

Nate glowers at me. "Be serious."

"I am."

"No, you're not."

"Okay, I'm not. I'm fine even with you ditching me for someone else."

Nate shakes his head but his mouth curls into a glimmer of a smile.

"Hey, what are we going to do for our birthday?" I change the subject with the finesse of someone learning to drive a manual transmission. (Years ago Nate tried teaching me. It didn't go well.) And yeah, it's also a bit of a set-up. I want to see if Beth has already popped the B&B question. And maybe it's also a bit of a trap because if he and I make plans, then he'll be forced to choose between me and Beth if she surprises him for the same weekend. Pathetic, I know.

"We could have a small party," I say when Nate doesn't respond immediately.

"Small as in your place or small as in my place?" My place small is six, eight people max. Nate's house allows for inviting friends I barely know.

"Here?" I say, then point up since here obviously doesn't mean at the store. "Or we could just do something the two of us." Such a setup. Way to go, Callie.

Nate slurps in a lo mein noodle and points his chopsticks at me. "Interesting idea."

"Is that the idea equivalent of saying someone has a good personality?"

Nate laughs around another ingoing noodle. "No, it's a 'that's an interesting idea'."

I warm to the encouragement. "We could make reservations at some swanky restaurant, get a car service, do this up fancy." I wiggle to the word fancy and Nate chokes on the noodle.

"You are so weird."

"Takes one to appreciate one."

Nate nods but I can tell his mind has drifted elsewhere. I toss a packet of soy sauce at him. "Earth to Nate. Hellooo?" I contort to look him in the eye.

"What were you and Beth talking about last night?" He

asks, watching as a noodle slithers out of the chopsticks and back into the container.

"Well, duh, we were talking about you."

He bends to talk directly to the cat. "She's impossible, isn't she?" Lulu stretches up and head-butts him in feline agreement.

"Oh relax. She adores you and she's duly impressed with the flower arrangements. She thinks you're absolutely brilliant." I add a flourish to the final word and bat my eyes at Nate.

"Seriously, though," I continue, "she really does like you. And she really is very nice." There's that same odd mix of happiness and jealousy that I felt last night. The unfamiliar mix of pride and possessiveness. A lifetime of being his biggest fan. A lifetime of him being my person.

I wasn't prepared for the two complications: Beth and feelings that I suppose were inevitable.

"She is," Nate agrees.

"Having second thoughts?" I try to read the expression on his face but all I see is the grimace of heartburn. I told him not to order the spicy chicken.

Nate shakes his head. "She's amazing. In every way."

I hold up my hand. "No details."

Lulu stands and climbs up Nate's chest to rub on his chin. "Okay, okay, you're more amazing," Nate coos at her.

"Um, helloooo." I gesture at myself.

"You're okay, too." Nate grins at me.

"Way to make a girl feel special." And, I silently add to my list, a lifetime of friendship. This is what I love most about Nate. This is what I don't want to lose. Not because of Beth and not because of feelings that have no business mucking things up.

Our eyes meet for a heartbeat. "You are special. I wish you'd believe that."

"Yeah, yeah." I wave him off, uncomfortable under his gaze.

It's been Nate's life mission to boost my self-appreciation. It's not that I don't think I'm worthy, it's that I don't trust the longevity of that worth.

Nate stands abruptly, dislodging Lulu who meows her objection. He reaches for my hand and pulls me to standing.

"Come." Still holding my hand, he guides me to the windows at the front of the store.

"When did that start?" I ask in hushed awe. With just the fairy lights illuminating the main part of the store and the streetlights in the courtyard outside the shop, I feel like I'm in a snow globe.

"There were some flurries when I came but I didn't expect it to develop into this," Nate says.

In the two hours since he arrived, the world outside appears to have come to a halt. A good six inches of pristine snow blankets the sidewalks and the courtyard between the two rows of buildings, glowing in the. Lights from the ramen restaurant across the courtyard and from the wine shop two doors down. Flickers of light come from Tish's apartment. Candles I assume.

"It's beautiful." My breath fogs the window in front of me and I shiver. Behind me, I feel a wall of heat as Nate steps closer and another shiver travels through me.

If I tilt my weight onto my heels, I'll be leaning into him. The idea sends a spark of confusion, paralyzing all movement and thought. Nate tips forward, trapping the wave of heat between us. I exhale, allowing my body to relax into him.

"The Santa Fe meteor shower was better," he says, the puffs of air with each exhaled word tickle my cheek.

I close my eyes, willing the white world outside to transform into the vast nothingness of the desert at night by the time I reopen them. Nate puts his arms around me and I soak in his warmth. Just like in Santa Fe.

"But here we don't have to worry about being eaten by coyotes. Or crushed by orbital debris," I whisper.

I feel his laugh against my back.

"Would it be okay if I stay?"

I swallow, nod. "Of course."

And as we stand watching snowflakes that don't resemble stars but hold the same promise of wishes granted, I mentally adjust the flowers going into the next bouquet.

# 32

# IN NATURE, NOTHING EXISTS ALONE.
## — RACHEL CARSON

Despite talking every night since the snowstorm three days ago, I woke up with the "Wednesday will he or won't he" dread that's been plaguing me since Beth became the third entity in our Nate and Callie relationship. Not that Nate and I have a *relationship* relationship. Not exactly. Not yet. To my relief, within minutes of waking up, he sent a text confirming that he'll be over by 7 p.m. Not only that, but he said *we* will cook dinner *together*. So, yes, I'm totally reading into that.

We've talked about everything and absolutely nothing. Every time I see his name pop up, my insides do an unflattering, inappropriate jig.

To add to the excitement of the day, Jeff Barnet called to tell me that Fancy Fleur is still in contention for the Spring Tour. He'd made the case to the board of directors that considering our history with the program, we should have an automatic entry assuming we indicated interest, which we had, no thanks to Maggie.

Just as I was getting cozy with the idea of this being a great day, Beth called asking me to meet her for coffee. When the phone rang, I'd momentarily considered not picking up. But I'd answered and I'd been too surprised by her invitation to come up with a plausible excuse. So here we are at the coffee shop.

And so far, our conversation hasn't moved past the artistic brilliance of the barista and his foam art on our lattes. Lame. Uncomfortable. Safe.

I shift in the hard wood chair and nod a hello at a woman who walks by with a to-go cup.

"Friend?" Beth asks.

"Not exactly. She owns the yoga studio at the end of the block." Since opening the studio a year ago, Lauren has repeatedly offered the invitation "for a free session." "Yoga is not my thing. Last time I tried, I got a cramp doing downward dog and ended up in a whimpering heap. I plan on making that last attempt indeed my last attempt."

"I have a confession, don't judge," Beth says with a shy smile. "I fell asleep once during yoga and let out such a loud snore in corpse pose that I was asked not to return."

I can't help it, I fall a little in love with her at that moment. Then I remember what Nate told me.

"Nate says you talked him into going to hot yoga."

"Yeah. He's still holding that against me." She looks equally chagrined and amused. "One of the teachers at my school is obsessed with hot yoga. She'd been on me for months to go with her. I finally caved and agreed. I find it miserable and amazing in equal parts. Sounds weird, I know, but it doesn't matter how crappy my day was, I always come out of a class feeling more grounded."

I'd be coming out of a hot yoga class in a to-go cup, the warning label changed from "contents may be hot" to "contents may be stinky."

Michael places two fresh mugs on the table and winks at me.

Beth leans forward and whispers, "Did you order those?"

"Nope, he's lobbying for barista of the year."

"Ah. Do I need to warn Eric that he has competition?" Beth eyeballs Michael as he walks away. It's a nice view. And we're not the only two admirers he has.

"No, no competition."

Though Eric and I have exchanged a few texts, we've yet to confirm a time and place to get together. Totally me being noncommittal but he also hasn't pushed. A fact I'm both extremely grateful for and slightly offended by.

"Do I need to get on Eric's case?" Beth asks, conspiratorially. She picks up her mug, her sleeve slipping back just a fraction. Just enough to reveal the bracelet Nate bought her in Santa Fe.

Inside my sweater, the leaf pendant suddenly feels cold against my skin.

Nothing happened between me and Nate the night of the snowstorm unless you call falling asleep together on the couch with his arms around me "something."

Here in the coffee shop with Beth, the moon pendant gleaming like a full moon on a clear night, I'm torn with the guilt of happiness I'd felt snuggled against Nate. What had felt so natural now feels so wrong. How is it possible to feel such conflicting emotions? How is it possible to want such opposite results?

"No need to get on Eric's case." I make a promise to myself to set a date with him.

Beth watches me with a mixture of trying-to-figure-me-out and I'm-not-sure-I-trust-you. It's making me uncomfortable. More uncomfortable. Because I wouldn't be surprised if my face showed a similar mix of emotions. The worst part is that I both really, really like her and really, really don't want to like her.

"Can I trust you to keep a secret until I'm ready to tell Nate?" she asks.

The deafening noise of the coffee shop freezes in my ears.

She's pregnant. She's already married. She's defecting to France. I nod.

"Before Nate and I started dating, I applied for a new position at a different school. I've had a number of conversations with the administration and yesterday they called and offered me the job."

"Congratulations." It's the correct response, right? But why is it a secret?

"It's an amazing position. I'd be developing a magnet program for space studies. A few years ago, the school developed a program for biological sciences, linking students to internships and research opportunities with local labs and hospitals, opportunities that usually aren't available until college or grad school. Now they're seeing higher GPAs and more kids applying to and being accepted to top colleges."

"That's amazing." I'm waiting for the but. There's always a but.

"But it's in California."

That's a big but.

"Oh, wow," is all I can think of saying. My brain immediately kicks over a stone of hope: Beth moving to California would mean no more Beth.

"Yeah, timing kinda stinks, doesn't it?"

"Why don't you want Nate to know?" The best friend in me is feeling prickly that she's playing with Nate's emotions, leading him on until she's ready to leave.

"I want to tell him, but I was hoping we'd have time to settle more in our relationship, first. This will sound crazy, but I think I want to ask him to move with me."

I was wrong, this is a massive but.

"Oh, wow," I repeat.

"Do you think he would?" My heart softens momentarily at the look on her face. She's in love with him.

"Oh, wow." I'm a stuck record. "I, um, I don't know. He has a great job here. His mom is here." I'm here, I add in my head.

Beth pulls her lips tight. "Which is why I'm so torn about bringing it up. I was thinking I'd bring it up when we go away to the B&B."

Sneaky. Smart.

"Promise you won't say anything?" Beth implores.

I want to out her and I want to keep her secret. I really do hate her for not being completely hateable.

"I promise," I say. And I mean it. Because whatever conflicted feelings I'm having, I also know I'd never do anything to jeopardize Nate's happiness.

That doesn't mean I'm just going to sit around and let her ruin my life. I relax my left hand, fingers crossed under the table.

# 33

## PEOPLE FROM A PLANET WITHOUT FLOWERS WOULD THINK WE MUST BE MAD WITH JOY THE WHOLE TIME TO HAVE SUCH THINGS ABOUT US.

— IRIS MURDOCH

Since the moment Maggie got back from Santa Fe and walked into her house, she hasn't stopped moving, not that she's actually *doing* anything, at least nothing productive. Her suitcase is still parked next to the front door and she's still clomping around in her shoes, scarf still tied around her neck. She's plucked dead leaves from a handful of plants, only stopping long enough to eyeball me reproachfully.

"Mom, you're making us crazy," Nate says. I force down a butterfly of emotion at the word "us." It's silly because we've always been "us" when it comes to so many things.

Maggie ignores Nate, turning on me instead. "David says you've been talking regularly. Hearing from you helps."

It's been helping me as well. With Nate walking a tightrope between me and Beth, friendship and relationship, confiding in my dad has softened the blow of not having Nate at the other end of the phone whenever a thought needs to leave my fingers.

"How's he really doing?" I ask, because Dad's answers

usually skew to the keep-it-light side when it comes to discussing his health.

"Not great," Maggie answers, her eyes on the philodendron as she pokes her finger into the soil.

Nate and I came by three days ago to water and bring in the mail. By the pinched look on her face, our plant-sitting won't earn us a tip.

Maggie exhales, crushes the dead leaf in her fist and drops the pieces back into the pot. She moves to the chair next to the couch, sitting with a heaviness of a bold exclamation mark.

"I came back to talk to the two of you about my decision. I'll be returning to Santa Fe."

"For how long?" I blurt.

"Why?" Nate asks over me.

"It's where I need to be. Rose needs me."

Every word she's not saying lands on my heart like an overfed hippo. My father is dying. The one man my mother ever truly loved is dying.

"Going back for how long?" Nate returns to my question.

"For good."

"That's crazy," Nate says, shaking his head so vigorously, I worry he'll give himself whiplash.

"But your home is here. Your store. Us." While Nate's tone had shot up in surprise, mine drops into despair. All these years Maggie has been more of a mother to me than my own mom. She's been my friend, mentor, and boss. She's given me a home and a family. I may not be a lost 16 year-old anymore, but I'm not sure I know how to live without her nearby.

"What about the store?" I ask in a whisper, afraid of floating the idea into the universe that Fancy Fleur could be sold.

Maggie sinks deeper into the chair. "Well, that's a conversation we need to have."

"Mom, you're not seriously thinking of selling?"

Maggie focuses on her fingers as they comb the tassels on

the scarf still wound around her neck. Another influence from my mother. Unless it's bone-chilling outside, Maggie hates having anything around her neck or on her head.

"I never thought I would," she says. "The shop has been my life. When Rose left, I struggled to understand how she could leave so completely. How could someone walk away from everything they'd built?"

It's the same question I'd mused and obsessed over. Our house may not have been the grandest but it was perfect. Everything in it had been purchased with purpose. There was a story behind every item in it. And then one day, my mom left. All she took with her was a carryon with the bare minimum of clothes. The house and all the possessions Mom had lovingly acquired were sold. Just like that.

Maggie inhales sharply. "Rose and I had a few ugly fights about the way she left. I never really understood how she could do what she did. I'd look around my house, my store and attempt to picture leaving it all behind. I hated Rose for being able to just walk away."

A gasp of surprise scratches my throat. When I'd complained about that very thing after my mom left, Maggie had given me a stern talking to. She'd made it clear that I had no place criticizing my mother, that I didn't understand what she was going through or how difficult the move was for her. From where I sat, Mom's move seemed like an escape, like she'd done it without even a peek in the rearview mirror.

"So why now?" Nate asks.

"Because for the first time, I see that her decision wasn't about what she was leaving, it's about what she no longer needed."

A stab of hurt deflates my lungs with a whoosh. I was one of the "things" my mother no longer needed?

For the first time since she sat down, Maggie makes eye contact with me. As though reading my mind, she says, "Your mom needed to let go of the hurt. She needed to let go of the person she'd become as David's wife."

"And as my mother," I add.

Maggie shakes her head. "No, never that. But in her mind, finding herself would never happen in the life she'd built with David."

"I don't understand, Mom," Nate attempts to circle the conversation back to the move of the moment. Maggie's move.

"My life isn't just about this house or the shop or even the two of you. I've done my part here. It's hard to explain but these last few weeks felt like an awakening. I don't need this anymore. I need to find the next version of me."

Next to me, Nate stiffens. "You've been around Rose too long. No offense," he adds looking at me.

"None taken."

"This isn't about Rose or because of Rose. Starting the store after your dad died was a leap for me. I couldn't have done it without Rose and David. They gave me the strength to believe in myself. This chapter in my life has been amazing but I'm ready for something else. I need something else."

She lets that thought settle before pushing off from the chair. "Now, if you two will excuse me, I'm going to take a bath then order dinner. Don't wait around." She shuffles down the hall and calls out, "lock the door behind you."

Nate and I stay stuck to the couch in shock, although no doubt for different reasons. I don't think Maggie has ever dismissed anyone, much less Nate like that before. And my brain is paused on "next chapter." I love that idea. And I'm absolutely terrified to turn the page and discover that I don't have the strength to go after my own next chapter.

# 34

## FLOWERS DON'T WORRY ABOUT HOW THEY'RE GOING TO BLOOM. THEY JUST OPEN UP AND TURN TOWARD THE LIGHT AND THAT MAKES THEM BEAUTIFUL.

— JIM CARREY

I tuck my hands deeper into the pocket of my fleece jacket as Nate and I move silently through the noisy aisles of the farmer's market. It's early for us for a Saturday, although for the hard-core farmer's market attendees, it's prime time. At this hour, the freshly roasted coffee beans smell richer, warmer and the bread has a beckoning softness.

To say that neither of us slept much last night after Maggie dropped the news would be ridiculously obvious. Nate and I had spent the better part of the night texting, unable to settle our thoughts. How could Maggie up and move? The abruptness of her decision has my mother's influence all over it. Maggie would never do something this impulsive, especially not when it comes to her beloved shop.

Not that I know what she's actually planning on doing with the shop.

Somewhere around 3 a.m., Nate and I discussed the possibility of me buying the store. At 4:18 a.m. we started brainstorming alternative career paths for me. And by 5:23 a.m. I was ready to plant myself on Maggie's doorstep and beg her to reconsider moving.

"Are we looking for anything specific?" Nate asks, as I continue to walk aimlessly around the stalls.

Normally, I would have already bought coffee from the micro roaster and a croissant from the bakery. We would have picked through the flowers from one of the local farms and bought cheese from a nearby dairy. Today, I march past Mark from the dairy with only a half-smile and nod hello, and I avoid Avi the baker.

"My sanity," I answer Nate. "More like your mom's sanity which she clearly left here before her trip to Santa Fe."

Nate snorts but it's not a laugh or acknowledgement or derision.

"She can't move. That's nuts," I grumble.

"It is. But I also kinda get it."

I stop and stare at him. "Who are you and what did you do with my friend Nate?"

Nate takes my arm and moves me out of the path as a man holding a cardboard tray with four coffees charges past.

"Don't you ever wonder if there's something else out there for you?" Nate asks. My eyes follow his gaze to the mysterious "out there" which turns out to be the bee tent.

"No," I answer with the conviction of a verbal foot-stomp. I mean, I have wondered, but not in the drop-everything-in-my-life way.

Nate isn't buying it. Of course, he's not because he sees in me what I refuse to see. "Is this really enough, Callie? Is this where your true happiness is?"

"You sound like my dad." I sidestep the questions and a small furry dog that's about to pee on the patch of grass by my feet. I glare at the dog's owner who's busy on her phone pretending not to notice.

"Well then, two of the smartest people you know think there's more out there for you," Nate gives me a smug smile.

"I need new people in my life." I do an abrupt turn and head to the bee tent, becoming instantly engrossed in the rows of candles and soaps, straws to put in tea, raw honey, honeycomb, and an assortment of flavored honey in cute little jars with mini dippers attached.

"You don't like honey," Nate says.

"I don't dislike it." I pretend to study a bottle of wildflower honey, then a lavender one. "I'm going to try these." I set a small bottle of lavender honey and three honey straws on the table and reach for my wallet.

We continue our walk, past a vendor selling photographs, another with bracelets made with handmade glass beads.

"Should I have gotten the wildflower honey instead of the lavender one?" I ask, my attention on the bottle inside the plastic bag. "Nate?" I look up when he doesn't respond.

A woman next to me smiles and shrugs. She's not Nate. I hate when he does this.

I scan the crowd for a tall guy in jeans and a light green sweatshirt. I find two, together. What are the odds?

"Good morning," Eric greets me when I've finally made my way to where he and Nate are standing.

"What are the odds?" Nate points from himself to Eric.

"That two space nerds would dress the same or that we'd bump into each other here?" I ask.

"Both," Eric answers, and I'm once again struck by his easy presence. Every time I'm around him, I'm taken in by the sincere intensity in his eyes. Nothing about this guy says he's my type, or, more correctly, that I'm his type. But whenever we're together, I can almost believe that he's truly interested in me.

The odds, I suspect, were somewhat stacked by Nate. Not

the sweatshirt part, but I wouldn't be surprised if he'd texted Eric to come to the farmer's market for a "chance" run in.

"What brings you here?" I ask, giving Nate the I'm-on-to-you stink eye.

"My realtor, actually. He called last night to tell me that there's a house about to go on the market and he wanted me to see it before it did."

"And?" Nate takes over the questioning but not before giving me a smug you-owe-me-an-apology look.

"It's almost perfect. There are things I'll want to change, but it's a good price and I love the location." He looks at me when he delivers that last bit. And once again, I can't help wondering what Nate's role is in this.

"Where is this almost perfect house?" I ask.

"Elm Street. It's the Carriage House with the green door and shutters in that small cluster of them by the lake. Do you know it?"

I nod. I know exactly the one. I feel Nate's eyes on me. The carriage houses skirt a common area with benches and flowers. The one with the green door backs onto the path that loops around the pond.

Nate and I had followed the construction, playing the what-if game over which carriage house we'd want to buy. Always the one with the green door.

"Are you thinking of making an offer?" Nate asks.

"Already did. I put it in right after touring the house. I'm waiting to hear from my realtor if they've accepted." He holds up his phone and looks at it as though willing the call to come in.

"That's a great location. And we'll practically be neighbors." I smile up at Eric. I feel Nate shifting next to me, the air between us being pushed out of the way. His hand touches my lower back. I glance up at his face, curious to this sudden claim on me which is when I see the vague shadow of someone inside Fancy Fleur. Maggie. Which means that whatever order I've made of the chaos she left me, she'll undo in the snap of a finger.

"Do you have time for coffee? Or breakfast? I've heard the crepe place is really good," Eric asks, looking from me to Nate.

"Yeah, it's good. Thanks, but I need to get to the store. Maybe tomorrow, though? Nate, you're free, right?" That was about as awkward as it can get.

"Ah, yeah. I could go for a coffee," Nate says.

"Awesome. And tomorrow?" Eric waits for me to respond.

"Sounds good." I take my leave before Eric can nail down a more specific plan for tomorrow. The more I'm around him, the less sure I am that I'm not interested.

"Hey, Callie," Nate calls after me. "I'll swing by in a bit for flowers. Is that okay?"

I suddenly feel like I'm being suffocated by an insidious vine. "Sure. I'll have something ready in an hour." Then, because damn the vine, I add, "Eric, how about lunch tomorrow?"

# 35

## A FLOWER'S APPEAL IS IN ITS CONTRADICTIONS - SO DELICATE IN FORM YET STRONG IN FRAGRANCE, SO SMALL IN SIZE YET BIG IN BEAUTY, SO SHORT IN LIFE YET LONG ON EFFECT.

— TERRI GUILLEMETS

I'm not usually a nostalgic person. I don't dwell on the past and I don't cling to "the good old days." That said, here I am on a Saturday evening, sitting on the floor of my apartment looking through old photo albums and my box of keepsakes.

When my mom up and left for Santa Fe all those years ago, Maggie cleaned out our house for the sale. I'd wanted to keep everything. Then five minutes later, I wanted to throw everything away. We finally compromised—she'd decide what to keep and what to get rid of.

It's a good thing I trust Maggie.

The photo albums were one of the few things she'd kept. When I moved into this apartment, she'd arrived with a box labeled "For Callie When She's Ready."

I don't look at the albums often. As a matter of fact, I can probably count the number of times I've opened one on both hands. The reminder of what we once had as a family is just too painful.

I flip through pages of photos, Dad and I lighting candles for Hannukah, Mom and I dancing with red feather boas around our shoulders. There are photos of mom and me at the beach, mom in a magnificent purple dress at the Kennedy Center, Mom curled up on the couch reading a book.

A pang of longing makes me stop at a photo of Mom sitting cross-legged on the grass in our backyard, her hair creating a brunette wave where she's placed it over her right shoulder. She's smiling at my dad, her head tilted in a why-are-you-taking-a-picture position.

On the next page is a photo of Mom next to a poster for Turandot, with an expression of joy and pride and confidence. An expression that, now that I'm looking for it, isn't apparent in most of the other photos.

There are only a few photos of the three of us, fewer of just dad. He was usually the one taking the pictures. I study a shot of the three of us around a birthday cake with a number three candle on it. There's another of us at a playground, Dad pushing me on the swing, while Mom leans against a tree, almost out of the frame. Dad, I notice is looking at her.

Those early pictures show the love of a young family. They also show the insecurity of a woman trying to fit in a world she doesn't feel welcome. Parenting was as natural as breathing for my father. For my mom, it was a constant reminder that she wasn't cut out for it. The closer dad and I got, the more shut out she felt. Then the older I got and less I needed (or thought I needed) from him, the more it became obvious that the bond they'd shared had been severed. Mom had shut herself off and my dad needed someone who would appreciate his big heart, someone who could help him heal that amazing heart.

From the shelf, I remove another album. Along the spine is a handwritten label—Summers. As a kid, I loved how my mom turned the bottom loop of the S into the shape of a mouth. I'd even lobbied my parents to change my name to Sarah or Sally or Sandy or anything that started with an S, just so my mom would write my name with the Smooch flourish. It was probably the closest I'd get to a kiss from her.

Lulu walks past me using the photo albums as a bridge from one side of the bedroom to the other. She stalls on a photo, her front left paw covering my face. The rest of the people in the picture, Nate and his oldest brother, Eddie, are on either side of me about to toss me into the pool. I can't remember whose pool it was or if I'd been laughing, happy or yelling for them to stop. I nudge Lulu along, earning a flick of the tail and a "rude" look from her.

I look at my face in the photo. Up close, I can see that I'm laugh yelling. In the distance I now see my mom standing, watching with a smile on her face but she doesn't look relaxed like the others.

Behind me, Lulu jumps onto my dresser.

"Hey, you know you're not supposed to be up there."

She, of course, ignores the reproach.

When I don't get up to address her highness, she knocks a perfume bottle off the dresser. Then proceeds to send a small bowl with the necklace Nate bought me in Santa Fe and a pair of hoop earrings flying my direction. Luckily her aim isn't the best and the bowl lands short of hitting me.

"Uncalled for," I say.

She responds with silence and another tail twitch.

"Do I need to call Nate to come over?"

Lulu turns to look at me as though daring me to do just that. Because, of course, that's exactly what both of us would want.

I can't, of course. He's out with Beth. He came by earlier to pick up the flower arrangement. It was a particularly inspired bouquet, if I do say so myself.

I'd included yellow zinnias for good memories, tulips for irresistible love, and sweet pea for blissful pleasure and its twist meaning good-bye.

My phone rings. I move a couple of photo albums looking for it, then realize I'd left it on the dresser.

"Hand me the phone?" I ask the cat who stares at the device jittering next to her. This, however, she declines to launch my direction.

I push myself up onto my knees and reach for the phone. Lulu slaps at my hand.

"Wench." I snatch my hand back and stare at my knuckles where her claw has left a scratch.

The phone stops ringing. I grab it before I get another feline flick.

One missed call from Dad.

I tap at his number then almost drop the phone when he answers before even one ring.

"Hi," he says, an exhale of relief accompanying the word.

"Hey. Sorry I just missed you. My phone was being guarded by a furry little monster."

My dad chuckles, the effort turning into a coughing fit.

"Dad, are you okay?" The alarm bells in my brain overpower the sound of his hacking.

It takes a long moment before he responds. "It'll pass in a minute. This happens from time to time. Tell me about you."

"What are the doctors saying?" I avoid his request. It's hard to know where to begin when it feels like you've experienced a year's worth of turmoil in a 24-hour period and none of what I'm going through is remotely worth burdening him.

"They're saying the same which is not much. I called to hear your voice, to hear what's happening with you. Please?"

I sink to the floor and lean against the dresser. Lulu, bless her wicked little soul, lays down and puts her paw on my shoulder.

"Do you remember the summer we rented the beach house in Delaware?" I ask, flipping to a page in the top photo album.

"What a question. Of course, I remember. It had that amazing deck in the back. Your mom was not pleased that it wasn't right on the beach but the moment she went out back and realized the property fit perfectly between the two houses that were on the beach and from the deck you could see the water and not have to deal with all the people on the boardwalk, she settled right down."

"Did she leave the deck during the trip at all?" I run my finger over a photo of my mother on said deck, a large floppy hat covering her face, her legs stretched across two deck chairs.

Dad releases a full David laugh and I catch myself smiling.

"Once, when we went to the seafood restaurant for dinner."

"That was a pretty amazing deck." Not only was the view perfect and private, but there was a pergola at one end that provided a shady spot to read and nap. Between the deck and the wood fence that separated the back of the house from the neighbors, the owners had planted a row of Pampas Grass. I remember lazy afternoons swinging in the hammock under the shade of the pergola, the decorative grass swishing in the lazy breeze, the waves creating a distant white noise that lulled me into believing the world was perfect. Even my mom had released her usual stranglehold on life.

"I spent years fantasizing about that house, wishing it was ours," I confess.

"Me too."

"Why didn't we buy it?"

"It wasn't for sale."

"Maybe they would have sold it if we'd asked."

"Maybe, but your mom wasn't, isn't, a beach gal."

"But we loved the beach."

"We did," he says, and I hear a tone of regret in the way he says it. Regret for not pursuing the house? Regret for the days when we vacationed as a family? Or maybe it has nothing to do with me and mom, maybe Steven had loved the beach as well.

I hear voices from Dad's end. "I'll call you later, Callie." Before I can react, the call drops.

I tap out a text to Nate:

Can we go to the beach for our birthday?

# 36

# WHEN YOU TAKE A FLOWER IN YOUR HAND AND REALLY LOOK AT IT, IT'S YOUR WORLD FOR THE MOMENT.

## — GEORGIA O'KEEFFE

Thursday, I've always felt, is a nasty tease of a day. It's almost the weekend but not quite. There's the promise of happy hour that rarely ends in happy (at least that's my experience). And for those of us who don't work traditional Monday to Friday jobs, Thursday is a reminder that the weekend is nothing more than more work ahead.

Granted, my outlook isn't being helped today by last night's dinner with Maggie and Nate. Partially because Maggie had ambushed me by including my mom via FaceTime. And partially, mostly, because Maggie is on a tear today.

Julia's head pops around the corner, her eyes wide with panic. "Um, Callie, can you please come to the front for a minute?"

"What's up?" I lift my arms, full of tulips, in case she didn't see that I, literally, have my hands full back here.

"You need to redirect Maggie."

"What?" The request is so bizarre that I'm sure I didn't hear her right.

"You need to redirect Maggie," Julia repeats, as if it will make any more sense the second time.

"Meaning?" The frustration of, well, everything, creates a thrum of noise that gets louder with each minute, like the alarm on my phone that starts with the soft tones of happiness and escalates to the chimes of hell.

"Meaning she's in some mood. Honestly, I've never seen her like this. And I'm afraid she's going to scare the customers away. She trying to talk someone out of buying the schefflera because she doesn't like where the woman is thinking of putting it in her house."

I look down at the flowers in my arms, weighing whether I want to people or flower.

"A plastic plant may be the thing," I hear Maggie say.

I dump the flowers into Julia's arms and speed walk to the front before the customer can stomp away.

"Hi. Sorry for interrupting but I couldn't help but overhear. Maybe I can brainstorm some plant ideas?" I plaster on the friendliest of smiles and angle my body so Maggie has to take a step back.

"I'm not sure you have anything I can use," the woman says, clearly offended by Maggie's plastic plant idea. She's elegantly dressed in black, wide-leg pants, a camel-colored turtleneck, and a camel duster. Her dark blonde hair is shoulder length with expensively natural highlights.

Underneath the refined elegance, I see a daffodil with its uncertainty and loneliness, a symbol of unfulfilled hope.

"Oh, I'm sure we can find you something. It's been a busy couple of weeks with deliveries and I have a jungle of options in the back room." I smile from the customer to Maggie, trying to soothe egos on both sides.

Maggie had fussed at the potted plants in the back but hadn't bothered to rearrange them. She'd scowled at the new addition of chairs and side table at the front of the shop. And she'd stalked around, looking at the various groupings of vases and knick-knacks Julia and I had set up around the store. We'd been quite pleased with the result. Maggie has yet to say how she feels about everything we've done.

"Tell me about the space you're looking to fill," I prompt the customer.

The woman looks at Maggie with narrowed eyes before turning her attention to me. "I've redecorated the study on the first floor to be a sunroom, removed all the heavy furniture that my ex-husband collected over the years, painted the walls a light, sunny yellow, replaced the heavy wood bookcases with white ones. I want a few plants in there to make it feel more tropical and friendly."

"Windows?"

She nods. "One wall of windows."

"Facing what direction?"

Her eyebrows knit and I'm mesmerized by the almost indiscernible wave that appears above them. At her age, and I'm only guessing, a few wrinkles and creases would be normal. At my age, I have more than she does.

"West, I think."

"I have two options that would work well in that kind of light." From the mini-jungle at the back of the store, I retrieve a medium-sized Yucca in a terra cotta pot and a Jasmine plant in a white ceramic pot.

Maggie shakes her head but surprisingly stays silent. She would have sent the woman home with a parlor palm. Or marching orders to the nearest home goods store for their plastic plants.

"This is Jasmine, right?" The woman leans down to smell the delicate white flowers. "And this is?" She fingers the tight, sword-shaped leaves of the other plant.

"It's a yucca plant. It stands for protection and loyalty. And the jasmine plant is supposed to attract luck and love.

The fragrance of the jasmine evokes positivity and confidence."

Though she'd given a slight snort of derision when I said "loyalty," her stance relaxes at positivity and confidence.

"I'll take them both." Before I can ask any follow up questions or make another suggestion, she hands me a credit card and walks toward the door. "I'll just bring my car closer."

"Well," Maggie says. I wait a beat to see what else she has to say but "well" seems to be the extent of it.

Feelings I've been tamping down like seeds in damp soil shoot through the surface. "What? If you want to yell at me for stepping in, do it now while there are no customers in the store. But you should be thanking me for saving a sale."

Maggie's head tips back at the force of my outburst. Talking back is not something I do. Ever.

"Since when do I yell?" Maggie looks genuinely surprised.

Every day of our childhood. Granted, the yelling was never angry or reproachful. It was probably the only way three rambunctious boys would hear her. Since she got back from Santa Fe though, she's looked like a volcano about to erupt at any minute.

Maggie takes the credit card from me and marches to the register while I help settle the two plants in the car and give her a quick tutorial on caring for them. The yucca is just tall enough that she has to open the sunroof to give it that extra little bit of space.

I watch as she disappears down the road, the green sword leaves dueling with the wind.

From the door, Maggie snorts a laugh. "Well," she says, turns and walks back inside.

That's two "well's." There will be a third.

Back in the store, Maggie is rifling through the cluster of plants. She pulls out a palm. "I would have suggested this one."

"You suggested a plastic one."

"I did. She'll kill the ones you talked her into."

"I don't think so. She needs to rebuild her confidence, find her way. Those plants will help her."

Maggie cocks her head and studies me. Here it comes, in three, two …

"Well."

Called it.

"You're not just good with flowers," Maggie says, a second before I lose my cool again.

"Maggie, you've spent far too much time with my mom."

"No, I mean yeah probably, but in all the years you've worked with me, I don't think I ever fully appreciated how well you read people."

"That's a compliment, right?"

She narrows her eyes and I brace myself. "I want you to think about buying the store from me."

This is not what I was expecting.

A laugh barrels up my diaphragm and lodges in my throat. Buy the store? She's kidding.

"You're kidding, right?" I can't buy the store. Despite what Maggie thinks she wants to do, I'm sure she's just under some magic spell of my mom's. She'll never sell the store.

"I'm not. You're already doing everything around here. It makes sense."

"It doesn't make sense at all. This store is yours. This store is you." Then there's the not so minor detail that I could never afford to buy the store. Despite a nice savings (thanks to Maggie letting me live upstairs), I don't have the kind of funds to purchase property in this community.

She pulls the chair out from under the desk and sits heavily. She suddenly looks tired and worn out. The last couple of months haven't been easy on any of us and I can only imagine the extra burden it's put on her. My mom is her best friend and she'll do anything for her. I know how that feels.

"It *was* me. I've loved every minute of owning this place. The best part, though, was the day you came to work with me. Callie, you are as much of a daughter to me as if I'd given birth to you myself. Nothing would make me happier than to see Fancy Fleur become yours."

Become mine. I look around as though seeing the store for the first time. Mine. I've always thought of it as ours. Mine?

I shake my head. "Maggie, I can't do this without you."

She reaches for me and I take the couple of steps to close the distance. She grabs my hands in hers and squeezes. "Of course you can. You have a gift, with flowers and with people. You deserve to make this place your own. I believe in you. Now you need to believe in yourself."

I do believe in myself. But I also know my limitations.

# 37

# SHE WORE FLOWERS IN HER HAIR AND CARRIED MAGIC SECRETS IN HER EYES.

## — ARUNCHATI ROY

It's not often that I blatantly ignore a request from Nate but in this case, I think it's justified. I've barely heard from him in a week. After he'd picked up the last arrangement I prepared for him to give Beth it's been a painful trickle of texts. Even Beth hasn't texted or called since our coffee date. Not that I expected her to but it's giving me a bit of a have-they-compared-notes-about-me prickle. Or maybe the sweet pea backfired with its secret mission of ending the relationship.

And so, when Eric texted asking if, by chance, I was up for drinks after work tonight, I said yes.

Why shouldn't I?

Around us, happy hour is buzzing. There's a hum in the air that reminds me of bees and it's making me twitchy.

Twitcher than I normally am on first dates. Third, if you count the two evenings with Nate and Beth.

"Callie?" Eric asks.

"Hmm?" I blink myself back to the bar where Eric and a

waiter stare at me expectantly. "Sorry. I'll have a ..." I don't know what I'll have. I motion at Eric.

"I'm having the Knotty Soda," Eric says with a smile and lift of the eyebrows.

Whoever came up with the names of the drinks here was having a good time. That could be a cool job. Wonder if it's something I'd be good at if I'm out of a job once Maggie sells, if Maggie sells.

"Same," I say.

"Great choice. I'll leave a menu, just in case." The waiter leaves us on an island of awkward silence amid the chatter and laughter of a bar full of people.

I do a slow visual sweep of our surroundings. Nate would have made a crack about the three guys at the bar. Something about the one with his tie hanging loose. "He wants everyone to know he can afford a Hermes tie."

And I would have pointed out that the guy in the jeans and sport jacket hasn't taken his eyes off his phone since the moment they sat down, nor has he said a word to anyone in his group. That would have led to wild speculation and an increasingly absurd pretend reality of what that guy's story really is.

"That guy over there hasn't said one word to his friends since they walked in." I motion for Eric to look. "What or who do you think is so fascinating on his phone?"

Eric studies the group in question for the length of a slow sip. "He obviously wasn't the one who had the idea to come here."

Eric turns back to me and adds, "This place is interesting. Robert, the realtor I've been working with, suggested it. Have you been here before?"

I shake my head. The Meadery opened several months ago and I've heard good things about it. Mostly from Tish. I look around wondering if she's here and can save me. She isn't.

I wait a beat, hoping Eric will take the cue and spin a story about Mr. Phone. He doesn't. I release a breath of disappointment. I can't expect him to slide into Nate's conversation patterns. Eric and I don't have the history Nate and I do. Of course, it won't be the same, but it doesn't mean it's bad either.

"Any word on the carriage house?" I suddenly realize I haven't heard any updates since Eric put in an offer on Saturday. It's been five days, surely something would have happened by now.

"Nate didn't tell you?

I shake my head. Nate hasn't told me much of anything lately.

"They accepted my offer. We're going to be neighbors." He looks genuinely pleased.

"Congratulations. Those carriage houses are adorable. At least from the outside. I've never actually been in one." Shut up, Callie. This sounds like a desperate plea for an invitation.

"Well then, you'll just have to come over. I could use help with plants. My roommate was the plant person. I'm afraid I'm pretty helpless when it comes to growing things."

"Happy to." I attempt to picture myself with Eric in the house I used to fantasize living in with Nate. Best friend Nate.

"So, buying a house means you're planning on staying for a while," I say with just enough of an up tilt in my voice to make it a question. Not that buying is any guarantee of permanence. Look at my dad, my mom. Look at Maggie. Nate owns his place but who's to say if he'll stay. Then there's me, unencumbered and nowhere to go.

"For now, yes. I like it here." Eric lifts his glass and I raise mine to clink back. Is he including me in the "like" column?

"You mentioned the other day that there were a few things you wanted to change about the house?" I picture my apartment and wonder what I'd change if I could.

Eric's face lights up and he launches into a list of projects that makes my head spin. "The main level could use an update.

The kitchen is dated and I want to open up the floor plan. The master bathroom needs to be gutted and redone. The previous owners had a giant corner tub in there which is nothing but a water hog. And awful carpet in the upper level. The attic space would make an amazing office but that's a bigger project."

I choke back an incredulous laugh. Gutting the bathroom and ripping out walls isn't big enough? "That sounds like more than a couple of updates. Will you do all of that before moving in?"

Eric shakes his head. "I'll probably do a lot of the work myself so one project at a time."

"Wow. All of that and a full-time job." I can barely deal with cleaning my tiny place on top of a full-time job. "I'm guessing you're better at fixer-uppers than assembling Ikea furniture?"

"I deserve that. And yes," He laughs. "I enjoy working with my hands. Not so much the Ikea furniture maybe. I find it relaxing. My previous house was a fixer upper. More fixer than anything else. I had to gut almost the entire place. But the end result was amazing."

The idea of hard, physical work being relaxing makes me shudder. I try to imagine coming home to a construction zone. Nope. The corner of my lip curls up picturing Nate tip toeing around power tools as though they're vicious Chihuahuas. He may be an amazing engineer, but he's not a handy engineer when it comes to home stuff. Then again, that could be strategic.

Now though, I attempt to picture the guy sitting across from me wielding a hammer, a tool-belt strapped around his waist, safety glasses on his head. Nope. I can't get past the crisp jeans, the expensive watch, the light blue sweater that fits him perfectly and matches his eyes. Everything about him is different from Nate. Different and new.

For the next two hours we talk about house projects (him), travel bucket list (him), fear of flying (me), why flying is safer than driving (him), the pros and cons of being a control freak (both of us with some input from our waiter). Eric is as easy to be around one-on-one as he was the few times we were together with Nate and Beth. But there's still an underlying something that won't quite settle in my head.

It could, of course, be linked to the fact that I've glanced at my phone every time a notification has buzzed. None have been from Nate. And it could be because, despite how attractive and attentive Eric is, he's not Nate.

# 38

**SHE SPROUTED LOVE LIKE FLOWERS, GREW A GARDEN IN HER MIND, AND EVEN ON THE DARKEST DAYS, FROM HER SMILE THE SUN STILL SHINED.**

— ERIN HANSON

Once upon a time, April first was one of the more epic days of the year for me and Nate. How could it not be? I mean, the Cameron brothers were forever trying to outdo each other. And as the sister-by-default, I was always in the mix of the chaos. Though usually Nate and I collaborated on how to best trick his brothers, there were a few years when he got me. And one brilliant year when I came up with a perfect Nate prank.

We've both always had a weaknesses for Oreo cookies. Nate always had a bag stashed under his bed, in a desk drawer, in a shoebox in his closet, in the linen closet behind Maggie's feminine hygiene products. The location changed regularly, although sometimes not before one of his brothers discovered the stash and snarfed half the package.

We must have been around 14 when I had the brilliant idea to mess with the Oreos. I bought a package and spent a frustratingly long time scooping out the cream filling and replacing it with toothpaste. I didn't ruin all of them, that would have been just wrong. Then I strategically repositioned the doctored cookies among their pristine pals. Nate being Nate always started at the top of one row and worked his way down, then up the second row, back down the last row.

It took a bit of searching to find the current hiding spot and then rearranging the Oreos to match the open container. Then it took a couple of hours, and a couple of sneak retreats to the Oreo stash before he'd finally landed on a doctored one. There'd been yelling and accusations. None of them suspected me. It was the first, and last, time I managed to pull off a prank.

So when Nate texts that he has to cancel our pizza and movie night because he's in the Bermuda Triangle, I play along. We abandoned pranks years ago, but once in a while we'll pull a half-assed joke. This, I assume, is one of those.

> Me: Don't get lost there.
>
> Nate: It's tempting.
>
> Me: *laughing emoji*

The three dots pop up and disappear, up and gone. Then my phone pings with an incoming photo.

> Me: Nice!

I do a quick google search and find a photo of a beach in Fiji and send it to him.

Nate responds with another picture of his feet covered in pink sand at the edge of brilliant blue water.

> Me: Ummmm ???????
>
> Nate: Not an April Fools joke. Sorry.
>
> Me: ARE YOU SERIOUS?

Nate: Don't yell at me. Beth surprised me with the trip.

My heart hammers in my chest. She talked about a B&B an hour from here. Bermuda is not an hour from here. And the fact that Nate waited until now, until he was in Bermuda to tell me burns worse than a wasp sting. Because there's no way he didn't know about the trip last night. He would have had to pack, to call in to the office. He could have texted as soon as he found out. Or even this morning if, by some chance, she'd waited until morning to spring the news on him.

Either way, I'm angry and hurt. And very annoyed. At Nate, at Beth, at myself.

But mostly at Nate. It's not like I would have made alternate plans, not like I had a backup date or two waiting. And it's not like this is the first time one of us has cancelled at the last minute. It's the first time, though, when it feels personal.

It is personal. He didn't just ditch me for dinner with Beth. He needed a suitcase and a passport for this ditch. And I'm furious at myself for feeling betrayed.

After pacing around my apartment for half an hour, I trudge down the stairs with Lulu weaving between my legs and cooing her approval at this change of plan. Time in the store, especially in the evening, is her special treat.

I flip on the fairy lights and take in the tranquility of the store at night. I do another scan of my surroundings, as familiar as any place on this planet. Tonight, though, I feel a thrum of unease, like the crackle of the air before a storm.

A knock on the window shoots my heart back into the apartment above me. I whirl around, ready to face my doom. Not that someone looking to break in and harm me would knock to announce themselves. So yes, before I can stop myself, I'm at the door.

Looking back at me through the glass is a smiling Eric.

"Hey, I was just walking by. I wasn't expecting to see you in the store," he says when I open the door.

I invite him in with a wave, waiting for my heart to settle back where it belongs and allow words, and air, to inhabit my body again.

"You okay?"

I nod. I'm breathing, but my words are still backed up. Lulu races to the door, sees Eric and puffs herself up before tearing off to the back of the store again.

"Guess I'm not who she was hoping to see."

"Don't take it personally. She reacts like that to me most times as well."

I lock the door behind Eric and usher him in. "What brings you here at this hour on a Friday night?" I ask, then wince inwardly at the awkwardness of the question.

Either he doesn't notice or is polite enough not to make me more uncomfortable. "I was meeting with the realtor and a contractor.

Which explains the neighborhood but not why he's walking by the store. I chide myself for the momentary thought that he came by looking for me.

"And?" I prompt, forcing my thoughts back to reality. He probably met someone for a drink after the meeting with the realtor.

"And I'll have to make some choices about what to tackle first unless I want to sell an organ or three to pay for the contract work."

"You do have quite the list." I mentally run through the projects he'd mentioned.

"Guilty. My dad says I should have been an architect with my fascination for house design."

"That didn't interest you for a career?"

"Surprisingly, no. I never even entertained the idea. My interest in it is more personal." I take the opportunity while he looks around the store to study him. I mean, I've looked at him plenty of times, but every time I'm around him, he surprises me with something new. Like the way the left corner of his mouth ticks up into a playful almost smile that's all flirt without the smarm.

"Hey, Eric, I have a pizza being delivered any minute. Would you care to join me?" I hear a voice, oddly similar to mine, ask. Then, because I am who I am, I quickly add, "although you probably have other plans."

"You don't have plans tonight?" Eric asks with genuine surprise and, for a second, I'm at a loss for an answer.

Boldened by the fact that the person I thought I'd be sharing the pizza with is on a romantic island with someone else, I say, "No plans and I'd love the company," then add, "Wait here, I'll bring us some beers." Even though he's been in my apartment before, I can't bring myself to invite him up when it's just the two of us. There's no denying he's attractive and there's no arguing that I'm feeling vulnerable. And there's little doubt that this will end in disappointment for me.

The pizza arrives as I'm returning with a couple of beers. And just then my phone lights up with a call from my mom.

"Do you need to get that?" Eric asks after the third attempt.

"No, it'll wait."

When she tries a fourth time, Eric asks, "Suitor? Should I be jealous?"

"Well, I'm not answering, so ..." I finish the sentence with an eyebrow raise and smile. Look at me being flirty. "But no, it's my mom." And there went my game.

"Are you and your mom close?" he asks.

"Define close?"

Eric laughs. I like his laugh, it's easy and natural and inviting. "I guess that's my answer."

"Yes and no. We're what I'd categorize as reluctantly close."

"Explain," Eric says, swallowing a bite of pizza. "By the way, I'm impressed." He points at the pizza.

"No crazy combinations this time. These guys have the best margherita pizza." I keep the part that it's Nate's favorite to myself. After a minute, I say, "Families are complicated." Anything more and I'll be sliding into overshare territory.

"That they are." From his tone I suspect he has his own familial complications. "But then there's Nate," Eric adds.

Because that's not complicated at all.

"Yeah. He's a character. We used to laugh that we'd end up in adjoining rooms in a nursing home."

"From what I've seen of the two of you together, you'd probably get kicked out for causing trouble."

"Probably." I shake away a mental snapshot of us sneaking out of the retirement home. At least that won't involve shimming across the roof.

"What about you and your family?" I switch the focus back to Eric.

"We're close. They live in Colorado. I don't see them as often as I'd like. My sister lives close to our folks so at least they have one of us nearby. And she has three kids, so Mom and Dad are happy. They've pretty much given up on me."

"Never married?" I probably should have asked the question earlier, but earlier he was just Nate's nice colleague.

"Nope. Came close once but it turns out we didn't want the same thing."

"She wanted 15 kids?" I tease. But I feel an odd pang in my belly. Not because Eric had that kind of serious relationship but because I never have.

"She didn't want any actually."

"Oh." That surprises me. It shouldn't. Wanting to be a mom isn't a requirement of being a woman. Look at my mom.

"Water under the proverbial bridge," Eric waves away the momentary tension.

"What about you?" he asks.

"I've always wanted 15 cats."

Eric laughs. I really do like his laugh. Our eyes meet over the open pizza box and before I can overrule my brain, my body follows his lead and we're leaning over what's left of a margherita pizza. Eric brushes aside a wayward curl and his lips, soft, warm, questioning, find mine.

And since I can't imagine any reason not to, I return the kiss.

Which turns out to be a lovely kiss except for one tiny detail —when I pull back and open my eyes, he's not Nate.

# 39

## JUST AS A FLOWER WHICH SEEMS BEAUTIFUL AND HAS COLOR BUT NO PERFUME, SO ARE THE FRUITLESS WORDS OF THE MAN WHO SPEAKS THEM BUT DOES THEM NOT.

— JOHN DEWEY

For the fifteenth time in the past half hour, I pick up my phone to check for messages and make sure I still have coverage. In the last few weeks, my father and I have gotten into a routine of checking in at 10:00 a.m. (my time) and then again at 3:00 p.m. (also my time) with a final goodnight around 9:00 p.m. (his time).

It's almost noon and I've yet to hear back from him. Maggie hasn't answered my texts and neither has Mom. For the second day in a row, Julia is sick and since I'm manning the store solo, we apparently have a flashing neon sign in the sky with an arrow pointing to our door. I've barely had a chance to catch my breath since opening. Luckily, that means I've been too busy to worry about why my father hasn't responded and too distracted to obsess about seeing Nate tonight.

Nate called Sunday evening when they returned from their romantic getaway. I'd declined his FaceTime request, with the excuse that I was in the tub. I wasn't. The idea of seeing him turned my stomach butterflies into idiotic moths, slamming around inside my chest cavity. Keeping busy helped me ignore most of his text messages so far today.

I deadhead an African Violet in the window of the store and top off the water of a spider plant hanging above it. I've swept the floor, dusted the shelves, rearranged the table display by the door, and switched out the water in every bucket in the cooler. Any more fussing with the flowers and they'll launch a mutiny.

Why hasn't my dad called? If something is wrong, Mom or Maggie would let me know. But the quiet is making me itchy.

I glance at the notepad open on the table where I've been trying to work on the plans for the Spring Tour. I've drawn the outline of the main floor of the Mansion, and I've drawn an arrow to the circle that represents the round table in the grand foyer. That's as far as I've gotten. Between customers and neurotic brain squirrels, I'm failing in the creative department.

The more I stare at the space I need to fill, the fewer ideas I have. If Maggie was here, I could focus only on designing. If she was here, I'd have someone to brainstorm with. In case I had any thoughts that maybe, possibly, I could run this business on my own, I'm now thoroughly convinced that I can't.

The front door chimes, announcing the arrival of a customer. "Can I help…" I say as I turn and stop mid-sentence.

"Hi, Callie." Even with her newly acquired tan, Beth's cheeks look flushed. Maybe with nerves?

"Beth." I involuntarily take a step back.

"Can we talk for a couple of minutes?" She does a quick scan of the store, whether to see if there's anyone else in here or looking for a sign that Nate and I were scheming on another arrangement for her, I'm not sure.

"It's just us." I send a silent plea to the powers above to bring another customer to the store, and soon.

"I owe you an apology. And I have a favor," Beth says. She

fiddles with the strap of her bag, looking everywhere but directly at me.

"Okay." It's not exactly an invitation. An apology won't change anything and I'm not sure I have much to give in the form of a favor.

"You must be mad at me about the weekend." When I don't deny or confirm, Beth swallows and continues. "It all came about suddenly. My old college roommate is a travel agent. Wednesday we were on the phone, and I mentioned that I was going to book a weekend away. Next thing I know, she's emailing me hotel reservations and flights using her vouchers. She's pretty amazing that way."

The only trip anyone planned for me was the Santa Fe fiasco. Well, not all of it was a fiasco. I mentally wave away the sudden vision of me and Nate together.

"Anyway. So, Nate was worried about disappointing you and I felt bad that the last-minute trip I pushed on him interfered with what you guys planned to do."

The anger brewing toward Nate subsides. I should have known he wouldn't be okay with disappearing on me like that.

"It's okay. It was last minute." It's as close to forgiveness as I can get.

"Nate mentioned that he's coming over tonight and that you guys are going to talk about your birthday. Would you allow me to plan a party for you two? My way of making it up to you. Please?" Her hopeful expression stops me from blurting out a big fat no. This will be our thirty-third shared birthday. The only people, other than us, who have ever planned one of those parties are our parents. The last person I want involved is the first person on my list of not-invited.

"There's really no need to do that. But thank you." I silently nudge the powers to get on with that customer request or make the phone ring or launch a battalion of cicadas. I'm not picky.

"It's no trouble. Really. I'd love to do this for the two of you."

Before I realize what she's doing, she crosses the floor and grabs my hands in hers. "I promise it won't be anything crazy. Trust me?"

Every nerve in body wants to scream no. But it's the same dilemma: for as much as I want to hate her, there's nothing to hate.

"Please?" She squeezes my hands and I find myself squeezing back.

"Okay," I concede. "No surprises though." I hate surprises. So does Nate, but she should already know that even if she surprised him with a trip to Bermuda.

"How was the trip?" I ask, dying to know how he reacted.

Beth literally swoons. I turn to mask the involuntary eyeroll. Because, wow, really?

"It was amazing. Far too short but it's so beautiful there. Have you been?"

I shake my head. No need to tell her about my fear of flying. Or the tiny secret that I've always had a fantasy of getting engaged under a moongate with the pink sand and turquoise water behind us. My eyes dart to her left hand. No new bling.

I would have known if Nate was considering something that drastic. Wouldn't I? Like I knew he was seeing someone?

Maybe they agreed that she wouldn't wear the ring until he told me in person. Is that what he meant this morning when he said he wanted to talk to me about something important?

Or, my brain flashes to the conversation Beth and I had in the coffee shop, is he going to tell me that he's moving?

"Did you tell him about the job?" I ask with a mix of suspicion and accusation.

"Not yet. The time just never felt right."

It seems to me that there's always a right time to share news like a major job offer. Unless things aren't quite as swoony between them as Beth wants me to think? Could there be cracks in paradise?

"Am I terrible for not telling him?" Beth bites at the cuticle of her pointer finger.

Yes, yes you are,

"You'll tell him when you're ready," I reassure. And the longer she waits, the more time I'll have to implement my un-woo plan. The next arrangement takes shape in my head: white camellia for admiration, yellow roses for affection and jealousy, two-toned carnations as a symbol of parting, and blazing star for happiness.

And tonight, I'll remind Nate how much fun we have together, the history we share, the connection that not even Beth can break.

# 40

# MANY EYES GO THROUGH THE MEADOW, BUT FEW SEE THE FLOWERS IN IT.
## — RALPH WALDO EMERSON

Something is different and it's not Nate's light bronze color. Nate has the enviable ability to instantly tan. I, on the other hand, only have to think "sun" and I burn. Which makes the fantasy of Bermuda rather ridiculous. But reality aside, engagement under a moongate is still my fantasy.

Maybe it's the pink polo shirt? I've never seen Nate wear a polo shirt. Or pink.

We're sitting on the couch in Nate's house, same spots as always, and yet it feels like there are miles between us.

It's not the tan or the pink shirt. It's not a post romantic getaway hangover. There's something he doesn't want to get into with me. It's written all over his posture.

I wish I could rewind to earlier today and suggest he come to my apartment instead or that we meet out. Being here, where he spends time with Beth is worse than being in the front row of a six-hour Wagner opera (no offense to Wagner fans). That happened once when Mom refused to tell me what performance we were going to. I had a bad feeling beforehand. I should have learned from that experience to listen to my gut.

"What gives?" I finally ask, just before I feel myself reach the edge of the patience cliff.

"What gives what?" Nate twists on the couch to look at me and it's the first time since I've arrived that he's looked directly at me.

Oh yeah, something is different. Something is very different.

"You said there was something important we needed to talk about but you've been avoiding actually talking since I got here." Way to shove the guy into a corner.

He sinks into the back of the couch. "Promise you won't punch me?"

"When was the last time I did that?" Despite the tension, a smile pulls at my lips. Tussling with the three Cameron brothers all my young life left an impression. I learned that fart jokes were an art form unto themselves, that you had to eat your favorite thing first rather than leave it for the finale lest someone steals it before you're done, and that sometimes a good punch in the arm gets your point across better than words.

"Last week." Nate rubs his right bicep.

What can I say, old habits die hard.

"You deserved it."

He huffs but doesn't attempt to defend himself. He may share the last of the eggrolls but he's not as magnanimous when it comes to the last glass of wine.

"I'm flying to Florida tomorrow. There's a problem with the upcoming mission and I need to be there."

"Okay," I answer, forcing my tone and face to remain neutral. Traveling for work is not a punchable offense.

He tightens the line of his mouth and adds, "I'll be away at least two weeks, most likely through the end of the month."

Two weeks means he won't be here for our birthday. "But

our birthday. Beth wants to plan a party." I am so whining and I so want to punch him.

Nate shifts on the couch as though sensing imminent danger.

"I talked to her just before you arrived. We'll have the party at the end of the month. Doesn't make it any less special."

Without permission, tears leak from the corners of my eyes. Not because of the party, I don't care about a party. I don't even want a party. But Beth knew about his trip before I did. He smoothed things over with her before talking to me.

"Hey, hey," Nate says, scooting closer and pulling me into his chest. The spark is immediate and surprising. And neither of us moves. I take comfort in his arms even though comfort isn't exactly how I would label this feeling.

"You never answered my earlier question," I sniffle into his chest.

Nate pulls back and looks down questioningly.

"Going to the beach?" Because suddenly, Beth doesn't matter.

He doesn't respond immediately, and I realize the irony of what I'm asking. He just got back from the beach.

"I could come to Florida," I say, perking up at the idea. Two birds with one plane ticket: birthday and beach. Three if you include the fact that we'll be a handful of states away from Beth. Unless ... "Unless Beth is going with you?"

Nate doesn't have a chance to answer. My phone lights up with a call from Mom. And even though I've called and left a dozen messages, I freeze. It's bad news. I feel it in the pit of my stomach. Nate reaches a hand and I give him my phone. I can't answer. I can't hear the words that I've lost him again.

"Hey, Rose," Nate answers before the call rolls into voice-mail. "Yeah, she's here. Okay, just a second." He taps mute and addresses me, "she asked me to put her on speaker."

"Okay," I choke out the word.

Nate unmutes the phone and says, "Okay, Rose, we're both here." He squeezes my hand, reminding me that I'm not alone.

"Callie, honey, your dad had a stroke. He's alive but it's not good. You need to come. Maggie has already cleared it with Julia. She'll manage the store for a few days." The softness in Mom's tone makes every muscle in my body go rigid.

Nate takes the phone off speaker and pulls me back into his body, wrapping his arms around me. With my head buried in his chest and my pulse raging in my ears, all I hear are muffled sounds in the distance.

I can't go anywhere right now. I need to finish plans for the Spring Tour. Three weddings are coming up next month and two in June. There's Mother's Day and proms, our birthday, and the beach.

"Yes, Rose. I've got this. She'll be on that plane." Nate's voice breaks through the noise in my head.

"You'll go with me?" I turn, wide eyed to Nate. I can't do this without him.

"Shit," he says, more hiss than word. "God, Callie, I can't."

"Please. Nate, I can't do this alone. Pick me this time instead of Beth." It's not because of Beth that he can't go, but my rational thinking has been temporarily suspended.

"I'll be back as soon as I can. This has nothing to do with Beth," he says, tipping my head up until I have no choice but to look him in the eye. His lips graze mine and he adds, "Trust me."

# 41

# WHERE FLOWERS BLOOM, SO DOES HOPE.

## — LADY BIRD JOHNSON

"Ladies and gentlemen, this is your captain. We'll be pushing back in a few minutes. We're just waiting for the final suitcases to be loaded onto the plane. Once in the air, our flight time to Albuquerque should be just about three hours and 44 minutes. We're expecting a smooth flight."

The woman in the middle seat next to me bends to retrieve something from the bag stuffed under the seat in front of her, and for a second her head is practically in my lap. Damn Nate's business trip. It should be him next to me instead of some stranger who smells like sandalwood.

Nate had walked me to my gate, apologizing for the two-hundredth time that he couldn't come with me. His flight is scheduled to depart ten minutes after mine.

My phone buzzes. Nate has sent a photo of his legs stretched out in first class. I snap a picture of my legs crammed against the side of the plane with my seatmate's head against my knee.

Nate: Making friends already. Good for you.

Me: I hate you.

Nate: I'm sorry. Really.

Me: I suppose you're forgiven

It's not like I can really be mad that he has this work trip. And he did pack a bag of Oreos for me. But I also don't have to like it. I can't like it.

This time I know what I'm getting into. And it's even worse than not knowing.

Nate: You okay?

Me: No

Nate: You'll be fine.

Me: I'll be fine

Nate: I'm only a call or text away

Me: I don't have an international plan

Nate: ???

I respond with a rocket emoji

Nate: funny

Me: At least I packed my sense of humor. Not sure I remembered underwear.

Nate: TMI

Me: Thanks for the Oreos

Nate: Least I could do

Me: Truth

Nate: Hey!

Me: laughing emoji

> Nate: You also remembered to pack your
> snark I see

> Me: Never leave home without it.

> Nate: Need to shut down. Safe trip. Love you!

> Me: Safe trip. Love you!!

I sink into the uncomfortable seat and stare out the window. The terminal outside begins to move away from the plane and I fight a flash of panic.

After talking to Mom yesterday, a pit planted itself deep in my stomach. It's not like I thought Dad and I had a lifetime ahead of us, but I wouldn't let my thoughts settle on a deadline. We still have so much to catch up on.

Never one to pad the landing zone, Mom had set my expectations to a 2.5 on a scale of ten with five being the fifty-fifty chance of survival. "There's no coming back from this, Callie. He's anxious to see you."

The bleak DC landscape blurs as the plane picks up speed then tilts up into the bleaker early April sky. I'm not one of those gloom and doom people. I can almost always find the bud of hope in any situation, but right now, I feel like I'm boob deep in a manure pile.

And this time, I don't even have Nate to toss me a lifeline.

# 42

## JUST LIVING IS NOT ENOUGH … ONE MUST HAVE SUNSHINE, FREEDOM, AND A LITTLE FLOWER.

### — HANS CHRISTIAN ANDERSEN

The noisy hush in the hospital room is setting my teeth on grind mode. Every beep or hiss of a machine has me bolting upright, waiting for an army of nurses and doctors to storm in. What sounds like panic inducing noises to me, however, appear to be normal for the medical staff because no one has entered the room in the half hour I've been here.

A pigeon on the ledge of the window scrambles to flight, knocking at the glass in his haste to get away. The arrival of a helicopter disrupts the cadence of the noises in my dad's room. Sun bounces off its shiny body, momentarily blinding me. I'm in a nightmare.

The weather outside feels like a betrayal. Sunny, warm, a hint of a breeze. Perfect in almost every way. I hate Santa Fe with all my might at this moment. I hate the stark beauty and the gorgeous weather, I hate how friendly everyone is. I hate that it'll be the last place I'll see my dad.

I settle deeper into the cardigan my mom insisted I take and tuck my hands inside the warmth. Warm but not comforting.

Dad stirs in the bed. I lean forward trying to decipher if he said something or moaned. It's a jumble of both. I reach for his hand. His eyes flutter open and his lips pull at the corners into what once would have been a smile. Now though, it's a quarter smile, quarter frown.

"Hi," I say when his focus settles on me.

"Hi," he manages to say. Just that one word feels like a monumental effort. He releases a shallow exhale that makes him wince.

"Should I call the nurse?" I release his hand and stand before he has a chance to respond.

Dad grabs at my hand. "No. Sit."

I do as I'm told but my eyes dart between him, the monitors, and the door, silently willing the nurse to come in anyway.

"Did you talk to your mom?" He asks, the words slow and deliberate.

"Not really." I'd asked questions, so many questions. She'd answered a total of two: Has the cancer progressed (yes) and how is he responding to treatment (he's not). And by "not" she'd clarified that he wasn't getting treatment anymore. This was a conversation I needed to have with my father, she'd insisted.

"She told you?" It comes out more relief than question.

I've gone through every emotion already today. Anger, grief, sadness, disappointment. I'd cycled through each and every possible combination when he left. And then when he didn't come back. And then again when the postcards stopped, and he completely disappeared from my life. Why then do I have to do this again?

"Why, Dad?"

His left eye, the one not affected by the stroke, narrows as he weighs my question. "It's time."

"How can you say that?"

He winces either in pain or at my tone or both. His eyes droop shut and he's once again asleep.

The nurse warned me when I first arrived that the medication made him sleepy. The stroke had been mild, she'd added, but he needed his rest. What she hadn't said was that, while the stroke may have been mild, the cancer was ripping through his body. Hard to celebrate the seemingly "positive" when I'm staring up at a massive lead foot about to drop on us.

The adjustment from hate-loving my dad to need-loving him again has been unsettling. And surprising. Very surprising. The shorthand we shared when I was young came back with the ease of slightly out of shape muscle memory. It was uncanny how he could read my tone, how I could pick up the unspoken cues, how we laughed at the same stupid jokes.

"This isn't going away, Callie." Dad's voice brings me back to the hospital room. "It's the universe's sick sense of humor."

I wait for him to continue.

He reaches for my hand. "I'm done fighting."

The resignation in his eyes makes me want to push harder. "You can't be done. There's more we can try."

"There isn't. I've made up my mind."

I open my mouth to protest but Dad squeezes my hand for me to stop. Talking is already a strain for him and, I suspect, he's had to justify his choice a couple of times already.

"I haven't come to this decision lightly. And you can be sure that your mom and Maggie have worked on me to change my mind. My beautiful butterfly, I need you to listen."

I nod for him to continue even though I don't want to hear that he's given up on life. Not when we've just found each other again.

"When Steven decided to stop treatments, I argued with him not to give up. But the treatments weren't going to make him better. He was so sick that he could barely function. Stopping allowed him to live the rest of his life on his terms. That's what I want."

I hear what he's saying but understanding and acceptance are just out of my reach right now.

"You could come to Maryland with me," I blurt. "We can make an appointment at Johns Hopkins."

Without opening his eyes, Dad lifts a hand to stop me. We have, of course, already had this conversation.

"I'm not going to Maryland," he finally says. "But I will be going to stay with your mom once they spring me from here."

I don't hide my surprise. I didn't really think he'd live the rest of his life in the hospital. But I also didn't really think about what his next step would be.

"With Mom? You're sure that's a good idea?" Nurturing she's not.

Dad's mouth ticks into a smile. "I asked her the same thing when she suggested it." He chuckles. "Your mom and I have quite a history. This could be the most amazing final chapter for us or an absolute horror of one. Look at the bright side, the cancer will probably get me before she has a chance to."

"Not funny."

"It kind of is."

Despite the topic and the hole in my heart, I smile.

"Any idea when they'll spring you?" I look at the tethers from machines to my father.

"Not for another couple of days. Hopefully not much longer." He winces again and taps the bed, searching for the call button.

The same nurse who smiled at me when I first arrived enters with a squeak of rubber shoes. "How are you feeling, David?" She fusses with the IV and toggles through a few numbers on one of the machines then jots something down on a piece of paper she pulls out of the pocket of her lavender scrubs.

"Pain," Dad says on an inhale.

"On a scale of one to ten?"

I bite my tongue to keep from asking why it matters. He's in pain, isn't that enough?

"Nine and three quarters," dad answers.

"You were supposed to call me at eight and a quarter," she says, tapping him lightly on the shoulder. "I'll be right back."

"Quick, before she returns with the magic potion, is Nate here with you? I'd like to see him."

"Not this time, Dad. He's on a work trip. We'll come back and see you as soon as he can get away."

The nurse returns and I stand to leave. Dad reaches for me and says, "Stay until I'm asleep?"

I nod and sit back down, my hand over his. It doesn't take long after the nurse injects the pain medication into his IV before Dad's eyelids shutter and his breathing settles. I anxiously watch his heartbeat. There are so many things we have to talk about and each blip on the screen is a reminder of all we won't have time for.

**43**

# FLOWERS WHISPER 'BEAUTY!' TO THE WORLD, EVEN AS THEY FADE, WILT, FALL.

— DR. SUNWOLF

I t's fitting that Maggie bought a house next door to my mom. They're happier when they're within yelling distance of each other. It used to drive my father crazy that Maggie and Mom would carry on a conversation from their respective back yards, raising their voices to be heard over rambunctious kids or mowing neighbors.

I met the couple living in the soon-to-be-Maggie's house during our previous visit. Visit, odd word for what that experience had been.

They're an elderly couple who bought the house "back when you could buy for normal prices," Mrs. Rice had said, tsking at the state of housing prices in the area. Their kids, she'd gone on to explain, had moved away years ago and now that age was catching up to them, she and Mr. Rice were considering moving as well.

"Where are Mr. and Mrs. Rice moving?" I ask.

My mom scoffs and Maggie *pfts* at her.

"They bought into a retirement ship," Maggie explains,

keeping tabs on my mom, her smirk deepening when my mom scoffs again, louder this time.

"Retirement ship?" I ask. That's one I haven't heard of yet.

"They decided to sell everything they own and live on a cruise ship with two other couples."

"That's, just, wow." I'm incapable of finding the words to express the horror of the idea. Living on a floating city sounds awful.

"Not a bad idea if you ask me," Maggie says.

Mom utters a final sound of derision before pushing herself up from the table and clearing the dinner plates with more noise than needed.

"You don't agree, Mom?" Obviously, but I can't see why it matters to her this much.

"It's not the floating retirement community. It's this one upturning her life with the same speed the Rice's did." Mom waves a fork in Maggie's direction.

Maggie ignores her and continues filling me in. "One day Mrs. Rice caught me at the mailbox, all excited because they'd just signed the papers on the cruise ship lease. One of those spur-of-the-moment decisions over a bottle of wine with their friends. I'm not sure what possessed me, but I offered to buy their house before we'd even removed our mail from the mailboxes," Maggie adds.

"It's insane," my mom grumbles.

"Mom, I thought you'd be happy to have Maggie closer?" I direct the question at my mom but I watch Maggie for a hint of the dynamics.

"Of course. But Maggie has her life." The emphasis on "her" makes me sit a bit straighter and tighten my focus on Maggie. She grimaces or maybe it's just a reaction to the drink she's taken a sip from.

"For god sake, Rose, we've talked about this. Back then I

wasn't ready to move. It was the right thing for you. Staying was the right thing for me. It's different now."

"It's not different. It shouldn't be. I will continue the way I've always done. But it's crazy for you to give up everything and move here."

Granted, I'd had similar thoughts when Maggie mentioned her plan. It made more sense to me for her to come and stay for a few months, then return to her life and her store.

"Maggie, what will you do here? Another Fancy Fleur?" I try to picture what that store would look like. All I see in my head is *our* store.

"She thinks she'll run my life," Mom says, returning to the table with refills for our coffees.

That's when I see it, the intense relief and gratitude of knowing she'll have her best friend by her side again, that whatever the next weeks, months, years bring, she won't be alone. And isn't that exactly how I feel about Nate?

"Well, this one is a full-time job." Maggie teases my mom.

"You could keep the store. Julia and I can run it."

"True. But the last few months have shown me how important it is to live forward. Despite the fact that she makes me batshit crazy, I'm happiest around Rose. We've been through everything together. And we're going to tackle whatever comes next together."

Mom shrugs in gratitude-laced resignation. Despite my anxiety over Maggie's plans, I can't argue with her reasoning.

And that's when I realize that, despite the craziness, it's time for me to embrace the idea of living forward as well.

# 44

## EVERY FLOWER IS A SOUL BLOSSOMING IN NATURE.

— GERARD DE NERVAL

"Do you want more coffee?" Mom asks, already out of her seat and moving to the counter. The three of us have been sitting at the breakfast table long enough that my rear end is numb. I've consumed more coffee than is normal even for me and somehow there seems to be no end to the strong black liquid.

"I've had enough," I say.

"I'll take more," Maggie says at the same time.

Mom refills all three mugs.

The call had come in a couple of hours ago. 7:24 a.m. to be precise. We had nowhere to go just yet. Dad wasn't waiting for us to visit.

"I don't understand what happened," I say into my unwanted coffee.

Mom and Maggie exchange a look but neither responds to me. I'm a vinyl record stuck on the same thread. I don't understand. I know what the doctor said when he called with the news. But it still doesn't make sense.

When we left the hospital last night, Dad was sitting up in

his bed. He'd been chatty, joking with the nurse and teasing Mom and Maggie about becoming neighbors again.

"I pictured you two in side-by-side units in a retirement home," he'd said.

"It's Santa Fe, close enough," Maggie said, rolling her eyes.

Mom's never-long fuse was already smoldering though. "Have you looked around? We're in the older bracket of the population."

Dad had winked at me, enjoying getting a rise out of Mom. "Two cougars on the prowl."

"That's gross," Mom said but I saw the corner of her mouth tilt up.

"He may be on to something," Maggie chimed in, enjoying the light moment. Not that she had any interest in dating, at least not that I'd ever seen, but she couldn't pass up the opportunity to tease my mom either.

"You're both sick," Mom had said, instantly wincing with the partial truth of her comment.

"He seemed to be doing better," I say, thinking back on last night. I look from my mom to Maggie to my coffee, hoping someone can shed light on how my dad went from joking around to dead in the span of a few hours.

I wait for tears, for the reality that he's really gone this time to sink in.

Mom pops up to refill the coffees again.

"Mom, stop," I say, taking the almost empty pot from her.

She huffs and marches out of the kitchen. I look to Maggie, who's watching my mom as she disappears down the hall.

"Have you talked to Nate?" Maggie asks me.

"He was already in a meeting. I left a message to call me back, no details." I'd debated not leaving a message at all, but that would have been an obvious red flag and I saw no reason to add to anyone's anxiety. He has his hands full with work.

Plus, I know Nate and he'll want to come immediately. But there's nothing to do here except drink Mom's awful, unending supply of coffee.

Then again, I could really use a Nate hug. My brain, traitor that it is, bounces to our last visit. To shooting stars and a kiss that should never have happened.

Mom returns, dropping a blue folder on the table. "David left instructions," she says with something that could be awe or annoyance. "He said he learned from the experience with Steven, and he wasn't going to put us through the same uncertainty and heartache."

"Pure David," Maggie says, and I melt at the admiration and love in her voice. Whatever hurt he caused when he left has been forgiven.

I fidget, waiting for Mom to tell me what the folder contains, how my dad expects us to move forward without him. *Again.*

Because in the short time I've had him back, I've come to look forward to our chats. I've come to rely on him again.

"Are you going to tell me or am I supposed to read what's here?" I ask. We're all staring at the blue folder as if we expect it to self-destruct if opened.

Mom exhales like a frustrated racehorse, a sound I remember well from my childhood whenever my father came up with a "I have an idea." Those ideas were generally a bit off the expected path and always a blast.

"His wish is to be cremated and that we distribute his ashes along the Oregon coast where he disbursed Steven's ashes." She delivers Dad's request with the resignation that most of his ideas elicited in her.

It never made complete sense to me how someone who could create amazing make-believe worlds for, let's just call them what they are, insane stories, would be so anti frivolous fun. I'll quiz Maggie later about this. Right now, we have another kind of crazy to address.

"Cremated?" I shudder, earning a get-over-yourself look from my mom and a sympathetic nod from Maggie. I've never known anyone who passed away and was cremated. Maggie had her beloved dog, Bruno, cremated and I still remember being wigged out by the idea that the large redwood box on the mantel in their family room contained the mass of love who was afraid of everything despite being as large as a pony.

"Cremated," Mom confirms.

"And then we're supposed to what in Oregon?" Another shudder takes over my body. I mentally flip through the postcards in the keepsake box in my closet for one from the Oregon coast.

"That part I actually like," Mom says. She collects her thoughts and continues, "At some point in the next few months, the four of us will take a trip." She tents her fingers over the folder and slides it closer to her. "He mapped it out for us."

"Four of us?" I ask.

"You, me, Maggie, Nate."

"Five of us," I correct her.

Mom nods, her mouth a tight line.

The loss settles around us, filling the empty spaces until there's no air left.

Mom stands abruptly. "I need to get to the hospital."

"I'll go with you," I say but don't move. The feeling of dread I'd had that first time after finding out Dad was in a Santa Fe hospital is a trip to Disney compared to what waits for us this time.

"Would you mind if I went alone?" Mom asks.

My brain ticks back to saying goodnight to him, to the promise I made that I'd show up today with his favorite raspberry mango smoothie. "But I promised him a smoothie," I say.

Mom holds out a hand and says, "Then let's go get smoothies." Except, I can barely see her hand or Maggie as she throws her arms around me. Tears I hadn't shed when Dad left seventeen years ago lead the stampede down my cheeks.

# 45

## LET US DANCE IN THE SUN, WEARING WILD FLOWERS IN OUR HAIR.

### — SUSAN POLIS SCHUTZ

"Happy Birthday," Beth singsongs when we walk in the door. Before I can formulate a reply, she thrusts a flute of champagne into my hand.

The entire week since I returned from New Mexico, I've waved off any attempts to discuss our birthday. All I wanted was for Nate to get home from his trip and spend a quiet evening with him, just the two of us. But Beth wanted to do something nice for us. And her something nice was to arrange a party. I gave up and gave in. But not before making Nate promise he'd keep a short leash on the plans.

Nate being Nate, he'd been ready to board a flight the moment he heard about my father. There was no point. He'll need that time off later in the summer when we go to Oregon. We've talked every day but today is the first time in two weeks we'll see each other. A party at Beth's house is not exactly how I want this reunion with Nate to happen. Especially not with Beth and Eric and several dozen people, most of whom I don't recognize.

Eric leans around me, one hand on the small of my back, and accepts the second flute Beth holds out.

"Wow. This is swanky," he says after we've both taken a sip of the bubbly and surveyed the layout of Beth's house.

"Yeah," I mumble, glad that Beth has already moved on to attend to some detail or another. Nate assured me this would be like every other birthday party we've thrown. This is nothing like any birthday party we've thrown. For one thing, there are balloons and streamers everywhere. I don't think we've had balloons or streamers at a party since we were six. There are food stations throughout the house and in the backyard, all catered, as well as bars with actual bartenders in the living room and on the patio.

"This must have cost a fortune," I whisper through a forced smile.

Over the chatter of voices inside the house, I suddenly hear music slinking in from the outside.

"There's even a DJ out there." Eric says, giddy as a schoolboy at his first adult party.

"A what?" I lurch to the side trying to see past a couple making a decent dent in the bowl of shrimp.

"A DJ. You know, someone who plays music for parties."

"I know what a DJ is, smartass. Why the hell does someone need to hire a DJ? And catering? The is so not what I expected." I squeeze my eyes shut and wish for magic red shoes that I can click together to take me home.

"This is nice of her." Eric still has his hand on my back which feels both comforting and suffocating.

I scan the room looking for Nate. This is supposed to be *our* day. This is so not *our* anything. This is Beth's something.

The bubbly liquid fizzes in my stomach, making me nauseous. I can't tell if it's the alcohol on an empty stomach or the swankiness on empty expectations. Together, they're a bad combo.

Someone across the room waves at me and I bolt in her direction.

"Happy birthday," Tish says, giving me a one-arm hug so as not to spill the purple drink in her hand.

"God I'm happy to see you. You may be the only person I know here."

"Um, hello?" Eric says from behind me.

"And you." I clink my champagne glass to his. I'm glad he's here. Despite my reluctance, I really do like Eric. We've gone out a couple more times and each date has been more pleasant than the previous. I know they're real dates because they end in a kiss. Just a kiss. A nice kiss. Not a Nate nice kiss, though.

"And him," Tish says, nodding in the direction of the patio.

I feel Eric's hand snake around me the same second Nate's eyes lock on mine.

"I'll be right back," I say with the warmest, most sincere smile I can force onto my face. The urge to run for the door and disappear makes my pulse pound in my ears.

It takes a few long minutes to weave my way through strangers until I finally reach Nate.

"Can we talk?" I ask at the same moment Nate asks, "Are you okay?" and at the same moment the DJ chooses to holler, "happy birthday," into a microphone. Why does he need a microphone? Beth's yard isn't large enough to warrant one.

Nate takes my hand and leads me back to a small water fountain and a two-person swinging egg chair. Nate indicates for me to sit, then slides onto the cushion next to me. It's cozy and it could be romantic, except for the noise in the background reminding me that we've snuck away from our own party, and except for the not so tiny detail that we're at Beth's house.

How many times have he and Beth sat here? I shake my head to dislodge the unwelcome image.

"I'm sorry," Nate says. For a second, I wonder if he's apologizing for the party. "I wish I could have been there with you." Not the party.

I nod, not trusting myself to speak yet. Every day of the five days I was in New Mexico, I'd wished for Nate to show up unannounced. For the grand, "I couldn't stand being away from you" gesture. He hadn't, of course. But that didn't stop me from secretly hoping.

The DJ starts another song, and I ask, "Why did Beth put this massive party together?"

"It's not massive. Come on, Callie. She wanted to do this. She likes to plan things."

"It's not exactly what I imagined this birthday would look like." What had I imagined? A proposal? A promise for a happily ever after?

"Me either." He gets quiet and I can almost hear the building blocks of words coming together. "Can I ask you a weird question?" I turn to look at him, waiting for the weird question. "All those years ago, did you think we'd make good on the pact?"

*Yes. No. Maybe. Of course. What a ridiculous idea. It's the only possible outcome.*

"Yes and no," I answer.

"Me too."

Curiosity gets the best of me. "Where's that coming from?"

"I don't really know. Seeing you walk in with Eric, his arm around you, I don't know. It stirred up something I've never felt."

Nate takes my hand in his and for a few minutes we sit in a comfortably uncomfortable silence, listening to the water gurgling in the fountain and the party moving ahead without us. My overstimulated insides want to push for more, to know exactly what he's feeling. I want to tell him about the dream I had in Santa Fe and the fantasies I've had every day since.

He's quiet for a minute before dropping the *but*. "But that's not who we are, is it? You've always been the perfect combination of best friend and sister, confidant and partner-in-crime."

I cringe at the word sister. The thoughts I've been having are anything but sisterly. And that kiss. Even now I feel it on my lips and in my very being.

"Partner-in-crime?" I force a smirk.

The corner of Nate's mouth ticks up in a smile. He releases my hand and wraps his arm around me, pulling me closer into him. "Just a couple of crazy kids."

Feeling emboldened in his arms, I ask, "Why can't it be who we are? Minus the brother-sister thing." Because why not? Who's to say this isn't exactly how life is supposed to unfold between us.

"I wouldn't be able to live without you," Nate answers immediately.

"Who said you'd have to?"

"If things don't work out?"

"Why wouldn't they? Nate, we know everything about it each other. We've always been there for each other. That wouldn't change." Look at me being all optimistic. Look at me attempting to live forward. Look at me threatening to topple the one steady thing in my life.

"But what if our feelings don't go beyond what we currently have?"

"Do you really believe that?" I ask pulling away from him so that I can read his face.

He tucks a piece of hair behind my ear, his eyes on my mouth. I catch my breath as Nate's fingers brush my lips. He doesn't believe it any more than I do.

Movement in the background snaps me to attention a quarter of a second before the words reach us.

"There you are."

Nate and I pull apart as though electrocuted and he springs up, sending the egg chair into a death spiral with me still in it.

"We were just catching up," Nate says, stepping toward Beth.

Before I can say anything or stop my world from, literally, spinning out of control, they're gone.

From the edge of the party, I watch Nate and Beth walking back to her house, hand-in-hand. I see Eric looking past them to where I'm sitting. I can't force myself to move. Whatever I think I want, whatever I think may be brewing with Nate, he's right. That's not who we are. And this isn't who I want to be anymore.

# 46

# A ROSE CAN NEVER BE A SUNFLOWER, AND A SUNFLOWER CAN NEVER A ROSE. ALL FLOWERS ARE BEAUTIFUL IN THEIR OWN WAY, AND THAT'S LIKE WOMEN TOO.

— MIRANDA KERR

I extract myself from the egg chair. This may not have been my choice for a birthday celebration, but it doesn't mean I can't turn this sour lemon into a flowering lemon tree.

From the patio door, I see Nate and Beth talking to a couple I don't recognize. Beth has her arm looped around Nate's and considering how animated she is, I'm guessing the couple are her friends. Their friends? Has Nate already been indoctrinated into Beth's inner circle?

Which takes me back to the original thought when I walked in the door. Why? Why am I even here? Because Nate insisted? Because Beth subscribes to the "keep your enemies close" approach to life? Or because she actually wants me here?

Beth didn't wander into the backyard at that moment by chance.

From where I'm standing, I have a good view of her house. It's exactly what I pictured. Okay, not at all what I pictured but now that I'm here, I can't imagine her living anywhere else. It's an older house that's been gutted and turned into a lovely, open floorplan. Large and light and perfectly put together. An adult's house, not a temporary apartment owned by someone else. Oh, and an apartment that I'll most likely lose, along with my job, in the near future. So, yeah, not at all like mine.

Beth squeezes Nate's arm, leans in to say something, then, all smiles, glides to a grouping of three people standing by the kitchen island. She motions at the row of wine bottles and one of the men picks up a bottle and studies the label.

The last party we had was three years ago at Nate's house. It was our thirtieth and since Nate's house number is 3030 we thought we were being clever having it there.

That had been our first attempt at a grown-up party with wine and mixed drinks and high-end beer. We had food and music. Looking around now, I have the feeling that I'm in a real-life game of "find the differences in these two pictures." The me that fit into our we're-legit party, now feels like a kid sneaking into her parent's soiree.

The room quiets and fills as people who'd been enjoying the cool evening outside come in. Someone dims the lights. In the kitchen, Beth lights candles on a birthday cake. On one side of the rectangle is an icing rocket. On the other side, an icing calla lily.

Nate scans the room until he finds me then motions me over. *Be a wildflower, not a wallflower*, I give myself a silent pep talk.

I stand to Nate's left leaving a slightly awkward but not entirely obvious gap between us. So much for the pep talk.

Beth smiles the smile of the happy hostess then begins singing "happy birthday to Nate and Callie." Someone steps forward from the crowd and points a cell phone at us. "Pictures," he calls out and motions for us to get closer. In my peripheral vision I see Nate shift but it's to his right, toward Beth. She flashes an adoring smile at him and my heart bounces off the spotless ceramic tiles at the way he looks at her.

Whatever that little moment in the egg chair was, it doesn't compare with what he shares with her.

While Beth cuts the birthday cake, I make my escape. Halfway to the siding door to the patio, and the bar on the other side of said door, Eric catches up with me.

"You look like you need this." He hands me a fresh glass of champagne and, putting his arm around my shoulders, steers me out of the house.

"Thank you," I mumble taking a long gulp, enjoying the sensation of the bubbles tickling the inside of my mouth.

Once we reach a quiet spot on the patio, Eric releases me. "Now that we have a moment to ourselves, I have something for you." He takes a small box from the pocket of his jacket and holds it out for me.

I freeze. I wasn't expecting a gift from him. I don't want a gift from him. A gift means that whatever is between us is actually a thing.

"Something small," Eric insists, thrusting the box into my hands.

I open the lid to find a sunflower pendant on a delicate silver chain.

"I love sunflowers. Thank you." I blink at the beautiful pendant. Sunflowers for adoration. It's a thoughtful gift, one I don't deserve.

"I was worried you left," Beth's voice cuts through the growing noise as the party resumes.

I tuck the small box into the pocket of my jeans and say a silent thanks to Mother Nature for making the evening cool enough that I wore a sweater which covers the angular bulge. I don't want Beth to coo over Eric's gesture. And I don't want

Nate reading anything into it. At least not until I figure out which relationship guidebook he's following.

"We have news," Beth says as she and Nate reach us. She's wrapped around him tighter than an ace bandage on a sprained wrist. Nate's expression looks as pained as if he really does have a sprained wrist.

"I accepted the job in California. Nate and I are going out there next month to find a place."

My mouth opens but the question burning my tongue flames out and, instead, I hear myself saying, "Congratulations."

"Whoa, that's huge. Congratulations," Eric steps in to save the conversation. "What does that mean for you?" He asks Nate with a friendly punch to the upper arm. This is definitely a punchable offense and mine wouldn't have been that gentle.

"Nothing yet. I'll help Beth get situated and then we'll see." Nate looks at me. I avert my eyes. I don't need his pity at the hurt I know is blazing on my face.

Eric asks the right questions about Beth's new job, the questions *I* should be asking. But the only thing I'm aware of are my hopes being trampled like unseen weeds. Somewhere between the career advancement of launching this new program and the horrific winter weather in Maryland, I find myself standing at the permitter of the conversation with Nate by my side.

"I wanted to talk to you before this became public."

"Why didn't you then?"

"Because Beth only told me this afternoon about the job offer." Why had she chosen today to talk to Nate?

"You could have said something when we were talking out here earlier." It's an accusation laced with hurt and defeat and betrayal. Not half an hour ago he made me feel like there was maybe, possibly a ray of hope for us.

When Nate doesn't respond, my insides tighten around my heart. "Well, congratulations. You got what you wanted."

"Callie," he touches my arm as I'm about to walk away. I force my eyes to leave the flattened patch of grass and look into Nate's confused eyes.

*Me too*, he'd said about us making good on the pact.

And then Beth broke the spell.

# 47

# LIKE WILDFLOWERS; YOU MUST ALLOW YOURSELF TO GROW IN ALL THE PLACES PEOPLE THOUGHT YOU NEVER WOULD.

— E.V. ROGINA

I follow Eric back into the house in search of another drink. Something more potent than a thin flute of bubbly hype. Celebration my ass. The only one celebrating here is Beth.

I glower at her. The perfect hostess, making sure everyone has a drink, everyone has eaten. Checking in with the DJ. And never once has she taken her eyes off of Nate.

Except now when she's staring right at me. Before I can find an un-awkward escape, she's at my side.

"Callie? Are you okay?"

I nod. I'm not but I'm certainly not going to let on that she's completely blown my life to shreds. Even if she hasn't done anything wrong. She's not the conniving other woman. That distinction falls to me.

"I owe you a huge thanks," Beth continues. "I put you in a bad position keeping my secret from Nate and you kept my trust. I really do owe you for that. And I know I got carried away with the party. I deal with stress by falling face first into a project that has nothing to do with what I'm stressing about." She motions at the kitchen. "Four years ago, after we had a lockdown when an armed man entered the school, I tore my kitchen apart and remodeled it."

I remember the news stories. The gunman had shot at the wall of pictures of the school administrators. No one had gotten hurt, and the incident was quickly eclipsed by another shooting at another school in another city.

"I didn't realize that's the school you're at." That's because I hadn't taken the time to really get to know her. At first, she was just another woman Nate was seeing. Then she became the woman I was losing my best friend to. Now, standing here with her, she's the woman who cared enough about my best friend to plan a special birthday party for him, for us.

Beth nods, her face revealing the horror she'd gone through. "I've never been so scared. And we were lucky. How screwed up is that?!"

I have no idea how to answer. The only words I can come up with sound trite and insignificant. I've never faced anything remotely close to that experience.

"Not that I'm comparing that to making a decision about a new career choice. But I've realized over the years that immersing myself into something productive that keeps my brain from fixating on whatever is freaking me out, is the only way I can sort through my thoughts and feelings."

One more tick in the why-I-want-to-hate-Beth column. Because, me, I ostrich when I need to deal with thoughts and feelings.

Like when my college advisor strongly recommended that I pursue a higher degree and went so far as to start the application process for me. He'd been so enthusiastic and supportive and for a few brief moments he had me believing I could do it. Until I was left alone with the looming deadline and placement test and somehow the dates came and went, and my short-lived ambition was forgotten just like the snipped ends of the flowers I put into my arrangements.

"Congratulations on the job. And thank you, again, for planning this party," I say, and I mean it.

"I know it's not what you would have done. Nate warned me this is too much, especially after ..." she stops mid-sentence. "I'm sorry about your dad. I can only imagine what you're going through. If there's anything I can do."

How much did Nate tell her?

I look to the patio where Nate and Eric are ordering drinks from the bartender. As though sensing my attention, they both turn, and I'm suddenly exposed in the spotlight where both of their gazes intersect. It's Nate's eyes I meet though.

In that moment, I see our future. I see *us*. And I see his eyes shift to the woman standing next to me.

"Thank you, Beth, that's very kind. If you'll excuse me though, I'm exhausted. I'm sure I'll see you soon."

I close the distance to Nate and Eric, focusing as hard as I can to avoid the magnetic pull of going straight to Nate's side.

"You look tired," Eric says when I reach them.

"I am. Can we go? I can also get a ride if you're not ready to leave." Part of me hopes he'll want to stay. Part of me wants Nate to watch me walk out of here with someone else.

"I can give you a ride," Nate says at the same time Eric says he's ready to go.

I accept Eric's arm and say, "No, you should stay."

As we walk away, I know Nate is watching us. And I know Beth is watching Nate.

# 48

# A ROSE'S RAREST ESSENCE LIVES IN THE THORN.

## — RUMI

A ringing phone, especially a call from my mom at 7:34 a.m., is not how I want to start any day. Today least of all. I'm still on my first cup of coffee, my brain replaying the events of last night.

Nate had texted three times, asking if I was okay, making sure I got home safely, checking that I was alone (not that he worded it quite like that). I responded to his first text after the third popped in. "I'm fine."

I hadn't been alone. For once, Lulu picked up on my mood and snuggled next to me. I said goodnight to Eric with a kiss on my doorstep.

"Callie, did you hear me?" Mom asks, overenunciating each word.

"English is my first language, Mom. You can speak regularly."

"You said, oh never mind. When can you get away for the trip to Oregon?"

I gulp down the rest of the coffee and pour a second cup. "I have no idea. June maybe? Or August? It'll depend on what happens with the store I suppose." Fortunately, or unfortunately, my brain has been preoccupied with my dad and Nate and I haven't given much gray matter to my future as it relates to the store.

"Hey, Mom," a thought pops into my head. "Where is ..." The thought may be there, but the words aren't.

"He's in the den," Mom answers the unfinished question.

I shudder. "Is it weird?"

"Yes. What's weirder is that I go in there every morning with my coffee and in the evening with tea or wine the way I did when he came from the hospital before the stroke." *Home from the hospital.* "I can't get used to a world without David in it."

"Me either," I say. He was out of my life for as long as he was in it. Even when I hated him, I took comfort in knowing he was out there somewhere.

"Do you think it would've been easier if he hadn't come back?" I ask.

"No," mom answers, a tremor in her voice that makes me wish I'd kept the question to myself. "As hard as it was to lose him a second time, I wouldn't trade those last months together."

I nod, not that she can see me.

"What about you?" Mom turns the question on me.

"Also no. Although it really does sting more this time."

"Having him back reminded us what an amazing human he is, was." She swallows loudly at the correction, and I feel the burn of tears.

"Mom, I need to go," I say, wanting to sign off before the emotional floodgates push open.

"Look at your calendar and give me some options please. And get dates from Nate." Without waiting for a response, Mom ends the call.

I drop my head into my hands. It would have been easier if he hadn't returned. I'd managed to fill that hole in my life.

Okay, not exactly, but I at least learned how to avoid the hole. Even if the leftover thorns still dug into me from time to time.

There's a knock on my door. I'm not expecting anyone, especially not at this hour.

"Hello?" I ask, still sitting at the kitchen island, a perk of living in a small apartment.

"Delivery," says a voice from the other side.

My heart, traitor that it is, skips straight to the door to fling it open. Luckily the rest of me has more common sense and I'm slower to let Nate in.

"Delivery?" I ask, leaning against the open door.

Nate lifts the cardboard tray with two coffee cups and a paper bag that can only hold one thing: fresh bagels.

"Did you think I'd forget?" he asks in response to my surprise.

"No. I just didn't think you'd come." We postmortem every party with lattes and bagels. This one feels different. This one feels like it shattered something previously unbreakable between us.

He walks past me and straight to the kitchen.

"Come on in," I say, closing the door.

Nate rolls his eyes at me. "You wouldn't turn away an everything bagel and a lavender latte."

"True. But you could have just handed them to me and gone."

"Why would I do that?" Nate straightens and crosses his arms across his chest.

I didn't mean for my tone to be so clipped. "Sorry, I'm tired. And just talked to my mom."

"Ah." Nate hands me the cup marked 'Lav'. "How is Rose?"

I shrug. I don't want to talk about my mom or my dad.

"What brings you by?" In 33 years, I've never once been standoffish or formal with Nate.

He winces as though I've just ripped a band aid from his hairy arm. Which I guess I sort of have.

"The party?" he attempts a quick recovery but the uptick in his voice is the giveaway that he's as unsure of where we are as I am.

"The party or Beth's announcement?" Damn, I need more coffee. I gulp from the cup he just handed me and wait for the lavender to mellow my mood.

"Both." He unpacks the bagels slowly, stalling. Yet another indication of how off track our friendship has veered.

"The party was nice," I offer an olive branch.

Nate raises an eyebrow. "Nice?"

"It was nice of Beth to plan it."

"She meant well."

She did. Or at least that's what I'm choosing to believe. I refuse to believe that Beth would orchestrate such an elaborate event just to lay claim on Nate. There's nothing for her to be insecure about. At least, nothing real.

Whatever feelings bubbled to the surface in Santa Fe are not feelings Nate wants.

"Did you have fun?" When in doubt, put the focus elsewhere.

Nate's left shoulder answers for him. *Sort of. Yeah. Not completely.*

"Why ..." I mimic his movement.

Nate searches for an answer in his coffee. "Bad timing maybe. There's just been so much going on that a party didn't quite feel right."

"Yeah," I say. "In her defense though, she probably thought we could use something happy."

Look at me being all Team Beth. Truth is, I spent most of the night thinking about Beth and Nate. And Eric. He made it clear last night when he brought me home that he wanted to come up. And I admit, my slightly inebriated brain challenged my over-bruised heart to a rousing game of rock-paper-scissors over agreeing or not. After a nice kiss that threatened to over-rule common sense, I came upstairs alone.

"Beth wants me move to California with her."

"It's what you want isn't it?"

"I don't know. I mean, yes but not this fast. Not this drastic." Nate wipes a glob of cream cheese that's poked out of the bagel and presents his finger to Lulu.

"You're spoiling her. And then she thinks I need to share my food with her as well."

Nate gives me a half smile. "Sorry, not sorry."

I sit across from him at the small kitchen table and reposition Lulu so I'm not looking down her backside. She flicks her tail at me but considering I've pushed her closer to where the cream cheese has plopped onto the paper, she's quick to forgive.

"We should talk about Santa Fe. And last night," Nate says. His body language says that's the last thing he wants to talk about. And suddenly, it's the last thing I want to talk about as well.

"Before you say anything, I have something I want to say," I preempt. He may not have said it outright last night, but I know Nate as well, better, than I know myself. I know we have new-to-us feelings but at the end of the day, we're still Callie and Nate. And that's not something I can live without.

"I think you should consider going with Beth. Let me finish," I say when he starts to protest. "I'm not suggesting you pack up your house into a U-Haul and follow her across the country immediately, but Nate, you wanted her. You got her. I helped you get her. Don't screw this up for us."

I attempt a smile.

"What if it doesn't work out?" Lack of confidence is what I do, not what Nate does.

"Then we'll put our collective charms to fix it. But it will work. Nate, you said so yourself, Beth is perfect for you."

Nate reaches for my hand and that same electricity that's been sparking since Santa Fe blasts through me. I pull away. As much as I want to throw myself at him, tell him to give us a chance instead, I am and will forever be his best friend.

"You said so yourself, Nate, this is who we are. This is what we do best." I stand abruptly, startling Lulu and Nate.

"Does this mean you and Eric," Nate doesn't finish the question.

"It means that I want you to be happy. And I think you'll be happy with Beth."

And maybe wildflower me needs to rethink Eric's role in my life.

# 49

## OPEN THE BLOOM OF YOUR HEART AND BECOME A GIFT OF BEAUTY TO THE WORLD.

— BRYANT MCGILL

Three hours later, I'm staring at the diagrams for the Spring Tour. Every idea I've had is either overdone or underwhelming. Creativity has abandoned me.

Partially because of my conversation with Nate this morning, partially because Eric just texted that he wants to come by, and partially because of the manila envelope peeking out from under the papers I'm pretending to be working on.

Maggie has an offer on the building. She sent me a copy and a request to talk before she decides. I've yet to open the envelope. I can't bring myself to look.

First, I need to deal with these arrangements. For once, I'm allowing the beauty of the stems to be enough. Lilies, orchids, ivy. Simple, elegant. No hidden messages. Soon, I'll deliver the first half to the mansion, then finish the rest tonight. I'll have time in the morning to take those over and fluff up anything that needs a boost before the mansion opens to the public.

I turn back to the large glass vase that will act as the centerpiece in the foyer of the Manor House. The vastness of the space requires an arrangement with presence. So far though, the feisty Tiger Lilies look more petulant than proud.

"You, my friend," I pick up a dendrobium stalk, "have your work cut out for you." I settle it in the vase.

"Think it's up for the job?"

I whirl around to see Eric. How did I not notice him come in?

"Julia let me in," he explains, seeing my surprise.

"I didn't think you were coming by until later."

"I met with the contractor. They'll start working on the carriage house in a couple of weeks."

"That's exciting." I'd pushed aside that detail. Eric and I are going to be sort of neighbors. Unless, of course, that envelope from Maggie contains an eviction notice for me as well as info on the new owner of Fancy Fleur.

"He has good ideas. I'm excited to see the transformation. And I'd love to take you over there if you're up for it. You did say once that you've always wondered what the carriage houses look like inside."

I had said that. I should want to go. I do want to go.

The phone rings in the front of the store and I turn toward the noise at the same moment Eric is coming in for a kiss. "Ouuff, sorry," I say as he puts his fingers to his nose.

"No blood. No harm done." But he steps back, either in self-defense or picking up on the change in temperature between us.

Not that there'd been a heat wave. The pre-Santa Fe Callie would have melted at the idea of handsome, amazing Eric being interested. At least once she got past the idea that he's only interested because Nate put him up to it. But for all his perfection, Eric has that one fatal flaw I always find in everyone: he's not Nate.

"Eric, I'm sorry, I don't think I can do this," I blurt. The moment the words escape and the moment I register the surprise on his face, I feel my face flame and lose color in an impressive display of horror. What have I just done?

Eric leans against the worktable. "It's Nate, isn't it?"

I cling to the Tiger Lily, willing its fierceness to rub off on me. "No. Yes. No." Way to drop the ball, Tiger Lily. "If I'd met you a year ago or maybe a year from now, I think it would have been different. So much has happened in a short time and there are more changes coming." I glare at at the envelope with the purchase offer on the table.

"What are the odds that I can change your mind?" He flashes a smile that would melt any woman's resolve.

"Not great right now. Maybe once my life settles a bit?" From a bucket of flowers on the floor, I extract a daffodil, a simple, happy daffodil. I hand it to Eric. "Daffodils symbolize friendship and luck. Two things I hope hold true for both of us. In Greek mythology they also symbolize the importance of self-love and that's something I need for myself right now."

Eric takes the flower and studies it as though it holds a secret. "We can still be friends though?" It's part question and I sense relief mixed with disappointment.

"I'd love that." And I would. Even though Nate will always be in my life, the days of Nate and Callie, Callie and Nate are numbered. Whatever emerges from this new version of us will be fine. I'll make sure it is. And that holds true for whatever grows from the friendship with Eric.

"Well," Eric says, pushing off from the table. "I won't keep you." Together we scan the work room and the flowers that witness this uncomfortable exchange. How many times have I complained to the gods of flowers that I'm never the one and here I am, sending away someone who wanted me to be his one.

But for all the doubts swirling inside me, I know at my very core that what I've just told Eric is the truth. If I have any hope of blooming, I need a spot without the shadow of anyone else.

# 50

## IF I HAD A SINGLE FLOWER FOR EVERY TIME I THINK ABOUT YOU, I COULD WALK FOREVER IN MY GARDEN.

### — CLAUDIA ADRIENNE GRANDI

Inspiration may not have been blooming, but I managed to come up with some beautiful arrangements if I do say so myself. I've already given Jeff the heads-up that I'll be by shortly with a delivery.

My phone pings with a text.

Nate: Can I come by?

Me: Since when do you ask permission?

Nate: You look busy.

Me: I LOOK busy?

"You do." I whip around to find Nate standing in the entrance to the back room.

"I was right, you never ask for permission. Why are you here, Nate?" I don't have time or energy or heart for another conversation. I just want to finish the flowers then fall onto my couch. Oh, and Thai delivery. Because tonight there's no one to suggest an alternate plan.

"I haven't been able to stop thinking about our conversation earlier." He buries his hand in his hair. "I don't know what to do, Callie."

Between Nate and Eric and the uncooperative lilies, my patience is tapped out.

"Do you love her?"

Nate swallows and that's when I see it. He's not here asking about Beth. Whatever grand speech I'd given him earlier, whatever grand speech I'd given Eric, all the excuses fall faster than the changing Autumn leaves.

"What do you want me to say, Nate? That I don't want you to go? I don't want you to go. I want you to be happy, but I don't want you to go. I know we're best friends and I know this is insane, but I don't want to be just friends anymore. I want Santa Fe."

Propelled by the boldness of the words and a day that'll go down in my journal with a mind-blown emoji, I close the distance and kiss him.

Nate's arms close around me, pulling me into him with a fierceness I've never experienced before. My heart slams against my chest and it feels like his heart is high-fiving back. As tender as the Santa Fe kiss was, this one is raw and needy and holy field of dandelions everything I've ever wished for.

A phone rings in the distance, the door chimes with someone entering or leaving, and I've just stepped on the orchid I'd been holding when I jumped Nate.

I pull away, resting my hand on his racing heart. I look up and catch my breath. I know every expression this man has, every tick and eyebrow twitch and yet for the first time, I can't read what he's thinking.

Did I just ruin everything?

*Please say something, please say something.*

He doesn't. His face is a blur of confusion and shock and something that's beginning to resemble horror.

I've ruined everything. I've ruined the one thing I can't afford to lose.

Nate takes a step back. His right hand I realize, still rests on my hip. He seems to realize it at the same moment and takes a further step back, taking his hand with him.

"I, um, oh god, Callie." He bends and picks up the orchid. Handing it to me, he says, "I have a huge favor. Can you please create one final arrangement for me?"

My heart recoils into its protective cave. "For?" My voice is as broken as the flower in my hand.

"A proposal."

I STARE ABSENTLY into the flower cooler waiting for inspiration. A proposal arrangement. I can see it as vividly as if it was already arranged and sitting in front of me. Except the arrangement isn't for Beth.

I lean against the doorframe of the cooler and look through the window into the shop. I've always loved this feature. I love that from the customer perspective it looks like a shop within a shop. Standing here never fails to perk my mood. Except today.

I step deeper into the cooler and pull out a bucket of roses and another of lilies.

To date, the arrangements I've prepared for Beth have been sincere. I agreed to help Nate and helping Nate was what I was committed to. It had been easy, even after my emotions started getting in the way, because I really do like Beth. Even my subtle attempts to confuse the woo universe with double-meaninged flowers wasn't a full-on battle cry to break them up.

I reach for my phone, the way I've done so many times in the last couple of months only to remember that he's not on the other end anymore. How odd to think that a man I didn't speak to in seventeen years, a man I wanted to hate for most of that time, is the one I long to ask advice from. He understood my feelings for Nate, understood them before I did.

I close my eyes and pull up the image of my ideal bouquet. Something that would take my breath away with its elegance and simplicity, something that exudes love and commitment, the promise of happiness and forever.

I choose the perfect white roses for eternal loyalty, heliotrope for devotion, and lilies for love. When I finish, I step back to survey my work. It's perfect. Perfect except for one small detail. I take one calla lily and position it in the center.

On a Fancy Fleur card, I write "My life forward is with you."

I wipe my cheek on my shoulder, capturing the tears before they can drop onto the crisp white card.

The flowers, however, aren't done with me. I grab another, identical glass vase and let the flowers create another arrangement.

The combination of light pink roses for admiration, zinnia for affection and memories is understated and tasteful. An anemone seems to reach out to me. Of course. Sincerity and abandonment in one perfect bloom. Anyone who sees this arrangement will be awed by its beauty. Only those who hear the flowers will know it's nothing but a heart breaker.

"Okay, then," I say to the two arrangements. "Go forth and do what you need to do."

I pick up my phone.

> Me: Arrangement is done.

> Nate: Thanks. Callie,

The three dots pop up then disappear. I wait, biting my lower lip.

Nate: Thanks.

What was he going to say before he changed his mind?

I type, I'll see you when you get here, then delete, letter by letter. I don't want to see him. I don't want to look into his eyes and know I screwed up our friendship by throwing myself at him. Instead, I type, *let yourself in*, and hit the send button.

I turn off the phone and slip it into my back pocket.

I look around at the beauty of the store, the anticipation of the flowers in the cooler, the perfect arrangements on the table. This is usually when I feel a ripple of happiness and pride. Today, the only thing I feel is a gnawing of dread.

Not only is my personal future sitting on that table, but my professional future as well. Next to the two bouquets sits the manila envelope. I haven't had the strength to open it.

If Nate is going to break my heart today, Maggie can wait until tomorrow.

# 51

# PERFUMES ARE THE FEELINGS OF FLOWERS.

## — HEINRICH HEINE

"Thanks for letting me come in this late," I say. I hadn't meant to bring the flowers over tonight, but I couldn't stay at home or in the store.

"Always pleased to see you. And I've been anxiously waiting to see what you had in mind for the main table," Jeff says, holding the door open so I can maneuver the large vase through.

"What do you think?" I ask, setting the vase down on the round mahogany table in the foyer.

"It's spectacular. Every year I think you've outdone yourself and every year you surprise me with something even more amazing."

My heart warms to his words. Despite not feeling the creative excitement that usually drives a project like this, I'm proud of the end result.

"I'm glad you stopped by while it's quiet," Jeff says. "There's something I want to ask you."

My stomach flutters. This community has the most gossip-fertile soil I've ever seen. He sees the answer on my face before he even asks the question.

"So, it's true?"

Maggie's absence hasn't gone unnoticed. Some people bought my story that she's on vacation. It was easier to say that than the truth. Others, who know her better, have chosen to at least keep the gossip over my unlikely excuses amongst themselves.

"It's true."

"Wow, I never thought Maggie would leave."

"Neither did I. And truthfully, I'm not sure she thought she'd leave either. That store has been her life for so long."

"Do you have time to join me in a drink? I was just enjoying the quiet by the fireplace." Jeff motions to the living room, the same room I'd extracted Nate from when he helped deliver the Paws Please charity event flowers.

"A drink sounds perfect." And while I hadn't banked on more human interaction today, the idea of a drink with Jeff really does sound perfect.

I follow him into the library and settle into one of the two chairs flanking the fireplace. Jeff pours me a glass of wine and refills his glass. Despite the late hour, he still looks as pressed and fresh as he did earlier in the day when I came with the first delivery. In his gray slacks, white shirt, and burgundy tie, he's a natural extension of this room. Matching colors, matching formality, and a matching ease that's both at odds with the stately mansion and somehow completely appropriate.

"How long have you been the Executive Director here?" I ask. Rifling through my memories of events we've worked, I can't remember dealing with anyone but him.

"Oh heavens, seems like a lifetime. It's been twenty, twenty-one years. Give or take a year or three." He smiles. And like almost every time I'm around him, I wonder how old he is. He's one of those men who just gets better looking with age.

"Do you ever think about doing something else?"

"Not really. A few years ago I sniffed around at the job

market outside these walls. But other than working as a curator in a museum, this is really the only job I can see myself in. The house is as much of a friend as the people I work with. Does that sound silly?" He strokes the armrest with his free hand as though reassuring the house that he'll never leave it. It's how I feel about Fancy Fleur.

"Would they ever sell it?" The original family who owned this property set up a foundation to oversee the mansion and gardens. But it's valuable property and who's to say a developer won't come along at just the right time with just the right offer.

"Nothing is impossible, I suppose, but I don't think they will. It's not just a historical building. It's the heart of the community."

Fancy Fleur is an important part of the community as well. We have so many standing orders with regulars who live walking distance. Every day neighbors walk by on their way to the coffee shop or a restaurant or being exercised by their dog. They all take a moment to look in and wave.

What will happen to Mr. Preston and his lavender roses? And Mrs. Cohen with her Shabbat bouquet. Will the new owners keep the name? Will they even keep it as a flower shop?

"Callie?" Jeff asks, pulling me back.

"Sorry. Brain chipmunks went AWOL."

He tilts his head, studying me. "What's going to happen with the store?"

I sink deeper into the chair, needing the support as I deliver the news even though I've yet to see what that actually is. "She has an interested buyer."

He looks as surprised as I felt when Maggie told me.

"Do you know who it is?"

I shake my head. I should have looked at the offer.

Jeff drains the rest of his wine. "What would the sale mean for you?"

"That's a great question. Maybe I'd stay depending on who's

buying it and what they want to do with the building." I have the sudden understanding of how a plant feels when it's being sized up a moment before it's pulled from the soil that's nourished it and kept it stable.

"Pity," he finally says. "I always assumed you would take over. Officially take over," he adds with a little wink.

That's what Maggie had said. It's what Dad said as well. Me? I never imagined myself as anything more than working *with* Maggie. Fancy Fleur is Maggie and Maggie is Fancy Fleur.

I look around at the arrangements I brought over. Arrangements I put together. Me. I pulled this off. My brain tiptoes through the field of accomplishments, not just since Maggie left for Santa Fe, but since I've become Maggie's second hand.

I've done the hard things, I've survived the harsh reality of losing my father once then again. My heart is still beating after exploding my relationship with Nate. I'm not a wallflower anymore.

"I need to get back to the store." I stand abruptly. "Thank you, Jeff. For everything." I set my wine glass on the coffee table and head for the door. I have to talk to Maggie. And I have to talk to Nate before it's too late.

I BURST into the store like I've been zapped by a lightning bolt. Which I kind of have. A couple of hours ago, I was resigned to losing it all. Now all I want is to catch Nate and rip that envelope to shreds. I skid past the buckets I'd left out earlier. Maggie would not be happy with me. For all of her chaotic organization skills, she kept everything in its place in the store. But Maggie doesn't want to own the store any longer.

The envelope is where I'd left it. I reach for it at the same time that I register the vase on the table. I'm too late.

I sink to the floor, envelope clutched in my fist. Outside the weather gods rumble their displeasure.

He picked my open heart arrangement. On the table sits the broken heart one. A reminder that we may have had feelings, but they weren't strong enough to take us from soulmates to heartmates.

My fist tightens around the envelope. I look down, surprised to see that Nate has scribbled "Call Maggie, urgent," on the front.

I twist to get my phone out of the back pocket of my jeans and press the button to power it back on. The phone goes into a buzzing frenzy as messages escape their captivity.

> Maggie: I need to talk to you. Call.
>
> Nate: Where are you?
>
> Maggie: Did you open the envelope? Call.
>
> Nate: Why aren't you answering?
>
> Maggie: Tick tock
>
> Nate: Callie, we need to talk.
>
> Nate: Please.

No, not please. The flowers speak for themselves.

But I may still have a chance with Maggie. I rip open the envelope and extract a piece of paper. It's an offer for the store. Maggie has included a sticky note on top: *It's a good offer. Make me a better one! (See page two)*

I look at the offer again. There's no way I can afford to match this offer. Not even Gringotts would give me that kind of money.

I turn to the second page and blink at it, waiting for the ink to disappear like something indeed out of Gringotts. In Mom's girlish loopy letters, she's written, *David left this for you in his will.*

The "this" has an arrow to a scrap of paper, clearly a photocopy, taped onto the page haphazardly. I squint at the blurry image. It's a bank statement. A bank statement showing a large sum. A bank statement in my name.

Under the clipping from the bank statement, mom added, *(See page three)*

The writing is wobbly and unsteady but there's no mistaking the swirl in the C that my father always added when he wrote my name.

My dearest Callie,

Leaving the first time was the hardest thing I've ever done. Not a day went by that I didn't think of you and long to be in your life. There are so many things I regret about those years, even as I know I couldn't have done them differently.

These last couple of months have been some of my happiest as odd as that may sound. I've loved every minute with you and I'm so proud of the woman you've become.

I realize it's a cheap shot to ask one last dying request but since you can't get mad at me now, I'm asking ...

Open your heart to the possibilities around you. Believe that you deserve everything. Trust in who you are.

Forever,
Dad

---

# 52

# LOVE IS LIKE WILDFLOWERS; IT'S OFTEN FOUND IN THE MOST UNLIKELY PLACES.

## — RALPH WALDO EMERSON

I'd spent the entire drive from my mother's house to the hospital whipping my anger back to the forefront that first time I saw him after seventeen years. Love aside, I hated him. I wanted to hate him. I wanted every second of every minute of every year he'd been away to fuel my anger.

Instead, I'd fallen for him all over again. He read me the way only Nate could, the way he had throughout my childhood.

God I'd hated how Nate and my dad would gang up on me those times I really just wanted to pout and feel the misery of youth. I couldn't hide anything from them.

Even after the years of silence between us, Dad knew the questions to ask, the questions not to ask, and the advice I didn't want to hear but needed most. And don't you know, he was right every single time. Well, right about everything but one.

He'd been right about me. He'd seen straight through the blustery proclamations that I was exactly where I wanted to be, fulfilled, happy, blah, blah. I was good at lying, especially to myself. He didn't call me out, just steered every conversation to the inevitable outcome.

I've made a career of supporting everyone I love from the shadows. Today, I turned in my resignation on that career. Not that I'm going to become a rebel. My insides are still quivering from the nerves of disappointing anyone.

Fancy Fleur has been my home, literally and figuratively, for most of my life. Maggie gave me a lifeline after college when I didn't know what direction to go. But that identity was always tied to Maggie. The store will forever be ours, but as of today, it's officially mine.

Dad, however, had been wrong about me and Nate. We aren't meant to be together. Not like that at least. I did my part helping him with Beth and I did it well. So well that I fell for him, too. But between being with Nate and keeping Nate, I'll still choose keeping him.

I pick up the heart-break vase and, cradling it in my arms, make my way out of the store. The sticky lock is even harder to manage with one hand. As I bend to set the vase on the ground, I catch a slight movement out of the corner of my eye.

Whirling around, I slam my elbow into the doorjamb. "Shit." Then, "Shit," as I almost knock over the vase, And then, "Shit, you scared me," when I realize it's Nate.

"Sorry."

"Why are you sitting on my stairs?"

Nate begins to stand, groans and sits back down hard. "My ass is numb."

"How long have you been here?"

"Two-ish hours."

"Why?"

"I need to talk to you."

I eyeball the vase on the step next to him. The arrangement he chose for her. "What for? You don't need my permission and I don't need an explanation. Just go see her, Nate. I'm tired."

Nate's body blocks the narrow stairs up to my apartment. I'm trapped between the outside storm and the storm Nate is about to unleash inside me.

"Callie." He reaches for my hand.

I pull away. Yes, I want to keep Nate, of course I want to keep him. He's my best friend. But for tonight, I need him to not be here.

"Please just go."

"Not until you hear me out."

I force air out of my lungs so I won't pop like an over-inflated balloon, and motion for him to continue.

Once again, he reaches for my hand and this time, I don't fight. But I'm also not giving in. My hand is as floppy as a three-day-old tulip stem.

Nate looks from my hand to our surroundings, dingy except for the mural on the wall behind me. "This isn't exactly where I imagined having this conversation with you."

I don't react. It doesn't matter where he breaks my heart.

"On with it," I say, irritation taking over. I'm tired, my feet are wet, and I want a big glass of wine. From above I hear Lulu scratching at the door. She knows we're out here, or more precisely, she knows Nate is here and she doesn't like being kept from him.

Nate tightens his hold on my hand, knowing I'm a flight risk.

"You have been my best friend since the day we were born. You know me better than anyone. You've seen me at my best and my worst. You've put up with my crazy times and you are the only person I know who can call me out and be right every single damn time."

Except for this one time, I want to say. But I don't. Because the distribution of the two last arrangements says it all.

"When I asked you to help me with the flower arrangements, I thought I knew what I wanted," Nate continues. "Beth is, was, perfect for me."

I blink at our hands, or his hand where mine disappears into his. *Perfect for me.*

Wait, *was.* He said was.

"I broke up with Beth." Nate drops my hand and turns to retrieve the vase from the step behind him. "When I saw the two bouquets in the store tonight, whatever doubts I had slipped away. You said everything I was afraid of feeling with these flowers. There will never be anyone who sees me the way you do. And there will never be anyone I'm more connected to."

The smell of the lilies I'd used for filler overpowers the space between us.

"Callie," Nate says, tipping my chin up and forcing me to look at him instead of into the flowers, "It's you I want to spend my life with."

"Wait, what?"

Nate thrusts the vase into my hands and pulls out the calla lily.

"This," he says. "This was the giveaway."

"Well, the flower and this." He leans across the vase and our lips meet, gently at first then with added urgency. Just when I think I'm about to drop the vase, Nate pulls away. "Damn, girl, if I'd known you could kiss like that, I would have kissed you years ago."

I set the vase down and step into Nate, strengthening my position as an expert kisser. Guess those teenage magazines were right. Being with the right person makes everything perfect.

A loud clap of thunder rattles the building and Nate and I pull apart.

"Are you sure?" I ask, because as much as I want this to happen, there's so much at risk.

"I'm sure. Callie, I love you. I've always loved you."

"I love you, too. Want to come upstairs?" I ask, feeling more shy than I've ever felt around him.

"Yes, but I need you to answer two questions."

"Okay," I prompt when he stalls. He really needs to get over this dramatic pause thing.

"One, have you talked to my mom?"

"That's the first question you have for me?" I ask incredulously.

"Yeah, I don't want her calling repeatedly and interrupting whatever we're about to do up there."

"Whatever we're about to do?" I laugh.

"I don't want to be presumptuous."

I kiss him again, cementing the whatever we're about to do as a given.

"Yes, Nate, I spoke to Maggie. You are looking at the official owner of Fancy Fleur. And now I don't have to move either." I look around the narrow, stairwell. It's not much, but it's truly my home now.

"Good."

"Question number two?"

"Will you marry me?"

From the arrangement, I pluck a pink Aster. "The emblem of Venus, the goddess of love," I say, handing the flower to Nate.

Nate takes the flower and tucks it behind my ear. "My goddess of love."

A flower cannot blossom without sunshine and man
cannot live without love.
— *Max Muller*

# AUTHOR'S NOTE

I'm a firm believer that books find their readers. And just as strongly believe that stories find their authors. Authors talk about the "story of their heart." Confession, this book wasn't that for me. *The Arrangements* started as a fun idea, something light-hearted and hopeful during a not very light or hopeful period (hello 2020).

There were a lot of starts and stops from the initial seed of an idea to this finished piece. Some more hopeful times, some far less hopeful times. This manuscript became a project of healing. It reminded me why I love writing. It reminded me that it's okay to believe. Mostly, through Callie and Nate, I was reminded about the beauty of friendships and discovery of self. So, even if *The Arrangements* didn't start as the story of my heart, it became the story of my soul.

It wouldn't have happened, though, without the encouragement and support from friends and family. Extra love goes out to Kerry Lonsdale, Camille Pagan, Alison Hammer, Kelly Harms, Erin Celello, and Erika Montgomery. All the thanks to Jodi Warshaw for her amazing editorial eye. To Alyson Delaney

Walker for being my gremlin slayer. And, of course Alex and my parents, Lea and Peter, for their unfailing love and forever being my why.

# ABOUT THE AUTHOR

Orly Konig writes hopeful stories with a dash of humor about finding resilience during life's messy detours. She is a passionate believer in the power of coffee, an animal lover, a crocheter of fun critters, and an unapologetic advocate for defining (and redefining) a confident, happy life. Orly lives in Maryland, sharing her personal space with two oversized and overfluffed cats.

You can sign up for Orly's newsletter on her website at orlykonig.com to be the first to find out about new books, give-aways, and other updates. And follow her on social media, because there's always something fun happening on social media.